I0594488

TAINTED

THE DRUID CHRONICLES
BOOK FOUR

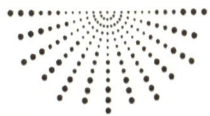

CHRISTINA PHILLIPS

PHOENIX 18 PUBLISHING

Copyright © 2013/2016 by Christina Phillips

All rights reserved.

This book is for your personal enjoyment only. No part of this book may be reproduced in any form or by any electronic or mechanical means, including information storage and retrieval systems, without written permission from the author, except for the use of brief quotations in a book review.

Thank you for respecting the hard work of this author.

This is a work of fiction. Names, characters, places, and incidents either are the product of the author's imagination or are used fictitiously, and any resemblance to actual persons, living or dead, business establishments, events or locales is entirely coincidental.

PO Box 4039, Mandurah, WA 6210, AUSTRALIA
EMAIL: Christina@christinaphillips.com
Christinaphillips.com
Cover Art by GetCovers
05/26

ISBN: 978-0-6487568-3-5

For Mum and Dad, always in my heart.

CHAPTER ONE

BRITANNIA, AD 52

 ntonia drew aside the silken drape at the window of her father's carpentum and scanned the flat Britannia countryside as they traveled along the straight Roman road. It was late spring, but the day matched her mood—cloudy, with a hint of restless despair on the horizon.

"Antonia." Her father clasped her hand, and his smile warmed her frozen heart. How she longed to make his dreams for her come true. But she was no longer a young girl with a glorious future ahead. She was a matron, past her prime. She feared her beloved father might never recover from the disappointment of his only child's failure to shine like a star in the Rome of his imagination.

She returned his smile. For him, she would endure this visit. For him, she would play the perfect Roman lady despite the fact her former husband had tossed her from his life with degrading disregard.

"My beautiful child." Her father sighed, and Antonia knew of whom he was thinking. "You're so like your mother. I see her face every time I look at you."

Her heart squeezed in her breast in reflected sorrow. She'd

never known her mother. But even after all these years her father still loved her. Still missed her. What must it be like to be loved so faithfully?

"I will find a man worthy of you," he said, and she tried to ignore the way her stomach churned, and chest constricted at the thought of being given to another man. "The noble blood of your mother runs through your veins. You deserve nothing less than to take your rightful place in the highest echelons of Rome. And befriending this tribune's foreign wife is the perfect way to achieve our ends."

If she had her way, she'd remain by her father's side for the rest of their lives. And she intended to have her way. But there was no need to distress him with her unconventional plans. Not when they were within moments of arriving at their hosts' villa, situated a few miles south of the town of Camulodunum.

"I confess I'm intrigued to meet this foreigner who appears to hold such sway over her husband." The tribune, Tiberius Valerius Maximus, was a member of one of the most powerful families in the Senate. It was a mystery to Antonia how he'd been allowed to marry a native of a conquered land.

Her father leaned closer in a conspiratorial manner, even though they were alone in his lavishly decorated carpentum. "There are rumors she is a barbarian princess from the wilds of Cambria. But don't let this concern you. If she takes a liking to you, I know she'll look favorably on finding a suitable match for you."

Antonia gazed into the anxious eyes of her father and swallowed the words of denial that threatened to spill free. She would use every weapon at her disposal to turn him from his dream of seeing her wed once again. Only as a last resort would she confess the ultimate reason that would ensure her continued freedom from the shackles of forced matrimony.

Once again, she turned to the window and saw a large white villa set back from the road. It was grander than anything she'd yet seen in Britannia, but was modest compared to the villa her former husband, Amulius Cornelius Scipio, had owned.

The land in front of the villa was cultivated but devoid of ornate statuary. As the carpentum slowed she glanced over the surrounding land and, although some attempt at order had been imposed, in the main, the estate looked little different from the countryside that surrounded it.

How strange.

As she contemplated why a Roman should leave his estate in such rural disarray, a rider galloped past the window, pulled to a halt, and leaped from the horse. Antonia tilted her head to get a better look and as she did so, the dismounted rider swung around and glared in her direction.

Their gazes clashed and Antonia's heart slammed against her ribs as her fingers clenched around the sill of the open window. His eyes were dark, and although a strip of leather bound his long, dark blond hair, loose tendrils whipped across his unsmiling face giving him a wild, savage appearance.

The carpentum drew to a stop but the rider didn't move out of the way despite how close he now was to her. Nor did he incline his head in a gesture of respect for her rank and Antonia continued to stare at him, mesmerized by the hostile air he projected her way.

Was he a slave of the tribune? Surely not. Even though he wore a neck ring, no slave would behave with such lack of deference to a Roman. Was he then a trusted servant?

She heard her father say they had arrived, but still she couldn't tear her fascinated gaze from the surly Briton. He held the bridle of his mount, his attention riveted on Antonia, apparently oblivious to the young stable lad who ran to him.

Unease crawled along her spine, although she couldn't think why. She was in no danger from this Briton. *But why does he continue to stare at me?*

With slow deliberation, the Briton's lip curled in open disdain and shock punched through Antonia's chest at his sheer, unabashed nerve. Was this the way he treated all visitors to his master's estate? Or just her?

Heat flooded her cheeks as she realized how blatantly she'd been staring at him in return. Hastily she averted her eyes, smoothing her blue woolen palla as she rose to follow her father.

She was no longer a girl who might blush and giggle at the bold stare of an undisciplined man. She was a divorced woman of twenty-five and had no wish to draw the attention of any man, undisciplined or not.

Slaves unhooked the back door of the carpentum and she took a deep breath, still unaccountably shaken by the look of contempt the Briton had given her. She'd grown used to the derision heaped upon her head by Scipio, but what had she ever done to this stranger that he should look at her so?

And why am I still thinking of him? He would be gone now to his tasks. She would never see him again.

Her father stepped to the ground and as she held out her hand for a slave to assist her, awareness skittered over her skin. Before she could retreat in self-preservation, the Briton took her hand, and his grasp wasn't light as protocol dictated.

He gripped her fingers as though he possessed the right to touch her, to hold her, and for one terrifying moment Antonia had the mortifying certainty that she would stumble into his arms. Once again, their gazes clashed and once again, she was unaccountably captivated by the deep brown of his eyes.

And the unmistakable gleam of contempt that he made no effort to conceal.

By rights, she should pull free and reprimand him for his insolence. But instead, she remained paralyzed as his calloused fingers burned her flesh and sparks of fire danced in her blood.

His eyes darkened and the heat from his hand radiated along her arm, feeding the fire, and searing the breath in her lungs. *Blessed Juno, what's happening to me?* Writhing serpents blazed through her breast and coiled low in her womb. Liquid heat bloomed between her thighs, the fiery path a strange blend of pain and pleasure. She had never experienced anything like it in her life before. Yet instinctively she knew what this was, no matter how she tried to thrust the knowledge from her.

Lust.

The raw desire the Roman ladies of her acquaintance had whispered about during feminine gatherings. The graphic confidences shared, and stamina of lovers compared, during the many scented bathing rituals she'd attended.

She had always believed the scandalous tales to be amusing exaggerations. Yet between one shocked heartbeat and the next, all her preconceived notions of passion sizzled into ash.

"Come, Antonia." Her father's voice penetrated her dazed contemplation, and she wrenched her gaze from the Briton to focus on descending the two steps to the ground. She wouldn't let him see how his intensity affected her. Would not give him the satisfaction of stumbling, even though her legs shook beneath her gown.

Her father smiled at her, apparently oblivious to the way the Briton continued to hold her hand. *Why is he still holding my hand?* Without turning to him, although every nerve she possessed screamed that she should turn to him, Antonia pulled free from his burning touch.

And then she couldn't help but glance his way.

His dark eyes mocked her, the tilt of his lips confirming his low opinion of her. She couldn't imagine why his opinion should matter and yet she discovered it did. Unnerved, she tilted her head at him in an unmistakable gesture of dismissal, but she wasn't surprised when he didn't back away or lower his own bold stare.

Her father was speaking, threading her arm through his, and Antonia dutifully walked by his side as they approached the villa. But his words flowed over her head, unheeded. Because, fanciful or not, she knew the Briton was staring at her. She could *feel* the fiery heat of his gaze on her back, and she struggled not to look over her shoulder, just to confirm her suspicion.

Her flesh tingled where the Briton had clasped her hand and she battled the urge to flex her fingers. If she did, he would know the reason why. And it was of the utmost importance that she gave him no clue as to how deeply his careless touch affected her.

Her husband had stripped her of almost everything she possessed during their time together, but she retained a shadow of her former pride. And she had no intention of allowing this uncouth native of a foreign land to breach the flimsy façade of serenity she'd fought so desperately to maintain during the last torturous year.

They entered the villa's atrium where the exquisite mosaic floor, exotic stonework and beautiful statuary boldly declared the high status of its master. She forced a smile to her lips as the tribune, in his purple striped toga, came forward to greet them. How her father coveted that cursed purple stripe. How mistakenly he imagined there could be no higher honor for his daughter than to be welcomed within the elevated patrician rank.

How she longed to tell him of the putrid stink that seethed beneath that lofty veneer of civilized sophistication. And knew she never would.

The risk was too great.

As the tribune welcomed her father, she looked at the Roman's face and shock slammed through her. Why hadn't her father warned her? Only years of successfully hiding her true feelings prevented her from gasping aloud.

Ancient scars distorted the tribune's face, yet they were like nothing she had seen before. But despite the disfigurement, his haughty patrician beauty was enough to take any woman's breath away.

How fortunate she was immune to such base stirrings.

And instantly the dark, condemning glare of the Briton invaded her mind.

"Welcome to our home," a feminine voice said in perfect Latin and for the second time in as many moments, Antonia's senses reeled in disbelief. The tribune's wife sounded as though she'd lived in the upper echelons of Roman society her entire life. With her golden hair, slender figure and dressed in an exquisite stola, she wouldn't have looked out of place in the emperor's entourage.

"Thank you." Antonia inclined her head in greeting as a slave took her palla. "It is most kind of you to invite me."

"My wife has been looking forward to making your acquaintance," the tribune said, and Antonia watched, fascinated, as he turned to his wife and bestowed a smile of such love that her heart ached. Never had she seen a man look at his wife in such a manner. Men of Rome would never allow such feelings to show, at least not in public. What enchantment had this foreigner weaved around her husband?

"It's true," the foreign princess said as she turned back to Antonia with a smile that could surely rival Venus herself. "There are very few young women of Rome here and I'm most eager to learn all I can of your city."

"It would be my honor to enlighten you," Antonia said, and she tried not to stare at the princess' mismatched eyes. She'd never encountered such a phenomenon before, although it was whispered one of the sacred Vestal Virgins also possessed such an anomaly.

"Come. We will leave the men to their business and take refreshments in the courtyard."

Antonia fully expected the Cambrian beauty—no one in their right mind could call her a barbarian—to take her arm as if they were the dearest of friends. In Rome all the ladies in her social sphere kissed and hugged no matter how slight their acquaintance, but regardless of how she looked, this tribune's wife obviously knew nothing of such customs.

Was that the kind of thing she wanted Antonia to tell her about?

"You must call me Carys," the other woman said as they entered the large courtyard. An impressive colonnade surrounded the four sides giving protection from the weather and a central fountain, of Venus rising from the waves, was an oddly discordant note of formality in the otherwise wild, undisciplined garden. "And I shall call you Antonia."

"Of course." For all that Carys was a native of a conquered land and younger than Antonia, she was still the wife of an influential patrician. And Antonia, despite the blood of her mother, was nothing but a divorced woman, once again under the protection of her father.

There was no question that Antonia would presume to dispute anything Carys might request.

Unless it involved matrimony.

They sat on a stone bench and servants brought out an array of edible delicacies and arranged them on a low stone table.

"I hope you enjoy living in Britain," Carys said, and it was a shock to hear her call the province by its barbaric name. "I know we're going to be such good friends."

Antonia smiled, as etiquette dictated, and recalled the women she had once thought were her friends back in Rome. How quickly they had faded from her side once it became known that her husband no longer had any use for her.

"I'm sure we will be." But friends confided their deepest secrets and Antonia would never share hers with another living soul. How often had she thanked the wise Juno for preventing her from telling her intimate circle in Rome of her treacherous plans? If she'd followed her heart in that matter, they would have betrayed her to Scipio. And she had no doubt, he would have taken her life.

Carys' smile faltered and for one surreal moment, Antonia had the certainty that the other woman had guessed her thoughts. Heat shot through her, and she broke eye contact, smoothing the flawless silk of her stola.

She had to forget about the women she had once called her friends. Their fickle natures didn't matter and would never touch her again. There was only thing she had to concentrate on, and soon, with Juno's blessing, her stealthily laid plans would come to fruition.

Awareness prickled along her exposed nape, and in the same instance Carys leaped to her feet in a manner most unlike any Roman noblewoman. Antonia refused to grip her fingers together in her lap, refused to glance over her shoulder, and instead focused with deathly intensity on the tranquility of the tinkling fountain.

The Briton had *not* just entered the courtyard. Why had her thoughts instantly turned to that possibility? And besides, if he had, Carys would most certainly not have jumped up with such a lack of decorum.

And despite herself, Antonia glanced over her shoulder.

It was the Briton. Disbelief pulsed through her as she watched Carys rise onto her toes to kiss his face. Paralyzed, she saw his grim expression relax into a semblance of a smile as he wound his arm around her shoulders and gave her a brief hug.

Was he Carys' lover? Did the tribune know? Many of her former friends had enjoyed illicit liaisons with slaves or those in their husband's employ. But even the most brazen wouldn't display her unfaithfulness before a complete stranger.

"Come, Gawain," Carys said, still speaking Latin, as she tugged the Briton by his hand. "There's someone I want you to meet."

Antonia tried to ignore the way her stomach churned, and she gripped her fingers together despite her best intentions. Why would Carys wish to introduce her to this Briton? *Why do I have the sudden urge to be violently ill?*

"Antonia, this is Gawain, my beloved kin from my homeland."

Her *kin*? Antonia stared at Gawain's long-sleeved shirt and the braccae that encased each of his powerfully muscled legs. Outside she had merely noted his clothes were not those of a Roman but now she realized that they were, in fact, of good quality linen. How had she imagined for even a moment that he was a slave?

"Gawain," Carys continued, turning to the now unsmiling Briton—*Cambrian*. "This is Antonia, daughter of our esteemed merchant, Drusus Antonius Faustus."

For a long, agonizing moment, Antonia looked up into his dark eyes as insane images of fleeing this courtyard flashed through her mind. He towered over her, a threatening presence of pure masculinity, and everything about him radiated a raw, primitive danger. Only now did she acknowledge that the torque around his throat was nothing like a slave ring. It gleamed like silver and its intricate engravings were similar to those that adorned his savagely compelling earring.

"My pleasure." His husky voice and erotically seductive accent caressed her skin like a lover's touch and sank into her blood like a dreaded fever. His free hand reached for her, and panic thudded through her blood, squeezing the air from her lungs, and making it hard to draw breath.

Years ago, as a young bride, she had dreamed of a man such as him. One who could ignite her senses with barely a glance and cause her flesh to smolder with a single sultry word. But she had been a girl then. She was a woman now. And she couldn't afford to indulge in foolish fantasies that would lead nowhere. He'd made his contempt for her clear. His attitude now was nothing but an insincere display so as not to offend his kin.

She could ignore him. And disgrace her father's name.

But she had disgraced her father enough. It wouldn't kill her to allow this Cambrian to take her hand. She would endure his touch one last time. The gods knew she had endured far worse.

Yet it took every particle of nerve she possessed to unclench her fingers and raise her hand.

She caught the mocking gleam in his eyes as he took her hand in his calloused grip and lowered his head. Her mouth dried as his lips brushed across her knuckles, his touch deliberately possessive as though he knew full well how she battled not to tremble at the contact.

Then, still holding her hand, he looked up at her and the lust and fury blazing in his eyes scorched her like a furnace to Hades.

CHAPTER TWO

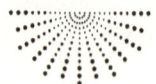

Gawain slowly caressed his thumb across the soft skin of the Roman's fingers and cursed how his blood thundered through his veins at the provocative touch. She looked at him with cool disdain, her blue eyes reminding him of a cloudless sky in the moments before a frost descended.

But she couldn't fool him. He'd seen her desire back on the road, before she'd managed to hide it. And now she looked at him as though he was little better than a slave. A native of a country her cursed emperor had conquered.

She attempted to free her hand and he tightened his grip. Her people might have subdued the vast majority of his, but no Roman dictated his movements. For an endless moment, he met her silent challenge and only when her eyes began to darken with reluctant acknowledgment of their mutual lust, did he finally allow her to pull free.

"Will you join us, Gawain?"

He knew Carys' question was pure formality. She didn't expect him to stay while she entertained a spoiled Roman female. He had no wish to stay. The news he had for Carys could be given to her later, but the way the Roman stiffened in response to Carys' question irked.

It was clear she wanted him to leave. Conversely, he decided that he would remain.

"Thank you." He offered Carys a sardonic smile and then ignored the pointed glare she sent his way. It was obvious she was going to berate him for his bad manners once her irritating guest had departed. He folded his arms and leaned against one of the pretentious Roman columns that surrounded the courtyard garden. "Do you intend to stay long on this primitive isle, Lady Antonia?"

She inclined her head in a regal manner and one pale golden ringlet trailed across the elegant curve of her shoulder.

"I intend to stay for as long as my father decrees."

Gawain tore his fascinated gaze from her cursed ringlet. Of course she would stay until her father told her otherwise. She was a Roman woman, and Roman women did only what their men folk commanded of them. But instead of responding to her comment, his gaze became fixed on the riot of curls and waves of her hair, held in place by glittering, gem-encrusted pins.

He had the savage urge to rip those pins from her and watch that glorious hair tumble in abandoned disarray over her naked shoulders. The image was so vivid in his mind that his cock, already aroused since his first encounter with Antonia on the road, hardened with anticipation.

She's a Roman. But it made no difference. He wanted her and by the gods he'd find a way to have her, and soon.

"Antonia only arrived in Britain six days ago." There was a hint of censure in Carys' voice. Did she know what he wanted to do with her fragile little guest? He smothered a grim smile. Carys might pretend to be the perfect Roman matron in public, but at heart she was a princess of Cymru. He had no doubt that she knew exactly what his intentions towards the Roman entailed.

"Is this the first time you've ventured beyond the cradle of

Rome?" He resisted the urge to shift position. It wouldn't do any good. The only position that would ease his discomfort was having Antonia on her hands and knees in front of him while he took her from behind. *While I plunge my hands into her golden curls and tangle her hair around my fingers.*

Gingerly he shifted his back against the marble column but as he'd already known, it did nothing to diminish his cursed erection. When Antonia deigned to favor him with a glance, it only increased the raw need pounding through his blood. She need only drop her gaze to see how much he wanted her. Would she feign shock at the sight?

"I was born in Gallia." There was a haughty note in her voice and her eyes didn't waver from his. "I didn't venture into the cradle of Rome until I was fourteen years old."

For a moment he was distracted from his fantasy of hearing Antonia scream in ecstasy as he hammered between her naked thighs. Not only had she repeated his less than complimentary words back at him. But he also detected a scathing undertone that was all her own.

"So you're not a Roman noblewoman born and bred?"

"Gawain." There was an edge to Carys' voice. "If you cannot be civil to Antonia then perhaps you should take your leave."

"Do you find my manner uncivil, Lady Antonia?" He offered her a mocking smile, daring her to respond. She might not have been born in Rome, but she was a Roman from the top of her elaborately curled hair to her daintily clad feet and in public, Roman women rarely spoke their mind.

"I find your manner unsurprising." Antonia smiled back at him, but her eyes were glacial. "And civility is a matter of perspective."

He managed to contain his own surprise at her response, but only just. He'd bantered with several highborn Roman women since leaving his beloved homeland two turns of the wheel ago.

But none of them had so bluntly inferred that they considered him a rude bastard.

But then, none of them had stirred his lust to the degree Antonia managed with barely a glance. He wasn't sure why that fact irritated him so much or why he felt the need to bait her with barbed remarks. Was it because he knew she hated the heat that flared between them? The knowledge that she battled, even now, to prevent him from seeing the need in her eyes?

Whatever the reason, her reply only stoked his lust further. And, gods curse it, that wasn't all. Her answer intrigued him on a level that no Roman had the right to touch.

"Your perspective," he said, "is one I shall enjoy exploring."

"Alas," Antonia's voice dripped ice. "My perspective is not available for such exploration."

"Indeed, Gawain." Only those who knew Carys well would recognize the fury beneath her level tone. "I can't imagine what you're suggesting." Her tone implied she knew exactly what he was suggesting and was deeply affronted by his nerve.

He tossed her a dark glance. She might think this fragile-looking Roman needed protection from his attention, but she was wrong. He could taste Antonia's repressed arousal in the fragranced air, could feel the fiery bonds of need that weaved between them. Could see the angry battle between lust and propriety behind the calm façade she presented to the world.

The other Roman women he'd had might not have stirred his cock so violently, but he'd been aware of their interest from the moment they'd met. In public, they behaved like model wives. In private, he'd shared their luscious charms and taken grim pleasure in the knowledge that those aloof foreign women had come apart beneath his invasion. It was a hollow satisfaction, but all he could gain, in knowing he invaded the women of Rome in response to how Rome invaded his own land and people.

Antonia was no different. Once he engineered a moment for

them to be alone, she'd discard her false pretenses and welcome his barbaric touch.

They all welcomed his barbaric touch. They swooned with orgasmic delight at the thought of bedding a primitive barbarian. None of them imagined it wasn't simply their bodies he coveted. None of them guessed it was the information he gleaned from their arrogant husbands that truly interested him.

Yet Antonia wasn't with her husband. The thought hammered through his mind, mocking his previous thoughts. And illuminating the reason why her presence so enraged his senses.

He wanted her. But he could learn nothing of use from fraternizing with her. Like all her contemporaries that he'd met, she might be frustrated, bored and eager for an illicit liaison despite how she attempted to hide her true feelings. But with all the others, while he'd never felt the need to decline their advances, he'd never experienced the urge to initiate such an encounter.

Yet he could think of little else when it came to Antonia.

"I suggest nothing, Carys." His voice was harsher than he intended. Gods. He might not care that Carys knew he desired the little Roman, but he certainly didn't want her guessing just how badly he wanted her. "If my words have offended Lady Antonia then I trust she will accept my apologies."

"Apologies are unnecessary." Antonia smoothed the white material of her long gown, her lashes lowered so he could no longer see her ice-blue eyes. "I'm not easily offended. Life in Rome is not for the faint of heart."

It was the second time she'd referred to Rome in less than glowing terms. Every other Roman woman he'd met had bemoaned the fact they'd been torn from the civilized center of the world and thrust into a primitive province on the edge of the empire. Shortly afterward, he impaled them, and they forgot their discontent as they gasped with delight at the pleasures available from willing natives.

Carys pounced on Antonia's comment and began to ask her questions about Rome. Gawain gritted his teeth and held his tongue. Carys cared nothing for Rome or its people. All she cared about was that her beloved husband and child and her goddess, Cerridwen, survived and prospered, and for that Carys would do whatever she had to. Even if she had to embrace the enemy in the corrupt heart of its empire.

He realized he was staring at Antonia's profile. She sat on the stone bench like a goddess in the flesh, the graceful folds of her gown enhancing the curves of her body in a sensual caress. Her cursedly provocative ringlet brushed her shoulder as she inclined her head at Carys, and a pale blush stained her aristocratic cheeks as though she were fully aware of his intense scrutiny.

She was beautiful, pampered and nothing like the kind of women he preferred. Did she even possess the knowledge of how to wield a bow, never mind the strength required to use one? He doubted she had the first idea how to use a dagger except as an implement to spear her food. Yet he couldn't drag his mesmerized gaze from her.

It made no sense. Except for the ethereal quality of her beauty, she was the same as every other Roman woman he'd had since he'd left the sacred Druid Isle of Mon.

None of them were warriors. None of them were capable of defending themselves against attack. Not once had he been unable to tear his gaze from any of them. He could scarcely even remember the last time white hot lust had seared his veins and the primal need to rut like a savage had thundered through his senses.

But this elegant creature, in her foreign gown and jewelry, bewitched him. Was it because she tried so hard to deny her desire? That had never affected him before. If a Roman woman was faithful to her husband, he'd never felt the urge to change her mind.

He had no idea of Antonia's marital status. He cared nothing for her marital status. But he would discover the game she played, and she would learn that he followed no rules but his own.

CHAPTER THREE

*A*ntonia forced herself to concentrate on Carys and her animated conversation. But every nerve quivered with acute awareness that the glowering Cambrian continued to direct his entire attention her way.

She wouldn't look at him. Let him imagine he could intimidate her with his pointed remarks and disdainful glances. If he wanted to direct his hatred of her people onto her, there was little she could do about it.

But she certainly wouldn't give him the satisfaction of realizing just how deeply his disregard affected her.

It's only lust. The shocking refrain wouldn't be silenced, no matter how desperately she tried. She, whose stomach heaved at the thought of submitting to another man ever again, found his brutal demeanor inexplicably alluring. And the Cambrian, despite his obvious distaste for all of Rome, appeared unable to stop looking at her.

Carys raised her eyebrows enquiringly and heat flooded Antonia's face as she realized the other woman had asked a question. *What were we talking about?*

"My lady." A feminine voice sounded from across the courtyard and Antonia breathed a silent sigh of relief at her reprieve, barely registering the odd way the slave addressed her mistress. "I'm sorry to disturb, but Branwen requests your presence."

"Oh." Carys leaned closer to Antonia in an intimate manner. "Branwen looks after my daughter. Forgive me. I won't be long." She stood up and Antonia focused on her fingers, clenched in her lap, and battled to keep the anguish that threatened to over spill her heart locked deep within her breast.

Her father hadn't mentioned that the tribune and his wife had a daughter. But why would he? A daughter was of no account in the wider Roman world, no matter that her own father had always showered her with genuine devotion.

And besides, her father was blessedly unaware that for one brief, glorious moment a year ago he had possessed a perfect granddaughter.

Buried injustice and raw grief stirred, no matter how hard she tried to keep her emotions contained. He would always be linked to her beloved daughter, even though he would never learn of her existence.

"Does your husband plan on joining you in Britain, Lady Antonia?"

Her chest constricted and the pain tangled with the ache engulfing her heart. The Cambrian stood by her side, unheeding of any pretense of propriety, and she didn't dare look up at him in case he saw the darkness in her soul.

"I believe that to be unlikely." Her voice was cool. She had learned to hide her feelings well during the interminable years of her marriage. She supposed she should admit that she was divorced and no longer belonged to Scipio, but it was none of the Cambrian's concern. "He's devoted to furthering his career in the Senate."

"At the expense of allowing his exquisite wife to travel unchaperoned?" There was a hint of mockery in his tone, and she couldn't help but glance his way. His legs were alarmingly close to her and for one heart-stopping moment, her gaze stalled on the unmistakable proof of his arousal.

Goddess.

She hastily looked away and caught sight of the slave girl who had brought Carys the message standing some distance off, beyond the fountain. A poor chaperone indeed. Yet somehow, the knowledge that she was all but alone with this tough Cambrian warrior didn't terrify her as she knew it should.

No. It didn't terrify her. But her heart thudded erratically in her breast, and she found it hard to draw breath. The heat from his body reached out to her and caressed her naked arms. A foolish thing to imagine and yet why else was her skin prickling in awareness? Why else did fire smolder her blood and cause her face to burn?

"I was adequately chaperoned on the journey to Britannia. And I'm safe enough under the protection of my father."

From the corner of her eye she watched as Gawain—*the Cambrian*—crouched by her side. He appeared determined to unnerve her. She refused to look him in the eye and focused on a nearby column with feigned fascination.

"Your father isn't here now, my lady." Was that amusement in his voice? She forgot about keeping her distance and turned to him. His smile faltered for a moment as though something in her expression shocked him, although she couldn't think what.

"Do you mean to threaten me with violence now my hostess is gone?" Perhaps she'd learned to hide her feelings, but something about this barbarian made it impossible for her to hold her tongue, the way a gently born Roman woman should. Hadn't her former husband told her that a thousand times in the early days of their marriage? And hadn't he then qualified his words by reminding her of her inferior heritage?

"Do you find my presence threatening, Lady Antonia?" The hint of mockery was back in his voice as though he didn't care if she found his attentions a threat. But the oddest thing of all was that, deep in her soul, she didn't fear that this Cambrian warrior would raise a hand in violence against her.

It didn't make sense. She could see his powerful biceps straining against his shirt and his physique put Scipio's to shame. And yet she had never felt this certain of her safety when in the presence of her former husband.

"Should I?" The question escaped before she could prevent it. Once again she watched, fascinated, as Gawain's eyes darkened and this time she made no effort to correct her errant thought.

His name was Gawain. She could call him that in her mind if she wished. No one would ever know.

"I would hope not." His voice was low, his accent enchanting, and an illicit quiver fluttered through her sensitized cleft. *Juno.* How could the mere sound of his voice do such a thing?

"Your suppositions are unfounded." She sounded breathless and there was nothing she could do about it. His dark eyes captivated her, and she couldn't tear her gaze away. "I do not fear you, Cambrian."

Once again he smiled, but this time it was a smile of masculine satisfaction without a trace of his former mockery. Strange little darts of desire attacked low, between her thighs, and disbelief spiked through her as decadent warmth slid sensuously through her damp channel.

Desperately she tried to concentrate on their conversation and not the exquisite sensations cascading through her breast and belly. But the man before her was the cause, and she couldn't look away.

"I have no wish for you to fear me, Antonia." She scarcely registered his lack of deference for her rank as the tip of his finger traced over her wrist. "I would never hurt you." His finger trailed along the back of her hand, perilously close to where her fingers clutched her gown on her lap.

Paralyzed, she stared at him. Did he know the effect he had on her? It was a mortifying thought. She struggled to regain control of her senses, the use of her voice. And only then did the scandalous impropriety of his touch finally occur to her.

She should pull her hand away. Stand up. Put distance between them. He might be kin of her hostess, but he had no right to touch her so. No right to cause such shocking sensations to ricochet through her body with little more than a smoldering glance.

But the shameful truth was, she enjoyed his touch. Even if all it comprised was the tip of one finger tracing across her knuckles. Where, earlier, his lips had also caressed.

Her lips parted, an involuntary response to her parched lungs. Was this how her former friends had felt when they first encountered a future lover? Could she have been tempted, as a young bride back in Rome, if Gawain had sought her out?

"I cannot fathom why you feel the need to tell me such a thing." She pulled her hand free and resisted the temptation to wrap her arms around her waist in a forlorn gesture of self-comfort. It had taken less than a year of marriage for her to recoil from the thought of enduring more sex from a strange man than she had already suffered from her insatiable husband. "Why should I imagine you might wish to hurt me? You don't even know me."

He leaned closer and a heady essence of wild forests and dangerous passion mingled with the undeniable scent of raw, masculine arousal. He was so close she could see amber flecks in his dark eyes, and the sight transfixed her.

"Not yet." His provocative whisper weaved through her mind, his meaning unclear. *Not yet?* The intensity of his gaze seared her and through the erratic pounding that distorted her reason, she finally grasped his intention.

Instead of outrage at his presumption, a flicker of excitement danced through her breast. It was insane that this virtual stranger could make her forget the indignities of her marriage bed so easily. But even as she knew she would never succumb to the desire that smoldered through her blood, she acknowledged its heady intoxication.

Perhaps, if circumstances were different, she might have forsaken her good sense and indulged in an illicit liaison with this Cambrian warrior. Perhaps, in his arms, she might finally lay to rest the unending nightmare of Scipio's demands.

How terrifyingly seductive.

"You presume greatly." She tore her gaze from his and once again focused, unseeing, on the nearby marble column. That Gawain was practiced in the arts of seduction was clear. That he considered her simply another Roman noblewoman to conquer was also, unfortunately, quite obvious.

She was too old and world weary to fall for his spurious, honeyed words. But still, knowing all this, she couldn't deny how much she enjoyed his undivided attention.

"Would you have me presume otherwise?" Deprived of her hand, his finger trailed a sensuous path along her forearm, and she fought the instinctive need to shiver in response. Was he so determined to have her?

Another thought wormed into her mind. If she wasn't so afraid of Gawain thinking her as incapable in bed as Scipio had often accused her, would she be so adamant in her refusal to verbally acknowledge his unspoken invitation?

The truth stung. She would finish this masquerade now and for all time. After all, she wasn't a neglected Roman matron seeking a thrilling diversion to pass the idle hours. She was, as much as she ever could be, free to make her own path in life. And that life did not include a lover, no matter how tempted she might be.

She turned to him, haughty words of dismissal ready on her tongue. And instead she was captivated by his long, dark blond hair that was so unlike any Roman man she had ever encountered.

His face was bronzed from the sun, and she guessed he was only a few years older than her. There was a predatory gleam in his eyes and an aura of triumph in the half-smile on his lips, as though he believed her surrender was both inevitable and imminent. His pagan earring, with its indecipherable engravings, sent a delicious, dangerous quiver along her spine, reminding her of just how different their worlds were.

Her good intentions wavered, and indecision simmered as hedonistic possibilities thudded through her mind. Did she dare embark on a fleeting affair? A brief interlude of passion before the next stage of her life began?

Gawain watched as Antonia's ice-blue eyes darkened with desire. She hadn't encouraged his advances in the manner he'd imagined but her continued aloofness had, inexplicably, only increased his determination to have her begging for his touch.

Except, far from waiting until she came to him, he'd been unable to keep away from her. Even now, his finger continued to caress her silky-smooth skin and it took more willpower than he cared to admit not to pull her to her feet and into his arms. And shatter that icy, patrician reserve she wrapped around her like a cloak.

It appeared she had no intention of answering his last question. Not that he wanted scintillating conversation with her. But Carys wouldn't leave her guest alone for long and he intended to ensure plans for an assignation with this beautiful Roman were in place before she returned.

"Antonia." He'd never initiated a clandestine meeting with a Roman woman before, but if that was what Antonia wanted then he was willing to unbend that far. She tilted her head, and he was momentarily distracted by her perfect ringlet brushing against her slender throat. He'd enjoy plunging his fingers through her immaculately styled hair, creating disarray where rigid order reigned supreme.

"Antonia." He said her name again, although he couldn't imagine why, and the foreign syllables caressed his tongue, his voice husky as vivid images of her pale golden hair, loosened from its torturous confines, cascaded over her naked breasts, blazed through his mind.

Her tempting pink lips parted, her breath erratic, and her silk-swathed breasts tested his self-control to his outer limits.

"How thoughtful of you to entertain my guest in my absence, Gawain." Carys' voice jarred his brain, and he watched Antonia blink in apparent horror that they had been caught in such an intimate encounter. She should be thankful he hadn't been in the midst of ravishing her lips when Carys returned. Another moment and he wasn't certain he could have resisted.

The realization that he might have succumbed to Antonia's charms without her lifting a finger to encourage him did nothing to dampen his cursed lust, but it did manage to blacken his mood. He stood, folded his arms, and then saw Antonia blanch as she caught sight of Carys' daughter.

An odd reaction. Did she imagine Carys would hand the babe to her and her pristine gown would become soiled?

"Antonia, this is my daughter. She's suffering with her baby teeth." Carys, besotted with her little princess, appeared unaware of Antonia's discomfort. For the first time Gawain wondered if she had any children of her own. Not that it made any difference to him. He wasn't interested in discovering the details of her life. He was only interested in possessing her body.

"How's my favorite girl?" He stroked the baby's soft cheek, and her smile of delight warmed his heart, as her smile always warmed his heart. It was ironic that the child of a Roman tribune had been the means of reminding him, three moons ago when he had first entered Camulodunon, that he still possessed a heart at all.

"She is very beautiful." Antonia's words sounded perfunctory, but he caught a strangely haunted look in her eyes. It reminded him of the look he'd seen earlier when she'd turned to him. He'd been taken aback, considering the bantering nature of their conversation, but it had vanished within a moment, and he'd almost forgotten about it.

"Yes," Carys said as she rubbed noses with her child. "The goddess has truly blessed my little Nia."

"Nia?" Antonia sounded confused and Gawain told himself he hadn't noticed the enchanting way she said the name. "Forgive me. Isn't her name Valera?"

"Nia is an ancient Celtic name." He offered her a mirthless grin when she looked his way. And his godsdamned erection, which had barely diminished since Carys had returned, hardened farther at the sight of Antonia's bemused expression. "*She* will not be kept in ignorance of her dual heritage."

He couldn't fathom why he threw that in Antonia's face. She was scarcely responsible for how the old ways were being insidiously eroded by the relentless spread of her empire. But she was responsible for his discomfort and although that was his problem, he was still irked by the fact she appeared utterly unaffected by the lust that steamed between them.

Except when he touched her. She was far from unaffected *then*.

Carys gave an impatient sigh and even though he didn't bother to glance her way, he knew she was giving him yet another pointed glare.

"You are correct, Antonia," Carys said. "Her Roman name is Valera after my husband, but we call her Nia Druantia, after my mother and her grandmother's sister."

"You named your daughter after your mother?" Antonia's eyes widened in clear disbelief. It was obvious such a notion had never crossed her mind before and Gawain smothered an impatient curse. Did no Roman woman possess the imagination to do such a thing? He disregarded the knowledge that no Roman woman possessed the right to do such a thing in the first place.

"Yes." There was a hint of defiance in Carys' voice that he'd come to recognize when she felt threatened. But how could she feel threatened by a woman such as Antonia? He understood Carys' need for circumspection when she accompanied her tribune into his social sphere. After all, like Gawain she was a Druid and if their secret was discovered crucifixion loomed on their horizon.

It was the reason he took extra care in his undercover activities. While he might not be concerned on his own behalf, he would rather cut his own throat than allow a shadow of suspicion to fall upon little Nia and her mother through their association with him.

"I very much fear," Antonia said, and once again she looked perfectly poised and as remote as one of the heathen Roman goddesses, "Rome is not as enlightened in such matters as your esteemed husband appears to be."

He couldn't help himself. "Rome could learn a great deal from the customs of its far-flung primitive provinces."

"I'm sure she could." Although he towered over her, somehow she managed to look down her aristocratic nose at him. He discovered the experience both irritated and aroused in equal measure. "Whether she wishes to is another matter entirely."

Her response silenced the caustic rejoinder burning his throat. He'd expected her to defend her cursed city, but why had he thought that? He already knew she didn't appear to mourn the loss of its glittering lifestyle.

Carys took instant advantage of his lack of response by handing Nia to Branwen, who had accompanied her into the courtyard, before sitting beside Antonia and engaging her in Rome-inspired conversation.

There were a multitude of tasks he needed to undertake. There was no reason for him to remain, listening to idle chitchat about a city he had no intention of ever setting foot in. The realization that he had no idea whether Antonia planned to follow through on their attraction gnawed his guts. But worse than that was the knowledge that if she didn't, he most certainly did not intend to let the matter rest.

CHAPTER FOUR

"*I* don't know what you think you were doing, baiting Antonia in that fashion." Carys gave him a regal glare after her husband and the merchant had finished their business and she returned from bidding her guests farewell. Branwen had taken Nia with her, and they were alone in the courtyard. "She's not a Roman whore you can bed simply because the urge takes you."

He shrugged and prowled the length of the courtyard garden. It wasn't as regimented as the other Roman courtyards he'd encountered in Britain, but it was far too confined for his tastes.

"You only met the woman this day, Carys. You have no idea what she's really like." Except Carys wasn't the only one who'd made such a swift assumption. Despite his low opinion of all things Roman, its women included, he was unable to level such an accusation at Antonia.

"I know a great deal more than you might imagine." She sounded the way she had back in Cymru, in the days before the Romans had invaded and all their lives had been turned inside out. "Cerridwen foretold Antonia's arrival long before the merchant informed Maximus of his daughter's plans. I won't have you using her as you might any other Roman woman. Do you understand?"

For a brief moment, a flare of dark longing seared his chest. Even after everything that had happened since the Romans had invaded, Carys was as intimate with Cerridwen as she had ever been.

Yet from the moment he'd left the sacred Isle of Mon and taken up with the rebels, his own god, Lugus, had been distant and unheeding of Gawain's worship. Not once had the great god given any indication that Gawain was traveling the right path.

But in time of war what other path could a warrior follow?

He pushed his unease to the back of his mind, leaned his forearm against a column and flung Carys a sardonic grin.

"I understand, princess. But Cerridwen doesn't dictate earthly pleasure. And I intend to use the Roman in any way I desire. Don't fool yourself that she's uninterested. Her arousal scented the air in a most intoxicating manner."

Carys frowned. Obviously, that fact had entirely eluded her. Then she shook her head, as if dislodging displeasing thoughts and pressed her hand against his chest.

"Dear Gawain." Her voice no longer held her previous note of exasperation. "I don't want to see you hurt again, that's all. Antonia is not for you. Please, don't get involved."

He laughed and threaded his fingers through hers. "Why do you imagine taking the Roman will hurt me? It's only sex I seek with her. Nothing of any importance. Within a turn of the moon or less she'll no longer be even a memory."

"Perhaps." Carys didn't sound convinced. He couldn't for the life of him fathom why she thought Antonia possessed the power to hurt him. No woman possessed that power. Not anymore. "But there's a reason Cerridwen revealed Antonia's existence to me, Gawain. And it certainly has nothing to do with her father's wish that I find her another suitable husband."

His amusement vanished. "Another suitable husband? How

many husbands do Roman noblewomen possess at any one time?"

Carys pulled free of his hold and shot him a look that suggested she thought he was being deliberately obtuse.

"The reason she left Rome," she said, as she began to pull the jeweled pins from her hair to loosen it from the constrictive Roman style, "is because her husband divorced her."

Why hadn't Antonia told him she was divorced? She'd deliberately let him believe she was still married. Why would she do that?

"All the more reason," he said, unsure why the fact Antonia hadn't confided in him irked him so much, "for me to sample her charms before she's auctioned off to another arse-licking patrician."

"If I have anything to do with it her next husband will not be an arse-licking *anything*."

He knew that was Carys' attempt to make him laugh, but he was too irritated. It was bad enough he lusted after Antonia in the first place. But to still want her, after knowing she'd deliberately deceived him as to her marital status, was just plain infuriating.

To compound it all, he couldn't fathom why the knowledge even gave him pause. It didn't matter. It wasn't her trust he wanted. Just her shrieks of fulfillment as he made her his.

And by the gods, he intended to quench this fire that raged through his blood no matter how Carys might disapprove. Antonia would part her thighs, he would have her, and then she would be relegated to the back of his mind where all his conquests languished.

"Now, Gawain." Carys' mood became eager. "Did you reach Mon? Did you speak with my mother about leaving the sacred Isle?"

He dragged his attention back to the present. "She's still determined not to leave until she can persuade all the Elders to agree to a mass exodus." After the Druids had fled Cymru, almost two full turns of the wheel ago, they had sought refuge on the sacred Isle. But he hadn't stayed long. He couldn't stand the thought of hiding from their enemies yet again and so he'd left to join the rebellion led by the Briton king, Caratacus.

And look what a bloodied mess that had turned out to be.

Lugus hadn't graced Gawain with his presence at any time during the rebellion or the bloodied aftermath. Yet what was he supposed to do? Remain on a secluded Isle while their people continued to suffer?

That was not the way of Lugus, the finder of paths and seeker of truth. It was not Gawain's way either. Yet he couldn't shift the knot of doubt lodged in his chest that his god not only disapproved of Gawain's actions but had also turned his back on his loyal Druid.

Not that Gawain blamed Carys' mother for her reluctance to leave the safety of the Isle. He knew that wasn't her primary motive for staying. She wanted to ensure the continuance of their Druidic way of life. It was the reason she hadn't left with him to join Caratacus. What had she told him? She didn't want a foreign king to unwittingly lead her people into a Roman-conspired trap.

Her foresight, in retrospect, was chilling. And reinforced the unsettling suspicion that Lugus truly had severed all sacred bonds with Gawain. Otherwise, why hadn't his god warned him of the treachery that laid in wait for the king?

It had been from that moment that he'd finally stopped trying to reach Lugus. When the time was right, his god would return.

Surely he would return.

Carys stared at him in disbelief. "But you told her of my vision? That Britain will burn and the Isle of Mon—it isn't safe, Gawain. I don't know why I feel that so strongly but surely she understands she can't stay there?"

"She understands, Carys." He took her hands. "She will leave,

I'm sure of it. But for now, she feels her place is to ensure as many of our people survive the Roman onslaught as possible."

Carys snatched her hands free. "Her place is *here*, with her daughter and granddaughter. How will our ways survive if all our Elders perish when the Isle falls?"

Gawain was silent. How could he comfort her when in his heart, where hope had long since died, he believed that their way of life was already ultimately condemned?

When Antonia arrived back at the townhouse, a grand establishment her father had commissioned in the most prestigious district of Camulodunum, it was a relief to escape to her bedchamber. Her father's incessant questions about the tribune's foreign wife on the journey home had forced her to face the fact that it wasn't Carys or what an advantageous friendship they might cultivate that occupied her thoughts at all.

Not that she had ever deluded herself for a moment that it was. Gawain's mocking smile and incendiary touch left little room for anything else in her mind.

She went to the window and looked out into the central courtyard. It was smaller than the tribune's, but meticulously tended as all Roman courtyards should be. But it wasn't the decorative statuary or exotic plants and flowers that captured her attention. It was the incongruous vision of Gawain in her father's domain, welcomed as an equal.

A foolish thought. Her father would never welcome a savage Cambrian warrior into his home, unless that warrior could be of use to him. And she certainly couldn't imagine any reason why Gawain would want to set foot inside a Roman merchant's dwelling, no matter how well-respected the merchant might be.

"Is anything troubling you, domina?"

Antonia glanced at her faithful slave, Elpis. They had always been close, but it was only during the last year Antonia had realized that, in truth, Elpis was more of a friend than any of the refined Roman ladies she'd met since her marriage to Scipio.

"No." Her fingers curled around the precious golden locket her father had given her to celebrate the day of her birth. A bittersweet celebration, since it was also the day her mother had died. Slowly she opened the locket. The likeness of her mother was painted on one half and on the other she'd illicitly commissioned the baby perfection of her daughter to be painted over her own portrait.

Her beautiful baby. The only child her womb had nurtured to term, the only one of the five she had conceived who had survived for longer than a few tortured breaths.

She swallowed, and traced a trembling finger across the perfect features. Her sweet Cassia Antonia, named not for her brutal husband but for her own mother and father. A small act of rebellion that had sustained her for the fraught hours after the debilitating birth, but a rebellion that paled into insignificance at what she had done next.

"You'll soon be reunited," Elpis whispered, her hand lightly covering Antonia's in a gesture that a friend might make, not a slave no matter how highly esteemed that slave might be. "A few more weeks, domina, and she will once again be in your arms."

A few more weeks, and she would be able to see Cassia whenever she wished. No more furtive journeys, avoiding Scipio's fawning dependents who would betray her without a second thought, to spend a few stolen moments with her baby.

Scipio believed their daughter was dead. He would never know the truth. And because of Antonia's lies, Cassia would enjoy a life away from Rome, away from her birthright, but a life filled with love and her mother's utter devotion.

Even if Cassia would never know that her adoptive mother

was, in truth, her birth mother. For if Scipio ever discovered her deception, she feared his rigid pride would never allow such devious disregard of his wishes to go unpunished.

When Cassia arrived, Antonia intended to devote her life to her precious child. She would never jeopardize her daughter's happiness by taking a second husband who might resent another man's child. And she would have no time for a lover.

But Cassia was not in Britannia yet. And the unsettling lust that had consumed Antonia while in Gawain's company still seethed through her blood. If she truly wished to sample sex with another man then now was the perfect, *the only*, chance she would ever have.

She looked at Elpis. They had been inseparable since the day her father had presented the young Greek girl to her on the eighth anniversary of her birth. Her very own slave, barely a year older than her, yet even then the bonds of friendship had somehow woven through the constraints of rank and heritage.

Elpis had been the one who'd comforted her when Antonia had suffered from terrifying nightmares of darkness and confusion, and the unshakeable certainty that her destiny balanced on a fragile thread. Elpis who had interpreted the mysterious feminine presence protecting Antonia as the great goddess Juno.

Elpis who had reassured both Antonia and her father that the unknown words she whispered while deep in the throes of sleep came directly from the queen of Olympus herself.

It had taken her too long to recognize the truth of their close relationship. She knew, in her heart, she should free Elpis but how could she bear it if the other woman left?

She pushed the thought aside. She needed Elpis and too much had happened over the last year for her to willingly seek any more disruption to her life.

So why in the name of Juno was she seriously contemplating taking Gawain as her lover?

"It cannot come quickly enough." She longed to once again hold Cassia in her arms. Was it very wrong of her to also want Gawain's strong arms about her? Just to experience the kind of sex she could give freely, without the demands of Rome chaining her to the bed?

"All will be well when she's once again with us," Elpis said. "But what else troubles you, domina?"

Elpis was too observant. What chance did Antonia have of hiding her plans from her? She didn't even want to. Elpis, after all, was her closest confidante and would sooner cut out her own tongue than betray Antonia.

She closed her locket and took Elpis' hands. "Do you still have the forbidden herbs?"

Elpis' eyes widened. It was obvious Antonia's question took her completely by surprise. For years, she'd encouraged Antonia to take the magical concoctions that would prevent conception. And Antonia had refused, until after the birth of Cassia.

Not that she had needed them, then. Scipio hadn't come near her since that blood-drenched night. But she had continued to take them, right up until the day she boarded the ship bound for Britannia. Nothing, not even the wrath of the gods, would have induced her to risk Scipio impregnating her once again.

"I brought them with us. And I'm certain I can find more in the markets if needed."

Antonia took a deep breath. If she had decided to step foot on this path, then she would make the necessary preparations before her doubts overtook her.

"I shall start taking them this day."

"Domina?" There was an unmistakable edge of concern in Elpis' voice, reflected on her face. "Did something happen to you that the dominus is unaware of?"

"No." Antonia could feel her face heating and she turned away from Elpis' penetrating gaze. "I wasn't attacked. But even though

I'll never marry again, I don't want Scipio to have been the only man I've ever known." She risked glancing over her shoulder. Reluctant understanding glowed in Elpis' eyes. "There was a Cambrian warrior, kin of the tribune's wife, who showed inter-est. I believe I will take him up on his unspoken offer."

CHAPTER FIVE

*G*awain leaned with studied nonchalance against a stone wall adjacent to the main market—the forum, the Romans called it—and glanced at his companion. The man was a close confidant of the Iceni king but Gawain had learned nothing from him that he didn't already know.

Although other Briton chieftains periodically rose up against their Roman invaders, the Iceni were content to be a client kingdom, a puppet of the foreign emperor. Before the Caratacus rebellion last summer, he would have railed against the Icenis stand, berating them for cowardice. But after the bloodied betrayal and his near escape from death from those who had pledged allegiance to Caratacus, the Iceni king's oath of fealty to Rome barely stirred an ember of anger in his chest.

There would be no large-scale revolt in this corner of Britain, despite how poorly the town was fortified. At least, not yet. Who knew how allegiances might change in the future?

At least the Iceni king didn't attempt to deceive anyone about where his loyalty lay.

"Life under Rome can be good," the man said. "My liege sees

no reason to jeopardize his relations with the emperor for no good reason."

Gawain could name a dozen good reasons without even thinking about it, but there was no point. Unlike those who rebelled, the client kings retained their lands and an illusion of power. Not for the first time, he questioned his actions in coming to Camulodunon after the fall of Caratacus, instead of returning to Cymru and continuing the battle.

But he knew why. If Caratacus with his army of warriors and Druids and a magical enclave that had hidden their whereabouts from the enemy hadn't been enough to defeat the Legions, how could small bands of untrained and poorly armed rebels hope to make a difference?

He'd hoped the Britons might be stirred to insurrection. Where better to hit the enemy than in this newly constructed capital? With their greater numbers, they might stand a chance against the Legions. But so far, the reality had fallen far short of his expectations.

And then, of course, he'd discovered Carys and her tribune were stationed here. How could he stir up a full-scale rebellion, even if such a feat was possible, when it would put her and Nia in danger?

His meeting with this man today was for no other reason than to gather information he might be able to use in the future.

A flash of a blue cloak in the milling crowd caught his attention and unthinking he turned. For a moment, the blue vanished but then reappeared and a jolt slammed through his chest.

Antonia.

Irritation spiked that such a fleeting glimpse of her recalled all the reasons why she haunted his nighttime fantasies. He didn't want reminding. The last thing he needed was her beautiful face, ice-blue eyes and pale golden hair invading his dreams.

He barely registered the other man's farewell. His attention was fixed on Antonia as she weaved her way through the crowd. In the three days since they'd met, he'd made no effort to contact her. He had attempted to convince his rampaging lust that he'd only found her so irresistible because it had been more than two moons since he'd last had a woman.

As he stared, riveted, at her elegant profile as she admired silken frivolities at a stall, he acknowledged the truth.

He still wanted her. And doubtless his desire-fueled nightly visions would continue until he'd sampled the real thing.

Without warning, she looked up from the ribbons in her hand and unerringly caught his gaze. She didn't appear surprised or startled at either his presence or his direct stare. Had she been aware of him before she'd deigned to acknowledge him?

He pushed himself from the wall and sauntered over to her. She didn't turn away, didn't attempt to break eye contact or disappear into the bustling crowd. She merely stood there, waiting for him.

Anticipation thrummed through his veins. She might not have arranged for an illicit assignation as his other Roman conquests had. But her surrender smoldered in the air, enhanced by the foreign spices and exotic delicacies on offer at neighboring stalls.

"Lady Antonia." He didn't offer her his hand. He knew she would never accept his kiss of greeting. At least, not in public. Instead he gave a half bow, unable to keep the smile of satisfaction from his lips. "I trust the day finds you well."

She inclined her head, a familiar gesture he recalled from their conversation at Carys'.

"Thank you." Her voice was as cool as he remembered and just as enchanting. For a moment he thought she intended to say more, but instead she dropped the ribbons she'd been holding back onto the stall.

He waited, but she appeared fascinated by a collection of glittering, colored beads displayed in a woven basket. Was she waiting for him to make the next move? If she'd changed her mind then surely she wouldn't still be standing here beside him, looking so remote and untouchable?

"Would you care for some company?" Gods, the stilted words all but choked him. If she were a Celt, he could come right out and say what he meant. But that hadn't stopped him with the other Romans he'd laid. They'd been superficially shocked by his blunt, barbarous manner but also delighted. So why, with Antonia, did he feel this odd need to coat his base intentions with honeyed words?

He'd not felt so restricted the other day. But when they'd conversed before, they hadn't been in the middle of a busy marketplace.

She gave him a lingering sideways glance. "Perhaps."

A delicate blush highlighted her cheeks, giving her an irresistible air of seductive innocence. It took him a moment to drag his mesmerized thoughts from such a laughable illusion. Antonia might be a seductress, but she was no innocent. He wasn't interested in innocence. And he couldn't fathom why such a thought had drifted across his mind in the first place.

Antonia was playing a game. She might have played it countless times in the past with various lovers. He had no objection. Not when the outcome remained the same.

"Do you often visit the markets?" He glanced at Antonia's companion, a young woman who, although doubtless a slave, didn't instantly drop her gaze to the ground when he caught her eye. Instead, she appeared to be scrutinizing him in a way he couldn't fathom.

He acknowledged her with a smile before returning his attention to Antonia who was now once again looking his way. If she made a habit of visiting the market it would be an easy matter to secure a room somewhere nearby for their mutual pleasure.

"Rarely," she said, demolishing that idea. "My father is convinced danger lurks for me on every corner."

"And what do you think? Does danger lurk for you at every corner?" Even as he spoke, he knew the answer. She was too fragile to defend herself against any form of attack. That was why she would never be allowed to wander the markets without her slave and, he was certain, a guarded litter to escort her through the streets.

But there were ways around such obstacles.

"Oh." A smile tugged at her lips. "Not *every* corner."

He laughed, surprising himself, but her response had been slightly deprecating and unexpectedly amusing. An intriguing combination for a Roman noblewoman.

"Do not fear. My sword is at your disposal."

She didn't simper or gasp in mock outrage at his words. Her smile deepened and with an odd sense of disbelief, he realized she read no sexual implication in his comment at all.

"I trust you'll never need to use it on my account."

Her words confirmed his suspicion. Unless this, also, was part of her seduction routine?

He leaned closer, enough to give them an illusion of privacy but not close enough to cause heads to turn.

"I look forward to nothing more than using it on your account, my lady."

A blush suffused her cheeks and he stared at her, transfixed. Anyone would imagine she was an untouched virgin, unused to such banter. Yet he knew that, despite their outward show of modesty, in private Roman matrons could be as earthy in matters of sex as his own countrywomen.

Unless Antonia truly was a virgin? Unease slid through his mind. He couldn't imagine why any husband would leave a woman as desirable as Antonia a maiden. Or was this the reason for her divorce? Because her husband had no interest in women?

"In that case, I have no objection to encountering your... weapon." Her whisper was so low he had to lean in closer to catch every word. Her elusive scent of woodland flowers teased his senses, stirred his blood, and made a mockery of his vow to withdraw. Her eyes no longer reminded him of winter's ice. They smoldered like a scorching summer sky. Virgin or not, he wanted her.

Relief seared through him. Antonia was good, he gave her that. For a moment he'd fallen for her façade of innocence.

"Then we should make haste with our introductions." He couldn't help but laugh aloud, both at his outrageous words and the look of bewitchment on Antonia's face. He knew she likely practiced that enchanting expression a dozen times a day to snare her lovers. It didn't matter. He had no intention of becoming ensnared but saw no reason not to enjoy her entertaining performance. "My weapon is primed to defend your honor."

Her eyes widened seductively before she lowered her gaze, her long lashes several shades darker than her elaborately styled hair. Her lush pink lips parted, and the tip of her tongue pressed against her teeth, and he fought the urge to fling caution to the winds and capture her provocative mouth.

She played her part to perfection. But he was disciplined and had no intention of losing control because of a Roman woman.

He watched her glance at her companion and was aware of the imperceptible message that flashed between them. Then Antonia clasped the other woman's hand.

"I'll meet you outside the temple shortly."

Satisfaction fueled his lust when her slave melted into the crowd, giving her mistress additional freedom.

Perhaps there would be no need to arrange another meeting. Perhaps Antonia intended to slake their mutual passion without further delay.

His cock thickened with renewed anticipation of possessing this Roman ice-maiden. And tonight the only dreams that plagued him would be of bloodied battlefields.

Antonia turned back to him. "I've been—" she began, but then

44

a great bear of a man stumbled into her, pushing her forward. Without thinking, Gawain wrapped his arm around her shoulders to steady her and pulled her against the safety of his body. For a fleeting moment, the seductive sensation of finest linen and softest wool molding her curves distracted him. Then instinct took over and his other hand whipped out in an unyielding fist and punched the drunken bastard in his face, sending him toppling onto the ground.

Even as his body responded to Antonia's erratic gasps against his throat and the erotic rise and fall of her breasts against his chest, he swiftly assessed the situation.

It was more than one solitary ale-sodden Briton who'd tripped over his own feet. A fight had broken out and was growing by the moment. He knew it would soon be stamped out by the legionaries and punishment administered. Once, in another life, he'd been the one restoring order to chaos. But since leaving Cymru he had, more often than not, helped instigate such disturbances in Roman strongholds. Small, insignificant rebellions but the inconvenience to the enemy had offered him fleeting satisfaction.

Had he been alone, he would likely have joined in the fray, but he couldn't leave Antonia unprotected.

He swung about, still gripping her against his body, and pushed his way through the now jeering and chanting crowd. He glanced down at her and saw the way she pressed her lips together, how she kept her arms wrapped around her waist and the trepidation in her eyes.

Instinctively, he tugged her even closer, even though they had now left the commotion behind and there was little chance of her being injured. How odd it felt to pull a woman to safety. Had he attempted to protect the woman he'd once loved in such a manner she would have laughed in his face, and then used her dagger to save them both.

As they hurried down a deserted alleyway, he waited for

contempt to weave through him at Antonia's inability to defend herself. But all he felt was an incomprehensible spike of heat deep in his chest, along with the strange compunction to keep on going until Camulodunon was far behind them both. Because only then could he truly keep Antonia safe from harm.

He halted and swung her around, so her back was against the rough stone wall. His last thought pounded in his mind, unwanted but not easily dismissed.

Antonia was not in danger. She'd been in little enough danger back in the market, but he'd seen an opportunity to get her alone and had instantly taken it. Why then did the insistent voice in the back of his mind urge him that this Roman patrician deserved more from him than a fleeting fuck?

She looked up at him, her eyes dark with need, and tendrils of pale gold hair that had escaped its prison curled around her flushed face. Raw lust stabbed low in his groin and his hands tightened around her hips.

"Gawain." Her voice was hushed, breathless, insanely arousing. Through the pounding in his head, he realized it was the first time she'd called him by his name. And his name on her lips sounded exotic, forbidden, even though she wasn't the first Roman woman to whisper his name in a Latin accent.

Beneath her cloak, he molded the flare of her hips, the curve of her waist and her uneven breath caressed his jaw with seductive promise.

"It seems Fate is on our side." His thumbs brushed the tantalizing swell of her breasts, and he forced his knee between her legs, parting her thighs. Curse her Roman gown for impeding his access. "I didn't imagine my sword would so swiftly be at your disposal."

Her hands flattened against his chest and her eyes never left his. "But what of—"

He didn't want to talk. Within moments, this interlude would shatter as the scuffle in the market was subdued and the onlookers dispersed. There wasn't time to take her in the way he craved. But there was plenty of time to taste, plenty of time to leave her as desperate for him as he was for her.

His mouth claimed hers. But as their lips touched the need to plunder, to conquer, to silence her words evaporated. Her mouth was open, but he didn't instantly invade. The exquisite sensation of her lips against his, so soft, so deceptively trusting, momentarily entranced him.

The tip of his tongue traced the seam of her lips and she trembled, her nails digging into his chest. She tasted of Rome, but there was something else that teased his senses, an elusive hint of summer rain in a distant forest.

Since leaving Cymru, he'd drunk Roman wine, used exotic aphrodisiacs from the East and inhaled sacred incenses. But nothing compared to the intoxicating taste of Antonia. He cupped her breasts through her gown, and she filled his palms with a hedonistic promise. Her breath hitched and he captured her gasp in his mouth, a sensuous whisper that caressed his flesh like nothing he had imagined before.

He moved in closer, pressing his body against her thigh and belly, his rigid shaft branding her through their clothing. How simple it would be to pull up her gown and thrust inside her wet slit. Yet he didn't invade with his tongue the way he imagined invading with his cock. Instead, he explored the tantalizing secrets of her parted lips, her smooth, even teeth an erotic barrier.

Yet no barrier at all. Her mouth was open, willing, and her hands slid from his chest to tangle in his hair. A groan razed his throat and one hand wrapped around her nape, the silk of her hair brushing his knuckles in a featherlight touch. Blood pounded against his temples, obliterating everything but Antonia's scent, her taste, her provocative touch. And then the tip of her tongue glided against his, an elusive caress he could scarcely feel. Yet white hot lightning seared his flesh and primal need arrowed through his chest.

He jerked back, panting. Her eyes were dark with lust, her breath as erratic as his. Her fingers still gripped his hair and her body meshed to his in excruciating abandonment.

If he'd taken her the moment they'd entered this alley, by now they would both be sated. But because of one cursed, illogical thought, he'd not followed through on his initial plan of a quick, mindless rut.

"Come with me." His voice was ragged against her lips, and he wound his arm around her waist while his other hand slid around her exposed throat. Her pulse fluttered like a trapped butterfly against his fingers, magnifying her vulnerability.

She attempted to speak, but the simple act appeared beyond her. He offered her a grim smile, his arousal making it hard to think logically, never mind convey his hammering thoughts.

"I'll find somewhere for us." It wouldn't be hard. There were plenty of rooms that were available for hire. For the right price. All Antonia needed to do was cover her face with her cloak. She would never be recognized.

Instead of complying, she remained rooted to the spot. "I cannot leave Elpis."

Elpis? "What?" He frowned at her as her hands dropped to his shoulders. She didn't try to pull away, but she wasn't making any move to go with him, either. Not that it would take any effort to simply sweep her up into his arms and march off with her. But he had no wish to draw unnecessary attention. Ruining her reputation was not something he craved.

"My slave, Elpis. I need to find her, to ensure she's unharmed." A thread of panic entered her voice and he stared at her in disbelief. Traces of arousal heated her face, her eyes were darker than usual and she clearly had trouble drawing breath into her lungs. And yet the first words out of her mouth were those of concern for her *slave*?

"You sent her to the temple." It took more willpower than he cared to admit not to ignore her words and ravish her lips the way he should have ravished her moments ago. "She was no longer in the market, Antonia."

Her hands slid from his shoulders and along his biceps in a slow caress. How could such a seemingly innocent touch cause his flesh to burn and balls to ache with tortured need? He'd been with plenty of women over the years. But one lingering caress from Antonia and his control threatened to shatter like that of a raw boy.

"I know." Her voice was breathless, seductive, and her fingers curled over his forearms. "But I cannot just leave her, Gawain, without knowing. And I didn't expect to... That you would wish to...." She didn't finish but gave him a tragic look with those beautiful eyes of hers, doubtless expecting him to fall at her feet and agree with her every whim. Was this how she treated all her lovers? Pushing them to the edge of their endurance, making them beg for her favors?

Once again, he swung her around and crushed her against the wall. This time he held her immobile with his body and cradled her face with his hands. She didn't scream, didn't try to escape. Just gazed up at him and for an eternal moment he forgot why he was mad at her.

Brutally he pulled his bewitched senses back together. "What didn't you expect?" He grazed her delicate skin with the pads of his thumbs and battled the urge to spear his fingers through her hair. "That I'd want to fuck you at the first possible opportunity?"

Beneath his palms, he felt her face heat. And despite himself, the notion that his coarse words had made her blush entranced him. How was it possible for her to manufacture such a response?

"That isn't what I meant." Her voice was soft, but he detected no tremble. "I thought you would wish to make suitable arrangements for a—an assignation."

He was suddenly aware that he had Antonia shoved up against a rough stone wall. That at any moment they might be discovered.

That he was behaving like the barbarian Rome accused his people of being.

He didn't care if she thought he was a barbarian. It was likely for that very reason she wanted him in her arms in the first place. And yet the realization that he was acting in such a manner irked him on a fundamental level he couldn't fathom.

Curse the gods, this woman made him think too damn much. All he wanted was to slake his lust. All she wanted was an illicit liaison before her father arranged another marriage for her. He was more than willing to oblige, but he had no intention of wasting his time playing an elaborate game of wooing and uttering meaningless, pretty words. If that's what she enjoyed, then she could find herself a sweet-tongued Roman with whom to pass her idle hours.

Even as the thought seared his brain, he knew the truth. He would likely give Antonia a measure of what she desired, if it ensured she would part her thighs. The knowledge infuriated him as much as it aroused him.

"Tell me something. Is it honeyed words you seek—or this?" He jammed his rigid length against her, fighting the need to rip her gown from her and take her where she stood. The image seared his mind and caused his blood to smolder with frustrated need. Why did he find it so hard to maintain his control with Antonia?

Her erratic breath fanned his face. It shouldn't affect him at all and yet every heated gasp stoked his lust with fiery torment.

"I have no need of honeyed words." Her uneven confession enflamed as much as if she'd grasped his cock in the palm of her hand. "Flattery means nothing to me. I only seek a—a momentary diversion with you."

His grin felt feral, but he couldn't prevent it as renewed desire pumped through his veins and gripped his vitals in a punishing embrace.

"Prove it." His mouth brushed hers, a fleeting kiss that burned his lips. "Tell your father Carys invited you to visit with her later this day. Meet me at the villa at the ninth hour and show me how much of a diversion you wish me to be."

CHAPTER SIX

*A*ntonia could still feel the imprint of Gawain's lips on hers as she entered her father's townhouse. Her face was warm, her skin tingling, and Juno help her, but if she felt this alive after just a touch how would she feel once Gawain had possessed her body?

"Domina." A slave approached and Antonia attempted to drag her errant thoughts back to the present. It was late morning and in less than four hours, she'd once again see Gawain. In the meantime, she needed to convince her father to allow her to visit the tribune's wife.

"Yes?" She gave the slave a distracted smile and hoped whatever query the woman had was easily resolved. She needed to bathe, to prepare her body and just as important, she needed to talk with Elpis as to the secrets involved in seducing a man. If left to her own devices, Gawain was sure to be disappointed.

Although she'd told Elpis of her assignation, there'd been no time to talk further. Antonia's father insisted she use a litter to and from the forum, and she could scarcely conduct such a scandalous conversation through the silken drapes while Elpis walked by her side.

"The dominus requests your presence in the atrium," the woman said. "The praetor wishes to extend his greetings to you."

The *praetor*? Why would such an important politician wish to greet *her*? She didn't believe for one moment he did. It was her father, hoping to introduce her to someone else who might be able to affect her entry once again into the elevated echelons of Roman society.

She took a calming breath as Elpis removed her palla and tidied her hair. Did she look half-ravished? She certainly felt it. But for her father's sake, she hoped she looked like the perfect, pure-minded daughter he deserved.

This perfunctory greeting wouldn't take long. There was plenty of time before she needed to leave. Plenty of time to agonize over the fact she was going to deliberately deceive her father.

She entered the atrium. Her father turned, smiling, and then the other man, dressed in a purple striped toga, also turned to her.

Antonia's heart slammed against her ribs, stifling the air in her lungs, squeezing her throat in disbelief. The praetor was not a stranger. He'd often visited Scipio in Rome. He'd always treated her with utmost respect and kindness whenever their paths had crossed. Yet despite his impeccable manner, she'd seen the lust in his eyes, and known that with the slightest encouragement he would have embarked on an illicit affair.

"Lady Antonia." Quintus Fabius Seneca took her chilled fingers and kissed the back of her hand. "It's a pleasure to see you again."

Antonia forced a smile to her lips and rescued her hand. "I did not know you were in Britannia, Praetor." Please Juno, let him be merely visiting the province. If he was now stationed in Camulodunum, the chances of Scipio discovering her future plans became alarmingly possible. But would her former husband truly imagine, for even a moment, the child she adopted was really his?

"A happy coincidence," the praetor said, and for some reason she didn't believe a word. He gestured to one of the ornate couches, indicating she should sit, as though he was the master of this townhouse and not her father. "It delights my heart to see you looking so well, despite the deprivations of this barbarous province."

From the corner of her eye, she saw her father flinch at the slight. His atrium was extravagant in the extreme and while it might not possess the spacious proportions of the grandest villas in Rome, Antonia was certain it ranked among the most lavish in Britannia. It certainly compared favorably to the one he'd had in Gallia, until he had moved to Britannia three years ago to capitalize on the sudden demand for luxury goods.

"On the contrary, I find this province to be most accommodating." As she sat on the couch, she tried not to let Gawain's mocking smile intrude into her thoughts. Now wasn't the time to let base lust dictate her words.

"Indeed, your father's establishment is most comfortable." The praetor offered her father a condescending smile, and Antonia bit her lip to stop herself from responding on his behalf. "And your loyalty, my lady, does you credit as always."

Antonia saw her father take a breath, undoubtedly to extol the extent of her loyalty to Rome, the Emperor and goddess knew what else. The last topic of conversation she wanted was one that centered around her, especially since the praetor knew far more about the state of her marriage to Scipio than her father ever would.

"What brings you to this far-flung outpost of the empire, Praetor?" Antonia folded her hands on her lap and prayed to Fortuna that he was merely traveling through the province and had no plans to stay longer than a few days or so.

"Duty, my lady." He clasped his hands behind his back and looked as though he prepared to address the Senate. "We are pledged to rid this primitive isle of the scourge of Druids and that is my mission. Not that you need to concern yourself with such unpleasant matters of state."

Scipio hadn't wanted her to concern herself with such matters, either. He'd been astonished, and not in a good way, when his young bride had voiced her opinions on politics, law, and injustice within his hearing. It hadn't taken her long to realize the extensive education her father had paid a fortune for was the last reason why Scipio had taken her for his wife.

But she was no longer Scipio's wife.

"Surely the Druids live in the wild forests of Cambria, Praetor? The last places they would flee are to Roman strongholds."

Instead of ignoring her or responding with a cutting remark as Scipio would have done, the praetor turned his full attention her way.

"With the fall of the rebel leader Caratacus last summer, the Druids were driven from their homeland." The praetor frowned and although Antonia wished he'd never set foot in Britannia, a part of her recalled why she'd enjoyed his attention in Rome. It was because, despite his innate air of superiority, he always considered her opinion worth the trouble of a genuine response. "We know many of them escaped to their barbaric Isle of Mona but it's my belief some of them spread across Britannia. The Emperor won't rest until every last one of them is crushed beneath the might of the Eagle."

"None would dare set foot in Camulodunum." Her father sounded outraged by the very thought. "The filthy cowards most likely fled north to the mountains of Caledonia."

"That is very possible," the praetor conceded.

"I wish you well in your mission, Praetor. All Druids should be hunted to extinction like the rabid dogs they are."

At any other time, Antonia would have loved to discuss the mysteries of the evil Druids, but her mind kept straying to Gawain. Had he meant that ultimatum? Or would she arrive at the tribune's villa only to discover it had been a cruel trick on his part?

If she didn't go, she would never know. And would spend the rest of her life wondering *what if?*

"Antonia?" Her father's voice jerked her back to the present. "The praetor enquired how you're enjoying the restricted social interactions here."

The pained expression on her father's beloved face told her that he was convinced she secretly hated everything about Camulodunum. Soon she would have to confide in him that she never intended to leave, but that was a conversation for another day. For now, both the praetor and her father had just given her the ideal opening regarding her clandestine meeting with Gawain.

"The tribune's wife, Carys, is most charming." If she were careful, she might be able to make it sound as though Carys had invited her without having to lie outright. She'd still feel bad about deceiving her father, but it would, after all, be for only a short while.

"The foreign princess." The praetor's tone gave nothing away of his private feelings on that matter. "She was the one who thwarted the mad Druid's plan in Cambria two years ago to over-throw the Legions."

Antonia stared at him, momentarily distracted from her purpose. "She was?" She tried to imagine the delicate-looking woman doing anything other than gracing her husband's Roman villa, and failed.

"It was the reason Maximus was allowed to marry her. The Emperor was most appreciative of her efforts."

"Another reason why no Druid would enter our great city," her father said.

She dearly wanted to learn more, but she couldn't allow this opportunity to pass by. "I've been invited to the tribune's villa this afternoon." She glanced at her father. "May I use the carpentum?"

Her father's face brightened, and guilt churned through her breast. But the guilt wasn't strong enough for her to retract her question.

"Of course. I'll arrange for a full complement of guard to accompany you."

Relief flooded through her, and she stood, inclining her head at the praetor. "It's been a pleasure to see you again, Praetor." She hoped they would never meet again, though. "Pray forgive my hasty departure."

Once again he took her hand. "The pleasure is all mine, my lady." His eyes never left hers and unease trickled along her spine at the desire he no longer made any effort to conceal. "I trust you and your father will honor me by attending a feast I'm holding next week."

Gawain found Carys in the room adjoining the Roman bathhouse Maximus had built in the villa's grounds. She'd just finished her daily teaching of local peasant children, and he couldn't help the glare he arrowed her way.

"The Romans will crucify you if they discover what you're doing under their aristocratic noses." Not to mention that she was flagrantly disregarding every edict passed down from the dawn of time that the ways of the Druids were sacred and not to be shared with any outsider.

"I'm only passing on the most basic of our knowledge." Carys shot him a frown of her own. "I'm not a fool, Gawain. I would never put my family at such risk. But Cerridwen's word must live on, and this is one way to preserve her wisdom."

He'd heard her arguments before, shortly after he'd discovered her whereabouts in Camulodunon. He still couldn't fathom that her patrician husband allowed her to continue with her passionate dream of educating the ignorant Britons, but Maximus, it appeared, was far from an average Roman.

"Why bother? The locals already worship the heathen gods of Rome."

"Yes, because their own priests have all been slaughtered or driven far from here." Carys gripped his arm, and he heaved a silent sigh. He knew what was coming next. "With your knowledge you could help turn the tide, Gawain. There's so much valuable information you can share with the populace."

"Unlike you, I don't have the advantage of Rome believing I led your tribune to the High Priest of Cymru in order to save their precious Legions." The High Priest had been insane with hatred for Rome, lust for Carys and the desire to wrench power from their gods and claim it for his own. It wasn't only the invaders who would've perished had he succeeded in his terrible vengeance. "And, unlike you, I no longer possess blind devotion to our fickle gods."

How could he, when the god he'd devoted his life to no longer acknowledged his existence?

"You'd rather stir up another rebellion."

He had no intention of discussing such things with Carys. The less she knew of his plans the better.

"Speaking of rebellion, I met the luscious Lady Antonia in the market earlier. It's likely she'll be visiting shortly. This room will do for my needs."

Carys stared at him, speechless. Gawain offered her a lecherous grin. "Before you leap to defend her honor, I didn't need to threaten or coerce. She appears more than eager to embark on an illicit liaison with a brutal barbarian."

"But—"

"For the sake of propriety, I imagine she'll inform her father that it's you she's visiting. These Romans have an odd sense of morality."

Carys glared at him. "After everything I said to you the other day, you're still determined to follow this path?"

He shrugged. "It means nothing. To me or to her. Your concerns are unfounded." Then he brushed a kiss against her cheek. He had, after all, known her for all of her life and she was the nearest thing he had to a sister. "But I thank you for them, just the same."

By the time Antonia arrived at the villa her nerves were in tatters. Elpis had accompanied her inside the carpentum and Antonia gripped her hands as she willed her limbs to stop shaking. If Gawain guessed how secretly terrified of this encounter she was, he'd laugh in her face.

"Are you sure about this, domina?" Elpis had become increasingly concerned as the journey progressed. "There's no need to continue if you've changed your mind."

But she hadn't changed her mind. She wanted to do this. She just wished she knew what Gawain expected of her. Elpis, it turned out, hadn't been that knowledgeable when it came to consensual sex and Antonia certainly hadn't wanted to ask the advice of any of her father's slaves.

"I need to do this." Not just for herself. She wanted her daughter to one day make a glorious marriage with a man she loved. How could Antonia offer her any advice if she had no idea what it was like to be with a man who didn't cause her flesh to crawl by the mere mention of his name?

She half expected Gawain himself to help her from the carpentum, but he was nowhere in sight. Was he allowing her a façade of respectability before her father's guards? Or was it because he had no intention of following through on their hastily arranged assignation?

Oddly, that thought calmed her nerves in a way nothing else

had. If he imagined to slight her by ignoring her, he greatly underestimated her. And if he supposed she'd be willing to over-look his arrogance and arrange a second illicit rendezvous then he most certainly would be disappointed.

Head held high, she followed the tribune's servant to the door, Elpis at her heels. There was still no sign of Gawain. Had he only wanted to see if she would take his bait? She stiffened her spine and hoped Carys was home and able to greet her. She would explain the reason for her unexpected visit was to invite the tribune and his wife to a feast the following week. Her father would be delighted.

She ignored the dull ache deep in her chest as she entered the atrium. She had feared Gawain might discard her the moment he'd had her. Wasn't it better that he'd discarded her before? At least this way she could retain a chilly veneer of indifference, should they ever meet again.

And then disbelief punched through her, stalling her thoughts, and she stared in shocked silence as Carys walked towards her. Her hair was braided like a primitive savage, her daughter perched on her hip and her gown was like nothing Antonia had ever seen before.

The Roman noblewoman had vanished. And in that instant Antonia understood how this woman could have thwarted a mad Druid.

"Antonia, welcome." Carys gestured her forward. "I've been expecting you."

"Thank you." The words slipped out, unthinking, as she tried not to stare at the extraordinary, bejeweled belt around Carys' waist. And then the other woman's statement penetrated, and heat flooded her cheeks.

Carys had been expecting her. That meant Gawain had told her of their assignation.

He intends to follow through on his promise.

"I'll show you to our bathhouse." Carys led the way through

the atrium. "My husband insisted on building one, although he assures me its splendor fades to insignificance besides the grand ones in Rome."

They left the villa and, directly ahead, Antonia saw a small building, marble columns flanking its entrance. Was that where she was to meet Gawain?

"The public baths are magnificent." Her voice was breathless as the prospect of bathing with him flooded her mind. She hoped Carys hadn't noticed. "But there is something to be said for the intimacy of a private bathhouse."

Not that she knew from experience. But several of her former friends had enjoyed scandalous affairs in such steamy surrounds.

"Very true." Carys shot her a glance she couldn't quite decipher and continued around the side of the bathhouse. She paused in front of another building that abutted the bathhouse and pushed open the door. "I will see you later."

Antonia stepped into the room, and was momentarily confused. She'd expected a secondary bathhouse, a hot or a cold room, or perhaps a small exercise area. Instead there were benches and a couple of couches as if this was another living area and nothing to do with the ritual of bathing.

A door opened to her left and she turned to see Gawain stroll in from the bathhouse. Her heart thudded against her chest, making it hard to draw breath, and the pit of her stomach trembled with strange, liquid heat.

He looked utterly foreign, a savage warrior, and sunlight glinted on the barbaric jewelry around his throat and at his ear. He smiled, a slow, seductive smile that sent tremors through her blood and did nothing to ease the constriction in her breast.

Except for Elpis, she was alone with a strange man, a man she had virtually propositioned in the street. A native of a conquered land who made no secret of the fact he despised her people. And yet it wasn't derision that glowed in his eyes. It was lust.

For her.

"Lady Antonia." His smoky voice wrapped around her senses, as potent as though he had wrapped his arms around her naked body. "You kept your word."

"Did you doubt I would?" She scarcely recognized her voice. She sounded like a sultry seductress. Perhaps, after all, Gawain would never guess what a novice she was when it came to playing such dangerous games.

He stopped in front of her, so close that the amber flecks in his dark eyes mesmerized her. "No." The word sank into her blood, igniting sparks of pleasure that skittered across her exposed flesh. "You want this as much as I do."

It was true. Why should she deny it? "Yes."

Elpis began to remove her palla, and Gawain took another step closer. "You have no need of a chaperone, Antonia."

For a moment, she stared at him, bemused. A chaperone? Did he mean he wished her to dismiss Elpis?

Such a thing had never occurred to her. She'd simply assumed Elpis would remain in the room, a familiar shadow, while she and Gawain had sex. But now the thought of being completely alone with Gawain had crossed her mind it was shockingly alluring.

She turned to Elpis. "You may leave."

Elpis hesitated, before she bowed her head and left to wait outside.

Gawain took her hand and brushed his lips across her knuckles. His warm breath seared her flesh, a lover's touch.

Soon he will truly be my lover. The knowledge caused damp heat to stir between her thighs.

"Did your father suspect anything?" He tugged her closer, his lips still grazing the back of her hand.

A sliver of guilt pierced her heart at how she'd deceived her father. "No." But even the guilt couldn't force her to drag her fascinated gaze from his mouth.

"Does your husband ever suspect your illicit liaisons?"

Scipio had never had cause to suspect her of any such thing.

But she had no intention of telling Gawain he had the dubious honor of being her first illicit liaison.

Yet she had to tell him something.

"I no longer possess a husband." It was easier to say that, than admit Scipio had divorced her because she had failed, so spectacularly, to provide him with a living son. "I belong to no man but my father."

Gawain gave her a probing look, and for a moment, she had the oddest sensation that he had already known of her divorce. But if he had, why would he have phrased his question in such a way?

He took another step closer, her hand still captured in his. The intense look in his eyes caused her mouth to dry and it seemed a thousand butterfly wings were trapped in her breast. "Soon you will belong to *me*."

CHAPTER SEVEN

*G*awain watched the enchanting blush suffuse Antonia's flawless skin. But she didn't break eye contact.

"I will belong to you for only a fleeting moment." Her breathless voice entranced as much as her blush. She was truly a mistress of her art. How many men had fallen for her air of innocence?

"I intend for our *moment*," he stressed the word and couldn't keep the mocking grin from his face, "to be anything but fleeting."

The tip of her tongue moistened the seam of her lips. He could almost believe his words truly discomposed her.

"That wasn't what I meant," she said at last. "And you know it."

He laughed out loud at her final thrust and wound his free arm about her waist. "I'm more than aware how fleeting our affair will be, Antonia. I would have it no other way."

She trailed the tips of her fingers along the front of his shirt, a light touch that branded his flesh with provocative promise. His cock thickened and it took more willpower than he cared to admit not to push her to her knees and invade her inviting mouth. She already knew how much he wanted her. He wasn't prepared to also let her know how far she tested his self-control.

"And is this how you usually conduct your clandestine affairs?" There was an irresistible huskiness in her voice and the hint of fire in her ice-blue eyes threatened to sever the tenuous threads that remained of his cursed self-control.

He unfastened her cloak and it fell to the floor. Her gown was of the palest blue silk and his palms skimmed over her delicately defined biceps, her skin smooth and warm beneath his touch.

"No. Usually I'm invited into my lover's bedchamber while her husband is occupied elsewhere."

Antonia tugged at the fastenings of his shirt. It was obvious she'd never attempted to strip a man who didn't wear the Roman toga.

She gave him a quick glance before she returned her attention to the ineptitude of her fingers. "I'll never invite you into my bedchamber."

He had no inclination to enter her bedchamber when they could meet here without the need for evading guards and bribing servants to silence.

"Rest assured I'll never attempt to persuade you otherwise."

She looked up at him again, and this time he could no longer resist. He cradled her face, and his thumb caressed the pink curve of her lips. Her uneven breath whispered across his jaw, and he caught an elusive hint of Roman mint as he lowered his head to her.

Her mouth opened but for a moment he lingered, her lips soft and tempting beneath his. Her hands fisted in his shirt as she rose onto her toes, and the tip of her tongue ventured between their joined lips.

Still cupping her face, his other hand slid up her arm and over her shoulder. The combination of sensuous silk and smooth skin collided with the raw lust pounding through his veins, and it was all he could do to stop himself from ripping the exquisite material from her body like a mindless savage.

Her tongue invaded, a torturous, tentative invasion that scalded his reason. She kissed with the innocence of an untouched maid, and yet her kiss aroused like a potent aphrodisiac. Desire speared through his groin, and he plunged his fingers into her hair, twisting the silken threads until her curls tumbled from their jeweled restraints.

She pressed her body close, her breasts against his chest, her belly cradling his rigid shaft. Her fingers mirrored his, tangling in his hair, the tips of her nails digging into the back of his head.

Her tongue continued to torment him with shallow, fleeting intrusions. Did she want him to burst into flame beneath her teasing touch?

A growl burned his throat and he thrust into her, devouring her shocked gasp as he claimed her delectable mouth. The evocative taste of fresh mint and exotic spices teased his senses and his cock jerked with frustrated need. His hand slid from her face to capture her vulnerable throat.

Her pulse hammered against his fingers, intensifying the pounding in his temples, the thunder of his heart. He wanted her naked, writhing beneath him, and his fingers were inside her gown before he realized his intention.

Panting, he pulled back. Whatever she imagined, he was no barbarian, and he wouldn't rip her gown to shreds no matter how much the image inflamed.

"Strip for me." It was a command, but it was agony to find the words to tell her what he needed. How much easier it would be if she understood his language. But even though he'd spoken in Latin she gazed at him in seeming confusion. He bared his teeth in a feral snarl. "Now."

Slowly she began to remove her gown. Her golden hair tumbled around her shoulders, giving her a strangely ethereal air. As her fingers fumbled, he wondered if she'd ever performed such a simple task for herself without the aid of slaves.

He didn't offer to assist. And with each tortured breath, she revealed another tantalizing glimpse of flesh. Finally her gown slid down her body to pool at her feet and his cock throbbed at the sight of her standing before him, a naked vision of temptation.

A blush highlighted her aristocratic cheeks, but she didn't drop her gaze in feigned modesty.

"Now you must strip for me." Her voice was low, and he imagined he detected a tremble, but it was likely another ploy she used to engage the devotion of her lovers.

"Patience, Antonia." He managed a mocking smile, but it almost killed him. He wanted nothing more than to pin her to the nearest available surface and thrust deep inside her, but she would learn no woman told him what to do. Even if she told him exactly what his rabid libido wanted him to do.

He raked his gaze over her full breasts, her nipples erect and inviting. Desire clawed through him, but he remained rooted to the spot through sheer Druidic pride. Her body was slender, beautiful, with subtle signs that she had borne children. His gaze shifted to between her thighs and his mouth dried.

A narrow band of pale golden curls hugged her plump lips. The hair was so fine, so delicate, it appeared translucent, and her mound enticed him to fall to his knees and worship at her shrine.

His hands fisted and he remained standing although the gods only knew how. "Turn around." The order was raw, brutal, and for the life of him he couldn't drag his mesmerized eyes from her dewy folds.

Without a word, she slowly turned and even without looking at her face he could imagine her smile of triumph. He barely cared. Because although she only half turned away from him, she looked over her shoulder and her provocative pose caused violent spirals of lust deep in his gut.

Her curls tumbled down her back to the dip of her waist, brushing against the swell of her arse. Gods, he'd never seen such a captivating arse. Firm globes of delectable flesh and he ached to taste, to touch. To grip her rounded cheeks while she rode him into a frenzy.

But not yet. He intended to savor this first time with her, and her practiced charms wouldn't sway him from his purpose.

Even if every frustrated sense he possessed thudded with the urge to *take her now* and explore her tantalizing body later, at his leisure.

Antonia wound a curl around her finger, a nervous reaction to the breathless desire fluttering through her breast. Gawain had barely touched her and yet her body tingled with arousal. Unable to help herself she slowly turned back to face him. Should she demand that he now strip for her? But it didn't matter what she thought because the dark passion in his eyes held her spellbound.

Without moving closer to her, he ripped off his shirt. The breath lodged in her throat. He had the body of a warrior god. Bronzed from the sun, scarred from battle, his muscles firm and molded like the finest sculpture.

She'd never imagined a man's body could be so beautiful. She ached to reach out and touch, to trace her fingers over his taut flesh and feel his masculine strength. Unlike with Scipio, the thought of exploring Gawain's body caused exhilarating whirlpools between her thighs and an exquisite sensation of damp heat trembled through her core.

Until she'd met Gawain, she'd never imagined wanting to see another man naked. Now, she couldn't wait. Riveted, she watched him unlace his braccae, her heart hammering high in her breast making it difficult to draw breath. With apparent disregard for the lust simmering between them, he slowly tugged them down his powerful legs.

Merciful Juno. Antonia stared, mesmerized, as Gawain straightened, and his breathtaking organ filled her vision. Thick and proud, his length caused another rush of heat careering through her blood, pooling low and bathing her sheath. She struggled to remain standing, to keep her hands to herself, not to gasp out loud with foolish awe.

But she couldn't drag her fascinated gaze away.

He cupped his testicles and the sight of his hand on his body sent molten waves of pure desire from her nipples to her womb. *And still he hasn't touched me.* Unfamiliar tugs of need tightened her cleft and this time she couldn't help but press her thighs together. The pressure only increased the sensation of fullness that surged through her swollen folds.

If he didn't take her soon, she feared she would collapse onto the floor.

"Do you like what you see?" There was a hint of amusement in his husky voice. She couldn't trust herself to speak so merely nodded. How much longer did he intend to make her wait? "Do you enjoy watching your lovers caress their cocks?" His hand slid up and grasped his root. Her fingers clenched around the curl she held, and her mouth dried to an impossible degree.

Did he truly expect her to answer him? How could she answer him, when Scipio was the only man she'd ever known? And he had never bothered with such exquisite foreplay. When he wanted her, he had taken her. She'd been married almost a week before she had even got a good look at his monstrous tool of torture.

"Does this arouse you, Antonia?"

She tried, desperately, to meet his gaze. And failed. She had never examined Scipio's loathed instrument. She'd closed her eyes, imagined herself back in Gallia. But Gawain—goddess, his shaft was a thing of untold fascination.

Gawain moved behind her and with his free hand grasped her hair and lifted it over her shoulder, leaving her back bare for his pleasure. With drugged reluctance, Antonia met his burning gaze and her pulses thudded at the raw lust he made no effort to conceal.

He'd take her now. Even though they had done none of the things her former friends had gossiped about, it didn't matter. Because she was more aroused than she had ever been in her life before, and for the first time she ached to be penetrated and possessed.

"Your eyes bewitch." He sounded as drugged as she felt, as if the words escaped without his knowledge. "You'll find me no easy conquest, Antonia."

She had no idea what he meant. She didn't care what he meant. Because his large hands curved over her shoulders and her eyes drifted shut as ripples of pleasure cascaded over her naked flesh.

He intended to take her from behind. Would he bend her over one of the benches or push her to her knees? She didn't care. So long as he did it quickly, before she revealed how much she wanted this and begged.

His thumbs began to massage her tense shoulders and her eyes sprung open in shock. His grip on her was firm, but now his fingers mirrored his thumbs and an involuntary groan of pleasure escaped.

"Relax, my lady." His smoky whisper brushed her ear as he leaned into her, and for a brief, glorious moment his broad chest grazed her back and branded her skin. "I have no intention of rutting with you like a wild beast from the forest. Not until you're ready for me."

Ready for him? How much readier could she *be*?

His hands worshipped her biceps and although she'd been massaged times without number in her life before, never had it felt like this. But then, never before had the masseur been a virile foreign warrior.

Another strangled groan escaped, and she pressed her lips together, but it made no difference. It was hard to breathe, hard to think. Hard to remain still and upright while Gawain's magic fingers turned her limbs to water.

"You torture me." The words sounded hoarse. She flexed her fingers in a futile effort to force her concentration away from the delirium Gawain's confident touch evoked.

"Good." His hands slid down her arms and involuntary tremors skittered across her flesh. Never in her wildest fantasies had she imagined her forearms could be so sensitive to a man's seductive caress. "I intend to torture you until you writhe at my feet for mercy."

She laughed, the breathless sound shocking her, and she only just stopped herself from slapping her hand across her mouth. Sex wasn't supposed to be funny. Was it?

"I see you doubt my prowess in this matter." There was no mistaking the hint of laughter in his voice and Antonia risked glancing over her shoulder. His dark gaze enslaved, and his fingers threaded through hers, pressing her palms against her taut thighs. "By the time we've finished, my lady, you will doubt me no longer."

CHAPTER EIGHT

*S*he didn't doubt his prowess in the slightest. But she had no intention of telling him that. His ego was inflated enough as it was.

"Perhaps it will be you, Gawain, who will end up writhing at my feet." The image of this tough warrior doing such a thing was so ludicrous that another inappropriate giggle bubbled in her breast.

Once again, he leaned into her, but this time the entire length of his body molded hers. His erection burned her lower back, so hard and hot, he seared her flesh. Her desire to laugh evaporated, along with her breath, and she gasped as his jaw scraped against her throat.

"I will have you where I want you, Antonia. Make no mistake." His raw whisper grazed her earlobe, an erotic promise. Or was it a threat? She didn't even care. "And you'll revel in it."

Yes, she would. She reveled already, and he had to know. She turned her face to him and his barbaric earring pressed against her cheek. Another sensuous ripple cascaded across her face and along her throat and her fingers clenched, despite how they were captured between Gawain's.

"We will have each other." Her heart hammered so wildly in her breast, constricting her breath, she scarcely knew how she managed to respond at all. But something compelled her. Something that had been beaten down during the years of her marriage, but that had refused to wither and die beneath the desert of derision and disregard. "I look forward to our mutual writhing."

Goddess, had she said that aloud? The way Gawain's body shook with silent laugher assured her that yes, she most certainly had. And he enjoyed her remarks. How shockingly easy it was to fall back into the patterns of her girlhood, when she had spoken before she thought. When she had believed, so naively, that all men would be as indulgent of her irreverent tongue as her father.

He untangled his fingers from hers and trailed an excruciating path up her thighs to her hips.

"So do I." His growl vibrated across her sensitized skin, and she closed her eyes as his lips claimed the angle of her jaw with nibbling kisses that stoked the embers to unbearable heights.

Threads of fire weaved across her flesh as he scraped the tips of his fingers over the swell of her hips and dip of her waist. She shifted against him, his erection growing even harder, and molten heat rolled deep in her slick sheath.

It was no good. He wanted her to beg.

"I believe I am ready." The words were uneven, her breath erratic, but surely coherent enough for him to understand. She wanted him now, before these exquisite sensations causing untold havoc between her thighs vanished.

His lips teased her earlobe, his warm breath dusting her skin like an elusive summer breeze. "I don't believe you are."

Her eyes widened. "I don't believe you know what you're talking about."

Again, an irresistible laugh vibrated through his body. "Do you always talk so much during intimate moments?"

"No." Her confession was out before she could prevent it. In truth, she had never uttered a word after the night of her marriage, when it became clear the only words Scipio wanted to hear from her while he claimed his rights were ones she would never voice. He may have owned her body, but he had never owned her mind.

Gawain trailed a fiery path across her belly and cradled her breasts. His hands were firm, roughened, and she hitched in an uneven breath and instinctively curled her hands around his forearms before she tumbled onto the floor.

"Then why am I different?" There was an edge of mockery in his voice, but it didn't disguise the throb of desire. His thumbs flicked across her erect nipples and a strangled moan escaped. How much more of this sweet torture could she take?

She moistened her lips and tried to gather her cascading thoughts. *What did he ask me?* "Why do you assume you're different?"

He nibbled a seductive trail of kisses across her shoulder, his lips and teeth creating a maelstrom of sensation that weaved over her breasts and circled her aching nipples. Her head fell back against his neck, thrusting her breasts forward, and his grasp became possessive.

"Because I'm the first barbarian to enjoy your charms?" As he panted the words against her heated skin, he pressed her breasts together, creating a deep cleavage. She knew he was looking at her and the knowledge caused another wave of heat to flood her quivering channel. It took more effort than she knew she possessed, but somehow she forced her head upright so she could witness the expression on his face.

As she had guessed, he was mesmerized by her creamy mounds and the dark crevice he had created between them. Entranced, she reached up and cradled his face, but he appeared unable to drag his gaze from her entrapped flesh.

"You're not a barbarian," she whispered. He was a foreign

warrior of a barbarous land, but that didn't make him a barbarian.

His gaze caught hers. His eyes were so dark his amber flecks had all but vanished. "Is that what you think?" His voice was raw with need, but she caught an underlying hint of something else. If it were not so insane, she might imagine her whisper had unexpectedly touched him.

"No," she breathed. "I know."

He didn't answer, but the feral smile that tugged his lips caused tingling flutters deep in her cleft. Without warning, he pulled her around so that she faced him, his hands spanning her waist. She stroked the angle of his jaw, delighting in the rough texture of his stubble, and then traced the exotic symbols engraved in his silver torque.

Everything about him radiated a savage, untamed power and yet she didn't fear him. As his hands sculpted the curve of her waist and swell of her buttocks, he lowered his head. Her breath caught and she dug her nails into his shoulder as he languidly trailed his tongue around her sensitive areola.

Her free hand tangled in his hair, the sensation of silken threads winding around her knuckles as evocative as the feel of his mouth and tongue and teeth on her breast. She stared at him, transfixed by the sight of him suckling her, as erotic tugs spiraled from the tip of her nipple to her wet core.

His warm breath grazed her breast and then he sucked her hard nub into his mouth. A shocking, brutal gesture that sent darts of primitive pleasure arrowing through her body.

"Gawain." Was that really her voice? "Please." *Take me now*.

With one last lingering lick across her erect peak, he looked up at her. A pagan god, with his tousled hair, heathen jewelry, and magnificent, irresistible body. "Soon."

It was a smoky promise she clung onto with the remnants of her sanity as, instead of claiming her, he trailed burning, provocative kisses over her aching breasts.

The grip on her buttocks increased as he parted her cheeks and she gasped, tightening her hold on his hair and shoulder. The grin he shot her was feral as he began to circle her exposed crack, each swirl of his finger bringing him closer to penetrating her vulnerable backside.

"Part your thighs." He accompanied his ragged command by thrusting his leg between hers and without thinking she obeyed, opening herself entirely to his determined exploration. Instinctively she tensed, but he didn't force his finger inside her tight heat. He continued to circle and dip, a mind-blowing torture of dark eroticism she had never dreamed could exist.

Slowly he edged down her body, his mouth worshipping her belly as he relinquished his possessive grip on her bottom. His hand clasped her thigh and despite the erratic pounding of her blood and the shocking stabs of desire his finger engendered, awe shivered through her as she watched him drop to his knees before her.

His thumb caressed her folds, a gentle touch, back and forth. Paralyzed, she watched as he leaned in and swept his tongue along her slick cleft. Liquid fire ignited and consumed her quivering core and a primal moan echoed in her ears.

She'd always wondered what it would feel like, to have a man's mouth on her there, to feel his tongue penetrate her silken folds. But nothing had prepared her for the reality. Not her former friends' gossip or her fevered imagination.

The scorching vibrations spiraling through her went beyond words. Beyond thought. She clutched at his hair, her anchor to the world, as the room faded around her. All she could see was Gawain on his knees, his face between her thighs, his bronzed, naked body worshipping hers.

He pulled back, just enough so that his jaw rubbed against her sensitized flesh. An inarticulate mewl of protest escaped at his abandonment. She dug her fingers into his scalp and felt as much as saw his savage smile.

"Let it go, Antonia." His demand was raw with lust. "I want you to come for me. Give me everything you have."

His words thundered in her mind, as potent as his heated touch on her body. But before she could even hitch in a jagged breath, he lubricated her taut behind with her juices and his finger once again stroked her virgin flesh.

"What?" she whispered, trying to form a coherent thought between the pounding of her heart and the white-hot desire that blazed through her veins. *What should I do?* she wanted to ask him, but the words lodged in her throat. It was impossible to speak, impossible to think. All she could do was feel. *But if I don't do something, Gawain will think me frigid.*

The tip of his tongue swirled around her clitoris, and she jerked in shock, clutching at his head, needing something to anchor her as indescribable streaks of pleasure consumed her sensitive bud. He teased and probed, his tongue an instrument of unimaginable delight. Her breath stuttered, the sound jarring into the sex-scented air with uncaring inelegance. Deep within her a strange pressure bloomed, bore down, then Gawain sucked on her clitoris and in the same instant, his finger penetrated her tight rosette.

She gasped and reared against his mouth. The sensation of fullness, of invasion, was beyond anything she had imagined. He rotated his finger, stretching her taut flesh and she hovered between pain and ecstasy.

Yet she didn't want him to stop. The feel of him inside her, where she had never been touched before, was worth any fleeting moment of discomfort. Her clit inside Gawain's mouth, the feel of his tongue and lips sucking her, caused her muscles to contract. She couldn't stop the ripples that claimed her cleft and swollen folds. *Didn't want to.* It was thrilling, *shocking* like nothing she had ever dreamed.

The world shattered into a thousand rainbow shards as her body convulsed with mindless delirium. Nothing existed but the wild spasms that vibrated her bud and licked through her trembling cleft.

Nothing but the man she clung onto with primitive need.

Gawain kept his tongue pressed against Antonia's quivering clit as she came inside his mouth. She tasted so sweet, of honey and spices and arousal so intense he smoldered with repressed lust. He tightened his grip around her waist to keep her upright as she trembled in the throes of her climax, and he eased his finger from her deliciously tight arse. Gods, had she never been taken there? The thought of being the first hammered through his mind.

Another time.

He was on the edge and didn't have the self-control required to initiate her into such dark pleasures. He needed her, and he needed her now. Without waiting for her shudders to subside, he lifted her in his arms, her naked body a torturous delight. With a feral growl, he snatched up a Roman towel, flung it onto the nearest stone table and then sat her upon it.

Brutally he pushed her knees apart and for one eternal moment stared, transfixed. Her pink clit was swollen from his tongue and her orgasm, and her slit tantalized with wet promise.

"Now," he said, as he lifted her chin and her dazed eyes locked with his. "You're ready for me."

She appeared incapable of answer, but he didn't need her to say anything. He gripped her hips, satisfied that she maintained eye contact, and pulled her to the edge of the table. Her arms slid around his shoulders, and he grasped his cock and rubbed his sensitive head over her slick flesh.

Her seductive little gasps and the way her breasts rose and fell with every erratic breath pushed him over the edge. With a primal growl, he rammed into her, and silken fire engulfed his shaft and scorched his reason.

He shoved his hands under her arse, her smooth cheeks filling his palms and squeezed her delectable flesh. She squirmed at his rough touch, and the friction burned his cock as he buried himself farther inside her welcoming sheath.

No hint of ice remained in her eyes as she focused on him as though he were all that existed in her world. It shouldn't have meant anything, and it didn't. Yet the thought caused the blood to hammer through his veins in primitive possession.

She wound her legs around him and his balls slammed against her tender flesh with every frenzied thrust. Exquisite quivers radiated along her tight crease, torturing his cock. He buried his face in the scented haven where her throat met shoulder and sucked her delicious skin into his mouth.

Mine. The word pounded through his head, illogical and unwanted. But the overwhelming need to mark her as his, to brand her for all the world to see, thundered through his smoldering senses.

Her choked gasp of protest—of desire—filled his mind with primitive satisfaction. *She is mine.* He grasped her arse, felt her legs tighten around him, felt her slick core convulse as another violent orgasm rocked through her.

His hips bucked and he hammered into her, flesh slapping, breath panting. Lightning clawed through his balls, his cock. A torrid maelstrom of primal need and base desire and with a guttural roar, he filled her with his hot release.

CHAPTER NINE

*A*fter endless moments, Gawain realized his face was still buried in Antonia's shoulder, his shaft was still embedded in her trembling slit and his fingers claimed her buttocks in a punishing grip. The knowledge drifted through his mind, languid and strangely comforting, yet an insubstantial whisper of unease edged the haze of euphoria.

Only when her legs slid over his hips in clear exhaustion did he finally raise his head to look at her. She peered back at him, her eyes dark with passion, her parted lips pink and deliciously swollen, her aristocratic cheeks flushed with the remnants of desire.

Her hair tumbled around her face in glorious disarray. His aloof Roman noblewoman looked thoroughly disheveled and thoroughly ravished. His gaze roved over her and savage satisfaction flashed through him at the sight of his mark marring her flawless shoulder. She wouldn't forget him easily when she left him this day.

He freed his hands, and she puffed out an enchanting little gasp as if her arse were sore. Slowly she slid her hands along his biceps and then clung onto his forearms as though she needed the additional support.

There was no reason for him to remain inside her body. No reason for him to clasp her waist. But somehow, he didn't have the strength to pull away.

Instead, he continued to stare at her perfect patrician features and waited for the mild contempt to weave through his mind. It happened without fail in the moments after he'd taken a Roman, no matter how beautiful or desirable she was.

He had taken her. He had conquered her. She was nothing more, now, than another Roman noblewoman who'd risked her reputation to taste the barbaric charms of a rough native.

Except Antonia had told him she didn't think he was a barbarian.

He shoved the thought aside with the derision it deserved. She hadn't meant it. Except a stubborn shred deep inside his chest knew she meant every word.

And still the contempt failed to materialize.

"That was…illuminating." Antonia's breathless voice jarred him back to the present. To the reality that he was still joined with her, when by now he should be retrieving his clothes.

"Illuminating?" What did she mean by that? "In what way, my lady?" He attempted to inject a touch of contempt into his final words, but the ability eluded him. And still he held her, her warm flesh an addictive drug.

She gave a breathless laugh and leaned closer, a bewitching smile now curving her edible lips. He gazed at her, transfixed, unable to put the physical distance between them that he knew he should. That he knew he should *want*. Yet did not.

"In all ways." Her ice-blue eyes sparkled with what he could only determine was mischievous glee. "You surpassed all my expectations, Gawain. Thank you."

Women, both Celtic and Roman, had said all manner of things

to him in the moments after copulation but Antonia's whispered confession rendered him speechless.

Logically he knew she was only spinning him a practiced line she had mouthed who knew how many times in the past. But she seemed so genuine. The knowledge that she could so easily manipulate his good sense with a few enigmatic words irked him.

"It was my pleasure." This time he managed a thread of mockery, although Antonia didn't appear to register it. With a reluctance that disgusted him, he finally pulled free of her welcoming clasp. "I'm gratified I exceeded the efforts of your Roman lovers, Antonia." Except he wasn't gratified. He was irritated by the comparison and couldn't fathom why.

She didn't answer him, but a small smile lit up her face, as though she were recalling the performance of all her lovers and still found him exceptional. Again, he couldn't imagine why such a thing should touch him. He didn't normally care if the Roman women he took reminisced on how different he was from their usual illicit distractions.

And then it hit him. It was because she had thanked him, as though he'd merely provided her with an entertaining service.

His illogical mood blackened further. Why did it matter if that's what she thought? It was, after all, mutual.

"Oh," she said, the word breathy and seductive and to his disbelief his cock stirred in primal response. "Yes."

Yes? He trawled through his mind until he recalled his last remark.

"Perhaps in the future, my lady, you can teach them the pleasurable tricks you learned from your *Cambrian* lover." He used the Roman word for his land deliberately, loading it with disdain.

It had to be a trick of the sunlight streaming through the windows, but it appeared her smile lost some of its radiance and a haunted expression clouded her eyes. She crossed her ankles and a shiver chased over her body, and in that blink of an eye, her air of sensual seductress transformed into reserved vulnerability.

"Perhaps." There was no trace of the teasing note she'd used earlier, or the dreamy quality that had so riled him a moment ago. She sounded as cool and remote as she had the day they had conversed in Carys' courtyard.

With a muttered curse in his own language, he snatched up another Roman towel and draped it around her shoulders. He had no idea why. It wasn't as if she were incapable of wrapping herself in a towel if she was cold. And he certainly wasn't her slave to anticipate her every demand.

She glanced up at him, clearly startled, and instead of stepping back as had been his intention he remained rooted to the spot, gripping the edges of the towel across her breasts.

"Thank you." She sounded uncertain, and an odd pain spiked through his chest. He didn't want her chilly patrician façade. He wanted the Antonia who teased and flirted. If that meant she wanted to maintain her incomprehensible illusion of innocence she projected so flawlessly, he would play along. It was a small concession for the pleasure they'd just shared.

A pleasure he had every intention of enjoying again. Soon.

He shoved the lingering remnants of his dark mood into the back of his mind. His reaction still made no sense, but he wasn't going to waste time mulling over it.

"I don't want you catching a chill and being confined to your father's townhouse for the next week."

She pulled the towel across her thighs and then looked up at him. "It would take more than a chill to keep me confined."

His lips twitched. It was so much better when she met him on equal ground without that unsettling whisper of elusive innocence she sometimes favored.

"I'm glad to hear it."

The tip of her tongue moistened the seam of her lips. Her seductive timing was breathtaking. "This liaison must be brief for many reasons, Gawain, but I would like to meet with you again tomorrow."

He realized he was still staring at her mouth. He also realized that he didn't care. "That can be arranged."

Her mouth curved into a smile of what looked relief. Except of course, she'd known he'd agree. Why would he not? He anticipated many days of enjoying Antonia's charms before he tired of her.

"I'll meet you at the public baths at the ninth hour. Will you be able to find us somewhere... suitable?" Her words were once again breathless, and he could almost believe she wasn't used to making such illicit assignations. Except she'd not only initiated their second meeting she was now dictating where it should take place.

Not that he had any objection. He'd enjoy the edge of danger her request would entail. He'd assumed Antonia would wish only to meet him here, at Carys', where they were assured of uninterrupted privacy, but it appeared her sense of adventure was greater than he'd given her credit for.

"As long as your delicate sensibilities can tolerate a primitive tavern room then yes, I can easily find us somewhere."

She smiled up at him, as though his gentle dig at her patrician heritage didn't disturb her in the slightest. Only then did it occur to him that he still hadn't retreated. That he still held her towel together at her breasts.

"My delicate sensibilities can withstand more than you might imagine." Her hand covered his in an oddly intimate gesture. "I'm not made of spun glass."

He laughed. *Spun glass.* Such a Roman term to use. He'd seen fragile glass creations and Antonia was wrong. Compared to Druid women she was, indeed, made of spun glass.

It was only when they finally pulled apart and Elpis returned to help her mistress look presentable that an odd realization hit.

He had compared Antonia, a Roman noblewoman, with his Celtic compatriots. And had not found her obvious deficiencies a source of disdain.

❋

After Antonia left, Gawain bathed in the river that bordered the estate. He'd used public baths in the past, but only to glean information from arrogant Romans who discussed their affairs without a thought that a native might understand their words, let alone act on them. He'd never used a Roman bath for pleasure and had no intention of ever doing so, no matter how Carys mocked him for his fastidiousness.

As he made his way back to the villa, he took stock of his situation. Staying in Camulodunon indefinitely had never been an option. When he'd first entered the Roman city, it had been with the burning desire to avenge the rape of Cymru, the betrayal of Caratacus and, obscurely, the devastating loss of direction he was experiencing from Lugus' continued absence.

But within days, he'd discovered Carys now lived here, and even if he had been able to raise an army of bloodthirsty warriors from these apathetic Britons, he refused to put Carys and her small family in such danger. She was a link to his past and if he could believe her idealistic vision, she and the many children she intended to have were the hope for the future.

As far as he knew, it was only the far north, beyond the traitorous Brigantes, whose queen who had sold Caratacus to the Romans, that remained free of the empire. Perhaps it was there, among the fierce Pict tribes and their advantageous mountainous land, that he would find a way to scrub the bloodstained guilt from his soul.

He entered the villa and caught sight of Carys. She was standing by a barely opened door that led into the atrium. When she saw him, she put a finger to her lips and jerked her head.

His warrior instinct alert, he went to her side, his hand instinctively going to his dagger. She was dressed as a Druid princess and when he heard the murmur of male voices from the atrium, he guessed why she was hiding.

It would not do for anyone of importance to see the tribune's wife as she truly was.

"…hoping to make the acquaintance of your wife."

"Carys will be sorry to have missed your visit, Praetor." Maximus sounded sincere, but Gawain was certain the Roman knew exactly where his wife was hiding and that she was not in the least sorry to have missed the official's visit. "Unfortunately, she is indisposed."

Carys scowled and Gawain bit back a laugh. *Feminine indisposition* was a favorite excuse when a Roman woman didn't wish to face a situation, but it was never something a Celtic woman would resort to.

"My sympathies," the other Roman said. Gawain leaned against a marble column. Obviously, Carys felt the need to stay and eavesdrop and what's more, she wanted him to, as well. "My late wife suffered greatly from the same malady."

Gawain grimaced, but Carys ignored him. He had no moral problems listening into private conversations when there might be information he could use to his advantage. But he had no interest whatsoever in this tedious exchange.

The strangled response from Maximus, though, almost made it worthwhile.

"So, Maximus," the praetor said, his tone turning brisk. "You've been stationed in this colonia for how long?"

"A little over a year." The tribune sounded restrained, and Gawain stifled a yawn and wondered if Antonia ever suffered from *feminine indispositions*.

"Long enough to have cultivated a good sense of the mood of the local natives."

Gawain folded his arms. Was the praetor concerned an uprising was imminent? If so, he need not worry. While the peasants might resent the Roman presence, their masters were content to bask in the condescending benevolence of the empire.

"The benefits of being under the protection of the Eagle are something they're coming to appreciate."

Gawain was sure Maximus believed that. It was hard not to draw the same conclusion at times. He was also sure Carys was going to make him pay dearly for saying such a thing within her hearing.

The praetor grunted in apparent approval. Gawain forcibly relaxed his fist, which he had no recollection of flexing.

"Do you believe they would knowingly harbor fugitive Druids?"

Ice slid through Gawain's veins, and he caught Carys' steady gaze. This was why she had wanted him by her side. Because she had known the praetor's visit directly impacted their survival.

"No." Maximus' voice was firm.

"No?" The praetor sounded taken aback, as if he hadn't expected such an uncompromising response. "Perhaps your view is clouded by your personal circumstances."

Gawain saw Carys stiffen and knew it wasn't her own safety that worried her. It was her husband's.

"The Emperor is assured of my loyalty." There was no inherent threat in Maximus' mild tone, but the threat was there, nevertheless. Gawain pulled Carys back against his chest and leaned forward so he could catch a glimpse of the praetor through the narrow gap.

He looked about forty, graying at the temples and was dressed in the purple striped toga of the aristocracy.

"I would never question the loyalty of the house of Tiberius Valerius," the praetor said. "But you're aware many of the Druids escaped justice two years ago when your esteemed wife thwarted their revered High Priest. I'm convinced many made their way into our prestigious city."

Carys threaded her fingers through his. As far as he knew, they were the only two Druids from Cymru in Camulodunon.

But was it possible Druids from other clans were here? Anticipation surged through his blood.

Of course it was possible.

"If that were the case we would know," Maximus said. "You will soon discover, Praetor, that the Eagle has a tight grasp of this corner of Britannia."

"I have no doubts at all. But our Emperor wishes to leave no stone unturned in the pursuit of our bitterest enemies. I relish the challenge of hunting them down." The praetor puffed out his chest like a preening rooster. Gawain relished the vision of wringing his neck like one. "But enough of this political talk, Maximus. I'd be honored if you and your wife would attend a feast at my townhouse. Just a small gathering, at next week's end."

CHAPTER TEN

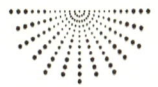

*A*ntonia remained frozen as the impenetrable blackness of the night seeped into her soul. In some buried corner of her mind, she knew this was only a dream, but it didn't stop the terror from pounding through her heart.

An unnatural breeze brushed across her arms, causing her to shiver although it wasn't cold.

My future hangs in the balance.

She knew she had to move. Knew it was up to her to make the decision whether to turn left or right on the rocky path beneath her feet. But if she took one wrong step, she would plunge to her death.

On the far horizon, an eerie silver glow bloomed, highlighting the ominous clouds that hung low in the sky. From the ethereal luminosity came the figure of a woman—no, not a woman, no mere mortal could radiate such a devastating otherworldly beauty. *Even in a dream?* But the thought was ephemeral because she knew who this goddess was.

Juno. Queen of the gods.

The great goddess approached, and a different fear clutched

Antonia's breast. It had been so long since Juno had honored her with a visitation that she had forgotten—

Forgotten that in her dreams, Juno didn't resemble the glorious statues or paintings in the temples dedicated to her worship.

She looked too young and wore a crown of flowers, like a goddess of spring. Yet the majestic power that swirled around her was not that of a minor goddess.

"Antonia." The feminine voice whispered through her mind, the power in that one word both mighty and terrible. *"You must bring them home to me."*

"Domina." Elpis' familiar voice penetrated the paralysis that gripped her, and she clutched her slave's hand as the lingering tendrils of the dream faded.

She looked up at Elpis in the glow of dawn. Her heart hammered against her ribs, but she couldn't quite recall what had so terrified her.

"Did I speak?" Her voice was hoarse and when Elpis bowed her head, dread knotted her stomach. "What did I say?"

"You spoke in Juno's tongue."

Antonia pulled her hand from Elpis and speared her fingers through her hair, digging her nails into her scalp. It had been years since she'd had the nightmares of impending doom. Years since foreign words had spilled from her mouth while her future was determined by faceless shadows.

Before Elpis had arrived, her father had been devastated by her inexplicable nighttime ravings. But the little Greek slave girl, who even now still worshipped Hera, the goddess of her people, had convinced them both that it was Juno speaking through Antonia, in the language of the gods.

As a child, she had accepted it. As she grew older, less so. If Juno was trying to tell Antonia something, why would she use a language no mortal could understand? But more than that, there was an uneasy certainty that, in the dreams, she could understand every word the goddess uttered.

"Why now?" She pushed herself upright and hugged her knees as if she were still that frightened child. "Juno hasn't spoken through me since the night before I left Gallia."

The night before she'd left for Rome, for her new life as Scipio's wife.

"I don't know." Elpis hesitated. "Perhaps it has something to do with the Cambrian, Gawain."

Antonia trailed the tips of her fingers over the tender flesh of her shoulder where Gawain had marked her as though she belonged to him. Although unease flooded her veins, she smiled at the thought. Truly, she had chosen wisely when she'd decided to take him as her lover. Already his touch had done much to eradicate the memory of years of forced submission she'd endured with Scipio.

"I cannot see how. Gawain has his own gods. Why would Juno return because I had taken a Cambrian lover?" As the words left her lips, a dreadful possibility occurred to her. Was it because Juno disapproved?

Her smile faded. No, surely not. Why would such a thing give the great goddess pause? Antonia was no longer married, so she wasn't even betraying her husband. And Juno knew how dedicated Antonia was in her desire to give Cassia a loving upbringing. Gawain was simply an intoxicating interlude.

No. She refused to believe the return of Juno had anything to do with her liaison with Gawain. It was a coincidence.

Her father joined her as she broke her fast in the opulent dining room. She hadn't seen him the previous day after she'd left him with the praetor, as he had been occupied with business. Self-consciously she checked that Elpis had arranged her stola so that Gawain's mark didn't show. How would she be able to explain *that* away?

Shockingly, the thought caused her lips to twitch with amusement and she hastily pushed some dried fruit into her mouth. Now, as her father reclined by her side and regaled her with the success of his current business ventures and the benevolence of the great Mercury, was not the time to lust over Gawain's sexual prowess.

She could do that later, when they were alone in a squalid tavern room.

Even that thought sent wanton heat blazing through her blood.

"The praetor thinks very highly of you, Antonia." Her father smiled at her, pride glowing in his eyes. "I didn't realize you were both so well acquainted with each other in Rome."

Antonia wasn't sure what her father implied by that, and was equally sure he was reading far more into it than he should.

"The praetor," not that he'd been a praetor back in Rome, "would often visit my former husband. But so too would many of the other senators."

Her father squeezed her hand. "You know, of course, that his wife died in childbirth over two years ago."

Of course she knew. His wife had numbered among her friends. If she had lived, would she, also, have turned her back when Scipio had made it clear he intended to rid himself of a useless wife?

"Her death was a tragedy." Antonia had mourned for her friend. But at least she had delivered a healthy son for her husband. Wasn't that all Roman patricians cared about? Her husband had never appeared distraught at her untimely death. But neither had he immediately taken another bride.

Perhaps, in private, he had cared. Despite how often his lustful eyes had glanced her way during the last eight years.

"He greatly admires you."

Her teeth lodged in the soft fruit, and she shot her father a probing look. Surely he wasn't suggesting—?

"I have high hopes that, with the right encouragement, he will elevate you once again into your rightful sphere."

She choked down the fruit. "I'm already in my rightful sphere. I have no desire to leave you again, Father." She took a steadying breath. Perhaps now was the time to tell him of her plans to not only stay with him, but to ultimately adopt a child. "The truth is—"

"The truth is you are too modest." Her father gazed at her lovingly and she stared at him, appalled. How could he imagine that the praetor might want to take her back to Rome? There was only one way he could do that, and it was if they were married. And she was certain that while he would have no compunction in taking her as his concubine, the praetor had no use for her as his wife. "After you left us, he made it very clear to me that he has your best interests at heart. You don't belong in a barbarous province, Antonia. You were born to grace the highest echelons of the empire."

"No, Father." She hated to upset him, but he had to face the truth. "My mother was born to grace the upper echelons of the empire, not I. You know as well I do that in the eyes of Rome, I am but the daughter of a merchant."

He winced at her blunt words, but she recognized the obstinate set of his mouth. "Your patrician relatives accepted you, Antonia. You were not cast out."

Unlike her mother who, when she had married outside her social sphere, had been forever ostracized by her powerful relatives. Not for the first time Antonia wondered if her mother would still have married her father had she not fallen pregnant with Antonia before the wedding night. Her father had never confirmed this fact and she would cut out her tongue before she raised the matter with him, but she'd worked out the truth long before she had left Gallia.

"Yes," she conceded. "My mother's relatives accepted me." But would they have accepted her if she had not possessed the coveted Roman ideal of blonde hair and fair complexion? She'd overheard their relieved whispers. Bristled at the knowledge that they had feared she would be a coarse, uneducated Gallia-spawned pleb.

Had she been any of those things, Scipio would never have noticed her. Would never have gone to such lengths to secure her as his bride. But it wasn't long before he took spiteful pleasure in reminding her of her lowly plebeian roots.

"I only want what's best for you." Her father sighed heavily, and guilt chewed through her breast at how she was deceiving him with Gawain. And how she would soon deceive him about his own granddaughter. "I cannot allow my own selfish desire to keep you by my side blight your future. The praetor is a powerful man. He has the ability to protect you against anything."

Antonia couldn't imagine what her father meant. She didn't care, either. "If you're right about him wishing to marry me then I must tell you now. I have no intention of doing so. Not to him or any other man."

There. She'd told him. Relief washed through her, along with a thread of concern. She hoped he wouldn't be too disappointed in her.

He patted her hand, as though she were still his pampered child who knew nothing of the wider world. "Perhaps not yet. But when you've had time to think on it, I know you will feel differently. When the praetor returns to Rome after his tour of duty in Britannia, I am determined you'll go with him—as his wife."

As she and Elpis approached the public baths, Antonia still couldn't get her father's words from her mind. "He's set on this course of action, Elpis. He's deaf to my protests."

"The dominus will never force you to do something against your will."

It was true. She knew it. And she knew how rare that situation was. Had her father been a patrician, a member of the class he so admired, her wishes would mean nothing to him. If he decided she would remarry, then there would be no discussion.

She knew all this. But it didn't prevent the spark of irritation that he was so set on doing something he believed was in her best interest, no matter how she tried to dissuade him.

"Beside the fact I'll never marry the praetor, surely my father knows that if I did, I would once again be among those who shunned me during this last year?" It was a horrifying thought. Not least because she knew the women who'd turned their backs on her would, upon such an advantageous remarriage, be only too eager to take up the severed threads of friendship once again. As if nothing had happened.

"The dominus doesn't know of the true circumstances of this last year, domina," Elpis said, and their gazes clashed.

No, he didn't know how she had been frozen out of the social gatherings and invitations. How, in the eyes of Roman society, she had become a persona non grata. If she told him, she knew he'd be devastated on her behalf. If she ever confided as to how Scipio had treated her, she feared the possible consequences of her father's fury.

It was best he believed Scipio had divorced her for purely political reasons. It wasn't a lie. It simply wasn't the full depth of truth.

She drew in a deep breath. The situation with her father would be resolved eventually. But now she was moments from meeting with Gawain. She pushed her father's ambitions to the back of her mind. Gawain was her secret fantasy, a fleeting diversion, and while they were together, she would not disturb it by thinking of reality.

They entered the building and swiftly Antonia exchanged her

blue palla for Elpis' plain one. It wasn't much of a disguise but since she was virtually unknown in the city, it would suffice.

Heart pounding, she slipped outside and instantly caught sight of Gawain across the road. He didn't acknowledge her. He merely turned and began to stroll down a side road.

She let out a ragged breath and glanced at Elpis, whose face was impassive. "Do you think me entirely wicked, Elpis?" she whispered, as they followed Gawain at a respectable distance.

"No, domina," Elpis said dutifully. "But I don't want you to end up hurt. And I fear this path leads only to heartache."

Antonia laughed softly. "I have no heart left to ache, Elpis. Everything I have is devoted to Cassia. This is simply…" She hesitated for a moment. It sounded wrong, somehow, to encompass everything Gawain made her feel into one clinical word. Yet it was nothing less than the truth. "Physical."

Elpis turned to look at her. "I hope so." Her tone was not that of a slave to her mistress. Worry clouded her eyes. "There can be no future with this Cambrian, domina."

Gawain disappeared around a corner and Antonia shot Elpis a scandalized glance. "I'm not looking for a future with him, Elpis." *Juno, where had that idea come from?* Elpis knew better than anyone else why Antonia would never tie herself to another man. "Cassia will be here within the month. The day she arrives is the day this affair ends."

CHAPTER ELEVEN

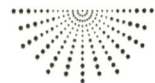

*G*awain waited just inside the tavern and watched Antonia as she approached. Even in this back street, where no patrician lady should set foot, she had an aura of confidence in her step and a smile tugged his mouth.

When he'd seen her across the square, as she left the Roman baths, something had tightened in his chest. He wasn't sure why. He'd been certain that she would turn up so it couldn't have been relief.

He leaned against the open doorjamb and saw her face light up as she caught sight of him. In that moment, she looked so young, so carefree, as though she wasn't risking her good name by meeting him here this day.

"Is this your idea of a disguise?" He tweaked the hood of her slave's cloak, which covered her pale gold hair. She laughed up at him and swayed towards him as if she intended to wrap her arms around him. But she didn't.

"Who will see me? Only you."

"Make sure it stays that way." The growled words were out before he could prevent them. Gods. He didn't usually care if his conquests bedded other men. But the thought of Antonia doing so did not sit well with him.

She raised her eyebrows. "I do believe we're talking at cross-purposes." She appeared to find that amusing if the quirk to her lips was anything to go by. "You have no cause to be jealous, Gawain."

That was taking it too far. He wrapped his arm around her waist and propelled her into the dark tavern.

"I'm not the jealous type," he said against her ear as he led her to the room he had hired. But the image of Antonia sharing her charms with another goaded his mind. "But while you're with me, don't even think about taking another lover."

What had possessed him to tell her that? He thrust open the door and allowed her to enter before him, aware that her slave remained in the passageway. She would be safe enough. He had given instructions, and paid the tavern keeper enough coin, to ensure they'd be undisturbed.

He kicked the door shut and watched Antonia as she slowly turned, examining the room. It was little more than a hovel. The thought irked him, even though it had been her idea to meet here instead of the luxurious surroundings of Carys' villa.

"This is quite charming." Her voice was breathless and from the subdued glow that came through the dingy windows her eyes sparkled with mirth. He took one step closer, ripped open her cloak and flung it onto the unsavory-looking bed.

"Do you often conduct assignations in such disreputable surrounds?" Perhaps she made a habit of it. The possibility stoked his ire. But why did it? Why did it bother him? Why did he give a shit where or how Antonia had taken her lovers in the past?

"Juno, of course not." She sounded scandalized. "This is the first time I've ever set foot inside a tavern. I confess it is quite exciting."

He laughed, even though he hadn't meant to. But she said the most extraordinary things, and in such a way that he was hard-pressed not to believe she meant every word. Maybe she did. Why would she lie?

"You're easily excited, my lady." His comment, and the unintended double entendre, sent another rumble of laughter through his chest.

"Oh yes." She gave him a sinful glance from beneath her lashes. "I'm very easily pleased, Gawain. I've never craved a great deal from life."

He pulled a jeweled pin from her hair and twisted it between his fingers, so the gems glittered. "I believe you." But what a gently bred Roman might consider the bare necessities would be unobtainable luxury for a noble born Druid. "So what is it you do crave from life, Antonia?"

Her smile faltered and for a fleeting moment he once again saw that haunting vulnerability cloud her eyes. *What is she hiding?* The demand thundered through his mind but before he could order his thoughts, before he could formulate the question, she gave a breathless laugh and shook her head, shattering the moment. Her ringlet bounced against her throat, captivating his attention, and she trailed her fingers along his jaw.

"No more than any other woman."

"Other Roman women." He covered her hand and pressed his lips against her open palm. Her gaze locked with his and he watched, bewitched, as desire darkened her ice-blue eyes.

"Are we so different from Celtic women?" Her question was barely above a whisper, and he caught an odd vulnerability in her voice.

"Yes." His hungry gaze roved over her aristocratic face, her intricately styled hair, the foreign gown she wore. But even if he dressed her as a Celtic noble, it wasn't the way she looked that divided them. "We live in two different worlds, Antonia. You wouldn't last a Roman month in mine."

A small smile curved her lips. "I didn't imagine you were so close-minded. How easily *you* could fit into the world of Roman politics."

Her words were unexpected. Once again, she appeared less than dazzled with her cursed empire and her attitude intrigued him. He slid his fingers through hers and tugged her forward. "Did you just insult me, my lady?"

"Do you have ambitions to infiltrate the Senate?"

She was laughing at him, but that wasn't all. She was laughing at her own culture, and he found it enchanting. "Do you think I'd succeed if I attempted such a feat?"

She tilted her head in a deliberately provocative manner. "I should like to witness such a thing. But I fear patricians are very fond of nepotism when it comes to matters of state."

"How fortunate I harbor no such ambitions, then." He slid the neckline of her gown off her shoulder and the savage mark of possession he'd given her the previous day riveted his attention.

"Is your way so different? Before the conquest would your chieftains welcome outsiders into their inner sanctum?"

His gut clenched at the word *conquest* but then an ice-cold realization speared through him.

Before the Romans had invaded, it was the Druids who'd held the power. Kings and chieftains had sought their wisdom and knowledge and deferred to them in all matters concerning the gods and portents.

It was the reason her emperor so feared and hated Druids. The reason he wanted to eliminate every last one in his cursed empire.

Druids did not, had never, open their sacred ranks to outsiders. The blood of the gods flowed through their veins and their magic passed down from one generation to the next. Occasionally an acolyte was accepted from the nobility or, rarely, the peasant class if they showed exceptional potential, but since the dawn of Creation, Druids had enjoyed an elevated, privileged status.

That didn't mean they were in any way similar to Roman patricians. The thought was abhorrent.

He frowned down at Antonia. She had only gently mocked his ways the same as she'd mocked her own. And she had no idea that he was a Druid, and therefore her bitterest enemy. But the unintentional parallel her words had drawn between their two cultures rankled, nevertheless.

"No, they wouldn't." It might irk to admit it, but in some things all peoples were united. "The ties of blood and links to ancestors are paramount."

"When our blood ties do not suffice," Antonia trailed her finger over the front of his shirt, a featherlight distraction that managed to shred his concentration. "We find adoption an appropriate solution."

He had the urge to laugh again, and all things considered, he wasn't sure why. How did Antonia manage to twist a conversation that had struck at the heart of his existence into something that tickled his sense of humor?

"Romans are a swamp of contradictions."

She rose onto her toes and brushed her lips over his. So soft. So irresistibly seductive. "Yes. I have always thought so."

He slid the tip of his tongue across the seam of her lips and wound his free arm about her waist, tugging her against his body so he could feel every delicious curve. "You also are contradictory."

"Good." She breathed the word into his mouth, and the familiar hint of fresh mint teased his senses. "How I would hate you to find me predictable."

This time he did laugh, and he tightened his grip on her hand and waist. Her erratic breath feathered his jaw and her breasts pressed against his chest in a delightful torture.

Predictable was the last thing he found her.

"Why are you still standing?" He untangled his fingers from

hers and palmed the firm globes of her arse. "I want you on your knees."

The vision of her on her knees before him, sucking him into her wet mouth, caused his balls to tighten with need. He would plunge his fingers through her artfully arranged curls, come inside her delectable mouth, and watch her swallow his hot seed. A strangled groan razed his throat at the potent image.

Antonia flattened her hands against his broad chest and the strong beat of his heart thudded against her palm. She loved the way he held her so forcefully, and the thought of him taking her from behind, while she knelt on the dirty floor, was intoxicating.

"First," she whispered, "I want you naked, Gawain. I want to explore every hard ridge of your body with my mouth." *Except his rod.* She thrust that notion aside with a shudder of distaste.

"On one condition." But already he tore his shirt over his head as if he couldn't wait for her to begin. Mesmerized, she drank in his magnificent, corded muscles and bronzed flesh and involuntarily the tip of her tongue moistened her lips.

"What condition?" Her voice was husky and her eyes locked between his thighs as he now slowly, maddeningly, tugged his braccae over his hips.

"That you also are naked." He kicked his clothes aside and a sigh escaped as she admired his proud weapon. She might not have any intention of using her mouth on that part of his body, but she couldn't wait to touch and stroke and feel its alluring texture.

"That doesn't seem unreasonable." With clumsy fingers, she unclasped the fibula at her shoulder, unable to tear her fascinated gaze from between Gawain's thighs. Already her core was damp and tender, and she fought the urge to squirm as she tugged free of her stola and pulled feverishly at her undertunic. She stepped from the pool of linen at her feet and cupped his strong jaw. "Now I have you at my mercy."

He cradled her hips, his hands hard and possessive and a delicious tremor claimed her sensitive folds.

"Not yet." He sounded on the verge of laughter again. She loved how easily she could amuse him. How different he was in reality from the first impression she'd gained when he'd appeared beside her father's carpentum.

She rose onto her toes, and her erect nipples brushed against his chest. His fingers bit into her and he tugged her forward, his shaft burning her stomach.

"You're not supposed to be touching me." Not that she wanted him to let go. But she also dearly wanted to explore his body and how could she do that if he drove her mindless with desire with barely a touch?

"That wasn't part of the bargain." His hands curved over her bottom, igniting a thousand dancing flames deep within her cleft. "You have a delectable arse, my lady. Did you know that?"

She laughed, shocked, and thrilled in equal scandalous measure by his unexpected observation. "I've never been told such a thing before." And then she couldn't help herself. "Have I really?"

His grin was the wickedest thing she'd ever seen. "One day soon," he said, and his gaze was so intense she couldn't have looked away if the world was ending, "your tempting arse will be mine, Antonia."

Her mouth dried. Her former friends had whispered of such delights, but it was something Scipio had never demanded from her. The thought of having Gawain take her *there* caused liquid heat to bloom low between her thighs and pump with erratic disarray through her blood.

She knew her face was flushed, knew her desire showed plainly in her eyes. But she didn't care. She stared up at him and the reflected lust that darkened his features aroused her as much as his erotic promise.

"You haven't answered, my lady." His finger caressed the outer edges of her crevice, an exquisite torture. "Does this thought excite you?"

"Yes." Her voice was low, hoarse, and did not sound like her at all. "Not today?" It was a question and her breath stalled in her throat in dark anticipation.

His fingers trailed up the length of her spine, while his other hand continued to hold her *arse* with predatory intention. Wet heat licked along her sheath, and she shifted against him, her nipples aching with need.

"No." His voice throbbed with passion and her hands fell from his jaw to cling onto his shoulders. He lowered his head, and his hot breath tantalized her ear. "I'll give you time to think on it, to imagine how it will feel when my cock claims your virginity."

CHAPTER TWELVE

*H*er nails dug into his rigid flesh and her legs threatened to collapse. If not for how he held her so securely, she knew she would fall at his feet.

Writhe at his feet. The image inflamed her overheated imagination.

"I trust you will not keep me waiting too long." The words were erratic, hard to articulate around the wild beat of her heart.

His teeth grazed her ear and she could imagine his sinful smile. "I'll keep you waiting until you're ready for me. Until you beg me for it."

His words smoldered through her veins, and she struggled against the urge to beg him for it now. If he could show restraint, then so could she. But it was hard to think of anything else but his breathtaking promise of hedonistic pleasure.

"Perhaps," she whispered, "you will be the one begging *me* for it."

His rumble of laughter vibrated through her, sending sparks of arousal across her sensitized skin. "There's a first time for everything."

She couldn't imagine Gawain begging for anything. But the seductive image of him begging for her favors entranced her, nevertheless.

Her fingers slid across his shoulders and along his powerful biceps, sculpting the muscled flesh. He relinquished his grip on her exposed bottom and stood before her, and when she glanced up at him, he had a half-smile on his lips, as though her tentative attempt at seduction amused him.

A wisp of unease wove through her mind. She might enjoy making him laugh, but there was a time and a place. And now, as she practiced her unsophisticated skills, was neither. He shouldn't be smiling at her. He should be battling the need to pin her to the bed.

"Is something wrong?" She heard the edge to her voice but couldn't help it. The thought of Gawain mocking her, the way Scipio had mocked her, caused her stomach to clench with distress.

"What could possibly be wrong?" His grin evolved, reminding her, obscurely, of a wolf eyeing its prey. "I'm about to be seduced by a beautiful woman. Every red-blooded man's fantasy."

His words stoked the embers glowing between her thighs and soothed the unease plaguing her mind. He wasn't laughing at her. He simply found sex an amusing pastime, and hadn't she discovered it could also be fun, the last time she'd been with him?

She had to answer him. Just because his idle comment had smothered her flare of panic, she knew full well that he'd meant nothing deep or personal by it. "Your practiced flattery will get you far."

For a moment, the muscles of his face tightened, as if she had insulted his honor. But it was gone in a flash and once again his eyes crinkled in apparent humor. "Then my mission is accomplished."

It was a perfectly reasonable response, and she knew she

should laugh. But something felt wrong, although she couldn't put her finger on it. Why did it matter that he was merely flattering her with his words? She'd always known that, right from the moment he'd set out to seduce her in Carys' atrium.

Hadn't she just virtually forced him to admit his ulterior motives? So why did the illogical wish weave through her breast that he'd never said such pretty words to another woman—that he hadn't said them to her simply because he felt he should?

This was insane. She had only limited time before she needed to leave him. Why was she wasting it by analyzing their conversation? Their conversation wasn't the reason she risked coming to see him.

Even if a part of her craved their conversation as passionately as she craved his body.

She pushed the errant thought aside. It had no place here, had no place in her life. Instead, she closed her eyes, pressed her lips against his chest and inhaled his intoxicating scent of primal danger and dark, unknowable forests.

Once again, she curved her hands around his biceps and his hard muscles and unforgiving strength sent delicious tremors cascading through her blood. She teased the tip of her tongue along the rough length of an old wound and felt him shudder beneath her touch.

Her fierce Cambrian warrior. The thought pounded through her mind, as potent as any exotic aphrodisiac.

Slowly her palms slid down his powerful arms, over his wrists, and flattened against his hands. How small her fingers were, compared to his. How easily he could bend her to his will, force her to do anything he desired. Except there was nothing she could imagine he would demand that she would not eagerly give.

Erotic shivers feathered over her body, and she circled her tongue around his erect nipple. His rock-hard shaft scorched her belly and his hands fisted, but he didn't grab her hips or spear his fingers through her hair. A thrill spun through her as she realized he was deliberately not touching her. Because she had told him he shouldn't.

A growl rumbled through his chest, and she abandoned his hands so she could explore the hard ridges of his body. Mouth still fastened over his irresistible flesh she pulled back so she was no longer crushed against him. The tips of her fingers caressed his abdomen, felt his taut muscles contract farther and it took all her willpower not to fall against him once again. How could she explore every delicious inch of him if his magnificent rod burning her flesh constantly distracted her?

"Bite me." His feral command thudded through her head, and she relinquished his nipple and looked up at him. He was staring at her, eyes glazed with lust, and he was no longer smiling. He looked in pain.

As she continued to gaze at him, mesmerized by the sight of her warrior lover poised on the edge of civility, he bared his teeth.

"Stop laughing and use your teeth on me, woman. Or I shall be forced to once again *touch you*."

She realized she was smiling. She also realized she couldn't stop. It might be an ephemeral illusion, but the feminine power that surged through her at both the look on his face and the agony in his words was exhilarating.

With slow deliberation, she returned her attention to his magnificent chest. She'd had no idea a man's nipples could become aroused in such a way, or that they might be as sensitive to touch as a woman's. Experimentally she lightly captured him between her teeth and his strangled groan thundered through her mind.

Encouraged, she sucked him between her lips and her nails dug into him as his heady essence of raw masculinity flooded her senses. His uneven breath dusted the top of her head and the erratic rise and fall of his chest enhanced the sensation of him inside her mouth.

She nibbled kisses across his chest, his light dusting of hair tickling her nose and lips and jaw. She flicked her tongue across his other nipple and then, daringly, sucked hard on his flesh.

Through the pounding of blood at her temples, she heard his seductive growl. Her hands gripped his hips as she slid sensuously down his body, no longer able to keep any distance between them, her sensitive nipples scoring a fiery trail along his rigid flesh.

Her nails scored across his taut buttocks—*his arse*—and with a breathless gasp she sank onto her knees. His mesmerizing erection filled her vision and her fingers tightened involuntarily as she gripped his behind.

"Antonia." The word was tortured. She knew he wanted her attention, but she couldn't drag her fascinated gaze away.

"Yes?" It was a throaty whisper, and clinging onto his arse with one hand her other glided over his hip.

"You are an enchantress." He made it sound like an accusation but still she couldn't look up at him.

"Yes," she breathed, because if he wanted her to be an enchantress, then she had no objection. Her finger trembled as she finally touched his rigid shaft, and the heat radiating from him scalded her enslaved senses.

"I've imagined you on your knees at my feet." His words were ragged. She held her breath and trailed her finger to his root. Merciful Juno. She gazed at his testicles in mute, reverential awe. Gawain's finger strayed across her face, as though he couldn't help himself. "The reality surpasses any of my fantasies."

She wanted to tell him that her fantasies were also surpassed, but it was impossible to speak. All she could do was admire the vision of masculine perfection displayed before her.

Her jagged breath sounded loud in her ears as she tentatively cradled his heavy balls. His fingers jerked against her face and then he twisted stray curls around his knuckles, sending darts of pleasure across her scalp.

"How long do you intend to torture me, enchantress?"

She licked her lips and breathed in his evocative, masculine essence. A heady, addictive scent of reined-in desire and impending sex. Ripples of need teased her damp cleft and her fingers tightened around his taut sac. If he expected a coherent answer, he was going to be disappointed.

Finally she released her death grip on his arse and dragged her fingernails across his hips, thrilled by the way her touch caused him to shudder with repressed desire. With infinite care, she curled her fingers around him, her breath hitching, heart hammering at her daring. He was so hard and hot and thick. She could feel his blood thundering beneath her palm, the sensation so arousing and astonishing she forgot how to breathe.

"Gods, Antonia." His hoarse voice penetrated her swirling senses but not enough for her to respond. "Take me now."

She dragged her gaze from his magnificent rod and looked up at him, her breath ragged. He gritted his teeth in a semblance of a smile and without warning plunged his hands through her hair, gripping her head in a merciless vise as he hauled her forward.

Her open mouth smashed against the length of his erection, and she attempted to rear back but Gawain's hold on her was absolute. Panic flared and she loosened her grip on him, flattening her palms against his thighs as he inexorably shifted their positions to his masculine advantage.

The familiar scream of denial lodged in her throat and a fetid wave of revulsion washed through her. Blindly she raked her nails along his thighs, her body rigid, her mind reeling.

No. No...

"No." Her voice cracked, and she sucked in a strangled gasp of air. She was no longer plastered against Gawain's length, and although his hands held her head, he had forced her to look up at him.

She couldn't look at him. She squeezed her eyes shut and wrapped her hands around his wrists in a vain attempt to loosen his grip.

"Antonia." His harsh voice whipped across her mind. She redoubled her efforts to escape before he forced her to—before he tarnished every memory they had made together.

"Release me." Her jagged command sounded pathetic to her ears and inwardly she shriveled. "I refuse to do it. You cannot make me." Except she knew only too well that he could make her. He might not have the right to force her to his will by virtue of a marriage contract. But he had the strength, and he could over-power her in the blink of an eye.

Her stomach churned. *Merciful Juno, please do not let me disgrace myself in front of him.*

"Look at me." His demand was absolute and against her will her eyes opened. He was kneeling in front of her, a savage gleam in his eyes, and to her infinite shame, she began to shake uncon-trollably. His mouth tightened in obvious distaste and his grip on her relaxed, but not enough for her to escape. "Curse the gods, Antonia. What's wrong?"

She tried to regulate her erratic gasps but failed. Gawain wasn't Scipio. Gawain had never raped her, and he wasn't forcing his shaft down her throat. He was asking her why she was behaving like a—

A useless, frigid encumbrance.

No. Her former husband had called her that, whenever she displeased him. But with Gawain, she wasn't frigid. With Gawain sex was everything she had always dreamed it could—*should*—be, and with this Cambrian warrior she had nothing to prove by way of producing a live, healthy son.

Her galloping heart slowed, her breath became less torturous. And still Gawain held her head and looked at her with that wild, intense expression on his face.

He had no idea why she was so panicked. The last thing she wanted to talk about was why, but she owed him an explanation.

"I'm sorry." Sorry for making a fool of herself. Sorry that Gawain had seen this side of her. When their affair ended, would this be all he recalled of their time together? "I cannot—I won't take you into my mouth."

Gawain stared into Antonia's panic-glazed eyes and forcibly relaxed his fingers. Sick disgust pounded through his gut at the knowledge he'd frightened her with his demand. But gods, she'd been on her knees before him. Her uneven breath had caressed his cock and he'd been certain that, within moments, she'd intended to wrap her delectable mouth around him.

His fingers trailed along her face. She didn't pull back with distaste, so he cradled her jaw.

"I'd never make you do something against your will." His pride was injured that she had even imagined such a thing and yet it dug deeper than mere pride. It speared to the elemental essence of who he was, and what Antonia thought he was. She had said he was no barbarian. But her reaction now proved otherwise. The question formed before he could prevent it. "Why would you think such a thing, Antonia?"

Her grip around his wrists relaxed, but she didn't release him. Instead, her thumbs gently caressed the back of his hands, but he wasn't certain whether she was even aware of her actions.

"I'm sorry." Her whisper tore into him. Why did she feel the need to keep apologizing? He was the one who was sorry. And he was the one who couldn't spit the words out. "In my heart I know you would never force me, Gawain. It wasn't you. It was just the memory of—of other times when I had no choice."

The disgust surged through him once again, but this time melded with impotent fury.

"You were forced to do this?" He enjoyed—more than enjoyed —a woman sucking his cock deep into her mouth. But the pleasure was mutual. The unsavory image of Antonia on her knees, being forced to accommodate a bastard Roman's lust hammered through his mind. "Who forced you?"

Not that it made any difference. He'd never be able to exact retribution. But the need to know clawed through his gut.

She looked at him, an odd expression on her face as though she found his reaction completely incomprehensible. "My former husband."

The savage urge to hunt down her former husband, hack off his raping cock and shove it down his throat pounded through Gawain's head. He fought against the rabid rage thundering through his veins yet couldn't rid himself of the insidious feeling that Antonia, a child of the empire, was as much a spoil of war as any of his enslaved countrymen.

And, as such, both deserved and demanded his protection.

He stared into her beautiful eyes and recalled the haunting shadows he'd glimpsed the first day they'd met. Had he discovered the reason for her fleeting moments of melancholy?

"And you've never tried to purge the memory of his actions with one of your lovers?"

Inexplicably, she blushed. And while the sight entranced him, it still confused him. But at least she was no longer shaking in fear or trying to push him away.

"No." Her voice was so hushed he could scarcely hear her. "I may have misled you in this matter." She broke eye contact and stared at his chest. "You are the first lover I've ever taken."

Her words punched through him, a physical jolt. He was her *first*? Her *only*? Why hadn't he realized?

But there had been many clues. He'd chosen to disregard them. The way she'd acted the first day they met. Her enchanting moments of innocence that he'd imagined were simply part of her practiced seduction.

The only man beside himself that Antonia had known was her husband. An inconsiderate Roman bastard who'd made her perform an act she hated. And he, Gawain, *her first lover*, had just attempted to make her do the very same thing.

He wasn't often speechless, but he couldn't think of a thing to say. Silence stretched between them and finally Antonia looked up at him, and the wary expression on her face speared through his chest.

He might not have a clue what to say to her, but he needed to say something. "I am honored."

Her fingers twitched around his wrists, as though she wasn't sure whether he mocked her or not. He clawed through his paralyzed brain to find something that would reassure her. And could think of only one question.

"Why did you choose me?"

"Oh." Her hands slid from his wrists but before she could do anything else, he captured them and pressed them against his chest. She frowned as if she didn't understand his action but that was no surprise. He didn't understand this overwhelming need to comfort her either. He just knew that if he didn't, he risked losing her.

Losing her? She was only a Roman noblewoman. He was only with her because she was willing and available. Except the thoughts were hollow and instead of reassuring him of the fleeting duration of this liaison, it left him feeling somehow... uneasy.

"Oh?" Gently he shook her captive hands. "Why, Antonia?"

She shifted on her knees and then sighed. "I wanted to experience sex with a man of my choosing. Until I met you, I had never found one who," she hesitated for a moment, "appealed to me."

Once again words failed him. Antonia knelt before him, naked and at his mercy in a squalid tavern room, her hair tumbling from its jeweled restraints around her shoulders. She was *only a Roman noblewoman* but in this moment, he knew her heritage meant nothing to him.

All that mattered was that Antonia was a woman and she had chosen him to be her first illicit lover.

He stood, tugging her to her feet. "Do I still appeal to you, my lady?" He injected a faint note of mockery, but only to disguise just how much her answer meant to him. He wasn't ready to end their liaison yet. Somehow he would show Antonia she had no need to fear that he would ever force her to do anything she wasn't more than willing to experience.

The actions of her despicable former husband would not dictate when or how this affair ended.

A smile illuminated her face, as though his question had, inexplicably, eased her mind. "You more than appeal to me, Gawain." Her voice was breathless, and the knowledge that she hadn't said those words to countless other men in the past heightened the seductive web her whisper spun around him. "Do I still appeal to you?"

He pulled her against his body so that she could feel how much she still appealed to him. "What do you think?" He wound his arm around her waist, and her chilled flesh caused him to silently curse. "You're cold."

She wriggled, and her erect nipples teased his chest as she slid her arms around him and held him tight. "I'm not cold where it matters."

He laughed and stepped back to the bed. "I would not have you cold at all."

"Then you had best warm me up, my Cambrian warrior."

Her *what*? Her Cambrian warrior? He grinned down at her, even though she'd called him by the hated Roman name.

"I'm your warrior, am I?" He lay on the bed and pulled her down on him. He wouldn't have her silken skin touch a common tavern bed.

"Yes." She flattened her hands against his shoulders as she

straddled his hips and smiled down at him in triumph. "And I am about to conquer you."

He molded her firm thighs and sculpted the curve of her arse and dip of her waist. Her eyes were dark with lust, her pink lips parted and her hair, half contained, half tumbling in disarray, gave her an air of irresistible ravishment. He battled the primitive urge to impale her and make her his. "Then conquer me, enchantress."

CHAPTER THIRTEEN

*A*ntonia gazed down at her wild Cambrian warrior. He had a half-smile on his face and his hands captured her waist in a touch so light it would take no effort to pull from his embrace. Yet his touch warmed her, not simply her chilled skin but sank into her blood, the very marrow of her bones.

She had no wish to pull from his embrace. As the tips of his fingers caressed the sensitive curve of hip and waist, a strange pain spiraled through the center of her breast. His reaction to her refusal to accommodate his desires, his obvious disgust with her former husband when she had gathered the nerve to confess, staggered her.

Her personal experience was limited but she knew, from feminine confidences, how dearly men enjoyed such practices. That Gawain hadn't insisted she continue or, almost as horrifying, ridiculed her, caused the odd constriction consuming her chest to weave deep into her heart.

Slowly she leaned closer and brushed her lips across his. He trailed a seductive path along her back, across her shoulders and down her biceps. Tiny rivers of fire ignited beneath his touch, causing heated tremors across her sensitized skin.

With a breathy sigh, she speared her fingers through his hair, and combed the dark blond length across the rough bed cover. His bronzed skin, foreign looks and the untamed air that radiated from him all combined to give the impression of a savage barbarian of a conquered land. She'd told him once he was no barbarian, but she hadn't fully realized the truth of her words.

Rome prided herself on being superior to all her provinces, the cultural center of all nations. But it had taken Gawain, a native of this far-flung corner of the empire, to show her the kind of respect she'd never received from her own husband, a patrician who could trace his lineage back to the founding of that great city.

She wound his hair around her fingers, grazed her cheek against his jaw and flicked the tip of her tongue over his pierced earlobe. He tasted as divine as a mighty god of Olympus and the absurd thought made her smile.

"What amuses you, my lady?" His deep voice sent desire rippling through her. She nibbled kisses across his shoulder and his arms wound around her, imprisoning her.

"You amuse me." She shifted in his embrace, her nipples hard against his chest, her breasts aching for his touch. "You enthrall me."

His body shook with silent laughter, and she abandoned his shoulder to watch his face. He caught her glance and she thought she might drown in the dark depths of his amber-flecked eyes.

"Your honeyed words," he said, as his hands stroked along her back, creating magical responses she had never dreamed might exist, "will get you far."

Enchanted by the way he had twisted her own words back at her, she untangled her fingers from his hair and flattened her hands either side of his head on the prickly mattress.

"How far?" She breathed the sultry question against his lips as she provocatively glided her tender folds over his engorged shaft.

He gave an agonized groan and finally cupped her breasts,

lifting them, pressing them together, rubbing his thumbs over their tortured peaks. She arched her back, filling his palms, delighting in the possessive way he held and stroked her body.

"As far as you desire." The way he growled the words at her she wasn't sure whether it was a threat or a promise. And when he pinched her nipples, sending sharp arrows of fire from her breasts to her core, she knew she didn't care. Either way would be an unforgettable, ecstatic adventure.

She lifted her hips and eased onto him. Her wet sheath stretched as she slowly sank down his thick organ. She could feel every inch of him filling her, possessing her and she couldn't tear her eyes away from his hypnotic gaze.

For seeming eternity, they remained utterly still, joined in the most primal of ways. Yet somehow, the connection was deeper, elemental. *Foolish* whispered across her passion-soaked mind but she ignored the voice of reason. Now, here, Gawain was hers and he encompassed her world. She wouldn't ruin the moment with logical reality.

He released one of her breasts and trailed downwards, across her belly. One finger slid between their bodies and caressed her sensitive clit. She gasped as shocking waves of pleasure vibrated through her cleft.

"Ride me, Antonia." His smoky command wrapped around her senses like temple incense, exotic and irresistible. "Make me come inside your tight slit."

A shudder ricocheted from the tip of her captive nipple to her swollen clitoris. Instinctively she tightened her internal muscles. He abandoned her breast and cupped her bottom, his hold both tender and possessive, and instinctively her hips began to move.

"Gawain." His name slipped from her lips, a heated caress. Her nails dug into the mattress as his finger continued to tease her silken peak. She quickened her pace, riding his length as he had commanded. She looked down at him, her captive warrior. His hair tangled around his face, his eyes were locked with hers. The rhythmic friction against her aroused clit and his rigid cock inside her sent fiery sparks cascading through her blood.

His grip on her rear became harsh. The intensity of his expression held her spellbound. He bared his teeth, a primal growl echoing around the room and savagely slammed into her.

Her balance tilted and she fell forward, but still he rammed into her, pinning her in place with one heavy hand on her arse. He was beneath her, but still he mastered her, his hand and his shaft molding her to his will. His finger circled her throbbing clit, an addictive torture, and she squirmed helplessly. Beyond the frenzied pounding of her heart, she heard his guttural roar and felt his hot release flood her channel.

Raw feminine power thundered through her veins. Mesmerized by the glazed lust in his eyes, captivated by his all-encompassing penetration, her sheath contracted around him. Her orgasm shattered through her, entrapping him, enslaving him, and milking him of every last drop of his essence.

She collapsed onto him, mind reeling, body quivering. He pulled his arm from between their slick bodies and held her close, a strangely comforting gesture. Slowly her erratic breath evened, and the world swirled back into focus.

Gawain still held her impaled on his shaft. She had no desire or energy to move. Instead, she shifted into a more comfortable position and smiled as he stirred within her wet cleft.

"And still I amuse you." He sounded sated, satisfied and infinitely seductive. "How easy you are to please, Antonia."

She trailed her fingers across his shoulder, her head against his chest. "So you delight in telling me."

His body shook in a silent laugh. She smiled again and idly traced her finger over his engraved torque. Then, for no discernible reason she could fathom, he suddenly stiffened and swore softly. She might not be fluent in the Cambrian language, but it was not so different in essence to the local dialect in Gallia that she had learned as a child.

She raised her head and looked at him. A forbidding frown darkened his brow, but she couldn't believe it was aimed at her. "What is it?"

"It didn't occur to me before, but now—knowing I'm your first lover—" He hesitated, and his frown grew even more ominous. She frowned back, bemused.

"What didn't occur to you?"

His big hand cradled her face. "I did nothing to prevent the possibility of impregnating you."

Juno. She stared at him in horror, and could feel her face flaming in shame. This wasn't a topic of conversation a woman had with a man. She attempted to respond, but words failed her.

Gawain's arm tightened around her waist as if he imagined she were about to flee. Perhaps she might have, if she weren't paralyzed with mortification.

"Antonia, the first time we came together I assumed you'd taken the necessary precautions. But just now—there was no excuse. I should have taken more care."

She wanted to curl up and hide. But she couldn't move because he held her so securely. There was no help for it. She would have to admit that she was protected.

Except Gawain wasn't her husband. He had no rights over her body in the way Scipio had. There was no possibility that he would dispense harsh punishment for daring to do such a thing without his express permission. Yet the thought didn't ease her mind, not when she had to explain such intimacies aloud.

"Gawain." Her voice sounded choked, and he appeared to find her response painful if the look on his face was anything to go by. Before she could squeeze another agonizing word from her throat, he gave a heavy sigh.

"Do not distress yourself, Antonia. I'll speak to Carys. She's a renowned healer and will know exactly what to give you."

Antonia stared at him, dumbstruck. She couldn't fathom whether she was more shocked that Gawain was so concerned for her welfare, or the fact that he so casually knew—and had no problem with—Carys' knowledge of such forbidden feminine things.

"Antonia." There was an edge in his voice now. "Everything will be all right. Trust me on this."

"There's no need." The words tumbled from her lips, and she studiously avoided eye contact. "Elpis is well versed in such matters. There's no danger that your seed will plant within me."

His silence unnerved her further and she risked glancing up. She wasn't sure what she expected, but it certainly hadn't been the satisfied smile that he bestowed her way.

"You were that sure of having me then, my lady?"

He was jesting with her? After the conversation they had just exchanged? She was quite sure Scipio would have beaten her senseless had he ever discovered she'd taken precautions against conceiving another of his children.

Gawain isn't Scipio. She knew this, of course. But the differences between them continued to astonish her. She attempted to gather her scattered thoughts.

"I simply wanted to be prepared for any possibility."

"Your foresight is admirable."

Amusement weaved through his words, and he played with her hair, winding curls around his fingers. The lingering strands of embarrassment drifted into oblivion, and she smiled back at him, warmth encasing her heart. "I'm glad you think so."

She should rise, call for Elpis, prepare to leave. Instead, she once again cuddled into him, relishing the way he held her tight as though he had no immediate thoughts of leaving either.

Idly she resumed tracing her finger over the elaborate engravings on his silver torque. Did the images mean something or were they—

Shock stabbed through her as she finally recognized what she was looking at. Tiny wings and twin serpents intertwined around a rod. Before she could think better of it the words tumbled from her lips.

"Why do you have the images of Mercury on your torque?"

He raised his head and gave her a pained look. "He's not Mercury. He is Lugus, an ancient Celtic god. Why would I place your heathen god around my throat?"

The same iconography—the wings and serpents—were repeated in his intricate earring. They weren't indecipherable at all. The images, so similar to Mercury's and yet, now that she studied them closely, possessed a wilder, more barbaric design, enhanced the danger of this illicit affair and renewed desire stirred between her thighs. Gawain was still inside her. Goddess, she loved having him inside her.

She leaned closer and nibbled his jaw, tasting his flesh and grazing her lips against his light stubble.

"Don't be offended." She didn't think he was, but also didn't want him to think she made light of his own beliefs. "My father has a special affinity with Mercury, so I'm very familiar with his images."

He grunted. "Perhaps it is Lugus your father worships."

Antonia laughed at him. Gawain resisted the urge to grin back at her. The god Lugus, finder of paths, a teacher and historian, had chosen him as acolyte while Gawain was a child. He could still recall his sense of pride and awe when his father had passed down the treasured torque when Gawain had celebrated his thirteenth winter. The heirloom had been passed from father to son for generations and Gawain had always believed that one day he would continue the unbroken chain.

But that was before the Romans had invaded. Before the woman he had once believed was destined to be his wife had turned her back on him.

Before Lugus had retreated into impenetrable shadows and his faith in his gods had faltered.

Yet he kept the torque around his throat. A reminder, perhaps, of when he had imagined his life's path was preordained. A link back in time to his ancestors. To his father.

"No." Antonia folded her arms across his chest to prop herself up. "My father is a wonderful man, but he doesn't easily embrace the gods of other cultures."

"Rome does not embrace." He wasn't sure why this conversation irritated him. It wasn't as if he felt especially predisposed to defend his own abandoned gods with Antonia. "Rome swallows and consumes."

"Oh." Antonia blinked and an enchanting blush highlighted her cheeks. He knew he was staring, but couldn't help himself. "Rome doesn't *always* swallow, Gawain."

For a moment, he didn't comprehend her meaning, but her blush deepened, giving her an irresistible air of seductive innocence. A snort of laughter escaped his throat and banished the hovering black mood as he finally understood.

"I wouldn't protest if you changed your mind." He trailed his finger along her heated face and an odd notion stabbed through his brain. He knew Antonia had deliberately twisted his words into a personal, sexual implication but he hadn't intended to offend her with his barbed remark. "You do know I don't blame you for any of your countrymen's actions, don't you?"

He'd never felt the need to say such a thing before when he'd been with a Roman woman. He might not personally blame them, but they were still the enemy, and he had no compunction in using his enemy.

But he didn't consider Antonia his enemy. He'd never wanted to have her simply for information he might glean, because she had no information. And while that had always been the truth, the added knowledge that she didn't flit from lover to lover to add illicit excitement into her existence stirred a strange element of protectiveness deep in his chest.

She was Roman, but he would not callously wound her with his views.

"Of course," she whispered, but there was an underlying thread of sadness, as though she knew, as well as him, that their opposing cultures would always stand between them.

The knowledge hovered, like an insistent wasp. Why did it matter? They wouldn't be together long enough for such a thing to matter. In fact, why was he still lying here, holding her in his arms? He had leads to follow up, elusive contacts to track down. If other Druids were, indeed, in Camulodunon, he intended to discover them.

But it felt too good holding Antonia in his arms.

Eventually it was she who stirred, reluctance showing in every move, and he pulled on his clothes before she summoned Elpis to assist her.

Once again, Gawain leaned against the door of the tavern, but this time he watched as Antonia walked away from him. She'd covered her head with Elpis' cloak, but nothing could disguise the fact she was a noblewoman. It wasn't simply the quality of her gown beneath the cloak. It was inherent in her bearing.

With a half-smile he followed at a discreet distance. He'd ensure she reached the bathhouse in safety and only then would he be on his way.

As she entered the main square, he decided he would catch up with her. It wouldn't ruin her reputation to be seen with him in such a public place, not when she was acquainted with his kin, Carys. But before he could put his plan into action, she was accosted by a Roman patrician in purple striped toga and flowing cloak.

His senses on full alert, Gawain sank back into the shadows of the side alley. It was not just any patrician. It was the one who'd been speaking to Maximus the previous day.

He watched as the Roman took Antonia's hand in a far too familiar manner. It was obvious they were acquainted and equally obvious that the Roman believed he had the right to not only kiss Antonia's hand but then take her arm in a blatantly possessive way.

What was the Roman saying to her? His head was inclined towards her, and he appeared to be admonishing her. Because he'd witnessed her leave a less salubrious quarter of town? Who did he think he was?

Irritation simmered. Not merely because of the Roman's behavior but because, deep in his gut, a sliver of guilt stirred. He should be the one escorting Antonia back to the bathhouse. He'd only agreed to this compromise after she'd reminded him that if her reputation was called into question her father would never let her out of his sight again.

He was further irked by the knowledge that had the Roman seen Gawain by Antonia's side as they left the alley her reputation would, most surely, now be in tatters.

The guilt, irritation, and rising unease at his reaction to this situation smoldered through his blood. Before the invasion, he'd enjoyed many Celtic lovers from the noble and Druid ranks. The woman he'd loved had been a powerful Druid. But even with her —especially with her—he'd never been consumed by this unnerving imperative to protect them from danger both seen and unknown.

As a warrior and member of the elite, he would have fought to the death to save their lives. They were his people. His fellow Druids would have done the same for him.

But Antonia was not a Celt, and she certainly wasn't a warrior. She would no sooner know how to wield a weapon than she would know how to assert her rights against her cursed empire and all it stood for.

Was that why he couldn't shift this insidious mantle of responsibility that seeped through his chest whenever he thought of her vulnerability? But if that was the case, why hadn't he felt this way with his Celtic lovers who had chosen not to follow the warrior path?

They had reached the bathhouse. The Roman finally left her, stalking off to the basilica, and Gawain tore his malignant glare from the man's retreating back to refocus on Antonia.

She stood beside a fluted column and was looking across the square at him. She caught his gaze, gave a barely perceptible shrug that spoke volumes of her opinion of the Roman, and then smiled at him.

The knot in his gut eased. He made no response but waited until she disappeared inside the building before finally turning away.

Now he could concentrate on hunting down elusive Druids.

CHAPTER FOURTEEN

*G*awain strolled with apparent nonchalance down the filthy back street. Thieves and cutthroats and worn-out whores infested this part of Camulodunon, a dank underbelly of the colonia into which no respectable Roman would dare venture.

For five days, he'd followed his instincts, seeking answers from those who didn't even realize they were being questioned. He'd pieced together random snatches of information, overheard conversations and seemingly unconnected snippets of gossip and speculation.

It was ironic to think that all the time he'd been gathering information on the mood of the local tribes on rebellion, fellow Druids had been infiltrating the colonia under his very nose.

A great hulk of a man emerged from the shadows and Gawain tensed, ready to draw his dagger in an instant. The other man made no threatening gesture, but his stance was not welcoming. But despite the rough clothing and unkempt beard of the silent man, an aura of power radiated from him.

Anticipation surged through Gawain's blood. He was certain he'd found the one he'd been seeking but he had no intention of assuming anything. He took another step forward and didn't miss how the man's fingers wound around his dagger in readiness. They were close enough to kill each other. But they were also close enough so that their words could not easily be overheard.

"By the benevolence of Annwyn, greetings." It was a formal, rarely used welcome between chieftains in Cymru. But Gawain spoke the words in the tongue of the ancients, the sacred language of the gods that only Druids understood.

The other man didn't show by a flicker as to whether Gawain's words made sense or not. For long moments they continued to maintain eye contact, senses alert. No one approached or called out to them.

They might have been alone in the alley, in the way all noise of life had stilled.

Finally the other man stirred. "By the gods of my ancestors, welcome." He also spoke in the language of the ancients and exhilaration pumped through Gawain's veins. He and Carys were not alone in Camulodunon. "My name is Rhys," the Druid said in their own tongue. The language of the gods was not for everyday conversation, after all.

"Gawain. Is there somewhere we can talk?"

Rhys indicated Gawain should accompany him and they made their way along the alley. "I've been aware of your presence since the day you first entered Camulodunon," Rhys said, and Gawain shot him a look of disbelief.

"Why didn't you make contact?"

Rhys turned a corner, and they entered a small square with a tired-looking market. Nothing like the prosperous market that graced the forum several times a week.

"You lodge with the tribune and his wife."

"The tribune's wife is from Cymru. We're kin by virtue of our clan. I'll protect the princess and her daughter with my life." It wasn't so much a threat as an explanation and when Rhys gave a brief nod Gawain knew that he had told the older man nothing that he didn't already know.

Gawain could only hope that whatever other information Rhys had discovered didn't include the fact that Carys was also a Druid. Not that she wanted to deny her heritage. But because the fewer people who knew, the safer she was.

"You've been attempting to stir a rebellion here." Rhys shot him a glance Gawain couldn't decipher. "I wanted to see how far you were willing to go. Two turns of the wheel ago, I also came to Camulodunon with the same desire. But, as you've discovered, the time is not yet ripe."

Rhys had been in the colonia since Gawain and the rest of his clan had retreated to the Isle of Mon? What had he been doing all this time?

His thoughts must have shown on his face as Rhys gave him a mirthless smile. "There's more than one way to undermine an enemy, Gawain."

It was late when he returned to the villa. Although both Carys and Maximus had offered him a room inside for his personal use, he preferred to sleep in one of the outlying buildings. Not that Maximus considered them buildings. Huts, he'd called them. Likely built years ago by locals, who had long since been evicted when the first wave of invaders had arrived. But it suited Gawain. Made him feel less constricted than being enclosed within a Roman constructed dwelling.

He kicked off his leather shoes, lay on the narrow, straw pallet that served as his bed and linked his fingers behind his head. Rhys had interrogated him although Gawain couldn't be sure that he had told the older Druid anything he hadn't already known. When Rhys finally disclosed the extent of the underground network of Druids that inhabited Camulodunon, Gawain hadn't been able to disguise his shock.

Even now, hours later, his mind still reeled. Why hadn't he been aware of their presence? Why hadn't any of them approached him? It certainly hadn't taken Rhys long to discover what Gawain really was.

But Gawain knew why their presence had eluded his senses. It was because he hadn't been looking for fellow Druids in Camulodunon. Not once had he sought guidance from any god but Lugus. He'd been so wrapped up in the failure of his mission with Caratacus and his own lucky escape from certain death at the hands of the Brigantes, that the possibility had never seriously entered his head.

And if it had, he certainly wouldn't have imagined them hiding with the dregs of humanity with no firm battle plan in mind.

There was strength in numbers. On his own, there was little he could do to change attitudes and will. But he was no longer alone. They could destabilize the enemy from within. Disrupt their love of order, destroy their cursed administration center. Carys would be safe. For her own reasons, she was determined that Maximus would return to Rome and Gawain would ensure she'd left Britain before any uprising.

Antonia's image pierced his brain and his thoughts slammed to a halt. *Antonia*. He gritted his jaw. He would ensure Antonia's safety. She would not be harmed.

But left to Rhys, there would be no uprising at all. His plans to undermine the mighty Roman Empire consisted of merely surviving. Of teaching their ways to those who could be trusted. Of ensuring their gods were not forgotten and their culture not erased.

It wasn't enough. It wasn't nearly enough.

"Gawain?" Carys' voice at the door jerked him brutally back

to the present. She pushed open the door without waiting for an invitation. "Can I come in?"

He remained on the pallet. "Is something wrong?"

In the fading light of day, Carys looked nothing like the Roman persona she perfected in public. How would she fare in Rome when she would need to keep up that façade without respite?

"No." Carys sat at the end of his pallet and wrapped her arms around her knees. "Although I doubt you'll take kindly to what I'm about to say."

"Why? Have you changed your mind about Antonia's visits here?" Since their assignation in the tavern, Antonia had met him at Carys' three times and the two women had struck up a tentative friendship. At least, it was tentative from Antonia's end. Carys, as faithful as ever to the obscure dictates of her goddess, had embraced Antonia as though she were a long-lost friend.

As though she were attempting to fill the gap in her heart left by her childhood friend, Morwyn.

He refused to think of Morwyn. The woman who had never loved him, never pretended to love him, yet whom he had fallen for, just the same.

"Of course not." Carys sounded dismissive of his concern. He heaved himself upright and leaned against a timber post.

"Then your uptight moralistic husband disapproves of my debauchery when it concerns Lady Antonia."

Carys smirked. "Maximus is not uptight." Then she sighed. "He doesn't approve. But he'd rather you meet here, where it's safe, than in a sordid tavern."

Gawain kept his mouth shut. He should have known Carys had told Maximus of that. Carys told her Roman everything. It was the reason he had no intention of telling her about Rhys or the discovery of Druids in Camulodunon.

Not that he doubted her loyalty. But Carys' loyalty was

continually torn between the heritage of her birth and the devotion she bore for her husband.

She would never betray her people. But keeping such a secret from Maximus would destroy her.

He took a deep breath and moved on. "Then what unsavory news do you have for me?"

She pulled a face. "The praetor somehow discovered your existence and extended the invitation to you to his feast tomorrow night."

Gawain snorted in disbelief. Spend an entire night in the company of that arrogant, Druid-hating bastard? Not to mention the overly familiar way he'd approached Antonia the other day. The next time they'd met, she had explained he was an acquaintance of her former husband but that certainly hadn't done anything to elevate Gawain's opinion of him. "I'm busy."

Carys gave him an insincere smile. "Doing what?"

He grinned back. "I haven't decided yet."

"That's unfortunate." Carys brushed nonexistent dust from her gown and then shot him a sly sideways look. "His other guests are Antonia and her father."

His amusement fled. Why hadn't Antonia told him? Logically he knew she had no reason to tell him such a thing. For all he knew she might dine with various high-ranking politicians every night. He'd never considered it before. And now the thought had occurred to him, he discovered the possibility irritated him beyond reason.

He also realized he had no intention of passing up the opportunity of spending an evening with Antonia at a social gathering. It would give him the chance to observe the praetor, to discover whether his only interest in Antonia was, as she had gone to great pains to stress, merely that of an old friend.

"In that case," he stared at Carys, daring her to comment. "I'll cancel my previous engagement and attend this cursed feast."

"I thought you might." Carys patted his foot before standing up. "And now I am off to collect my wager from Maximus. He was certain you'd refuse the invitation."

It was only when the door swung shut behind her that a discordant thought thudded through Gawain's mind. Why did he care what interest the praetor had in Antonia? He knew she would never take another lover while they were together. And when their affair ended, she could do as she wished.

But the sense of unease, of something off kilter lingered, and he couldn't place it. He only knew that the thought of that bastard Roman touching her curdled his guts.

Antonia threaded the brightly colored silk ribbons through her fingers as the stall keeper urged her to buy one of each shade at an exorbitant price. Tonight, she and her father were to dine with the praetor, and she wasn't looking forward to it. Especially since her father appeared to think the evening was a precursor to the praetor declaring his intentions towards her.

Well. He could declare all he liked. She'd given him no encouragement and there was nothing he could say or do that would change her mind. And that was assuming her father hadn't misunderstood the praetor in the first place.

She returned her wandering attention to the ribbons. "The blue will suit Cassia perfectly, won't it?" She glanced at Elpis by her side. "The shade matches her eyes exactly."

"She has your eyes, domina," Elpis said, her voice warm with affection. But who could fail to love little Cassia? She was a gift from Juno herself and no one who met her could fail to fall under her spell.

In less than three weeks, she would arrive in Britannia, along with the guardians Antonia had entrusted her daughter's safety to for the last year. Last night she'd broached the subject of adoption with her father. He'd been bemused, then awkwardly sympathetic and she knew he was thinking of the babes she had lost during her marriage.

But he'd never known of her final pregnancy. By then she had been too heartsore by her losses to risk raising her father's hopes once more.

Eventually he'd murmured something about how she would have her own children one day, when she remarried, and had then lapsed into a brooding silence when she'd gently told him she desired no such thing.

The seed had been sown. Antonia knew she could persuade him. And when Cassia arrived, her father would already be half in love with her and unable to do anything but fall in with Antonia's plans.

An odd prickle drifted across the back of her neck, and she frowned and glanced over her shoulder. Her heart leaped in her breast and warmth flooded her heart as, through a gap in the crowd, she saw Gawain at the other side of the forum.

She knew she was smiling. Knew she should try to be more circumspect, but she couldn't help it. Just looking at him caused her pulses to race. It had been two days since they'd last been together, and she wouldn't see him again until tomorrow.

The truth was stark. She'd missed him. Missed the mocking glitter in his eyes, the deep rumble of his laugh, his enchanting accent when he talked.

Ah, how she enjoyed their conversations. No subject was taboo. Roman politics, Celtic tribal traditions, and the cycle of feminine indispositions. She'd almost choked on the delicacies Carys had provided when Gawain had casually touched on that. But he'd been respectful, interested and shockingly informative and his uninhibited attitude delighted her.

A whisper of unease drifted through her mind. Even though she tried to ignore it, the thought weaved into her consciousness nevertheless.

Conversation wasn't the reason she was supposed to crave

Gawain's company. It was all about the sex. *Lust*. And yes, she missed his body, missed the way his hands and mouth made her feel, but it was so much more than that.

It didn't mean anything. So she liked him. Perhaps she liked him far more than she should for her peace of mind. But when she'd embarked on this liaison, she hadn't imagined he possessed such a complex, intriguing personality.

Three more weeks and the affair would end. She took a deep breath and attempted to banish the inevitable. She wouldn't think of that. Not until the last possible moment.

She passed the ribbons to Elpis to deal with and rose onto her toes to keep Gawain in her sight as the throng of bodies threatened to conceal him. Although he looked relaxed, a strange tenseness clung to him, as though he searched for someone without wishing to give himself away. Illicit thrills raced through her. Was he searching for her?

Perhaps they could steal an hour to be together. She took a couple of steps in his direction and then paused. Gawain's gaze locked for a brief moment on something across the square and instinctively Antonia followed his glance.

An eerie shiver scuttled along her arms although she couldn't fathom why. There was nothing unusual over there. Except for a fleeting instance, she had the absolute certainty that an unspoken message had passed between Gawain and a huge man dressed in peasant clothing.

Already the stranger had vanished into the crowd, and she shook her head, attempting to dislodge the foolish unease that drifted through her mind. There had been no unspoken connection. And even if there had, what did it matter? Gawain was entitled to communicate with whomever he wished. Even if across the crowded forum was an unusual way to do it.

Even if the entire exchange did have a dark aura of furtiveness about it.

She huffed out a breath and returned her attention to Gawain. But he, too, had vanished.

CHAPTER FIFTEEN

*A*ntonia stared in disbelief as Gawain entered the praetor's atrium, along with Carys and her tribune. It had never occurred to her that he might attend. Why hadn't he told her?

As pleasantries were exchanged, she tried to stop staring but wasn't sure she succeeded. But he looked so magnificent, despite the foreign clothes he insisted on wearing. Or perhaps because of them. They certainly enhanced the seductive aura of primal power that radiated from him, without him making the slightest effort to impress.

Or perhaps she was simply biased.

He certainly gave the impression that they were scarcely acquainted, offering her a formal half bow that turned her knees weak. It was just as well he hadn't touched her. She would likely dissolve into a puddle of mindless desire at his feet.

The image caused a wayward giggle to escape, and she hastily turned it into a cough before her lust disgraced her father's name.

"Allow me the honor of escorting you, Lady Antonia," the praetor said, taking her arm before she could bestow such honor his way. She resisted the urge to glance over her shoulder at

Gawain. She might have imagined it, but when he'd asked about her relationship with the praetor, she'd received the oddest impression that he had been jealous.

A foolish supposition. She didn't want Gawain to be jealous and why should he, in any case? Yet the feeling lingered and try as she might, she couldn't deny the frisson of pleasure at the knowledge Gawain didn't like the praetor's over-possessive attitude.

"This townhouse is not up to the standards of those in other provinces," he said as he led them into the dining room. "The quality of the mosaics is most disappointing but what can you expect from this barbarous land?"

Antonia sank onto one of the low couches and glanced at the other guests. Carys glared murder at the praetor's back, her husband held her hand as though he feared she might follow through and Gawain's face was impassive.

Her father simply looked resigned.

"Such workmanship takes years to perfect," she said, silently astonished at the way Carys schooled her features and once again looked like the perfect patrician wife. "Once local craftsmen have the opportunity to study under the masters then they too will be able to create art to rival any in Rome."

The corner of Gawain's mouth twitched in obvious amusement at her counterstrike. It was only as she resisted the urge to smile back at him that she realized she had been staring at him.

"Very true." The praetor nodded sagely and indicated his slaves should begin serving. "This is, after all, only a temporary lodging. Should I decide to remain in Camulodunum I'll have a villa built to my own specifications."

Antonia's heart sank at the reminder that he might choose to stay in Camulodunum. Could she persuade her father to return to Gallia, to the town where she'd grown up? He'd only moved to Britannia when it became clear luxury goods were highly sought after by the newly settled Romans.

Despite her best intentions, once again she glanced at Gawain. If she moved to Gallia, she would never see him again.

But as soon as Cassia arrived, their affair would end in any case. What difference would it make where she decided to live?

She tore her hypnotized stare from the oblivious Cambrian who sat upright on the opposite couch as if he were a royal chieftain entertaining a gaggle of lowly plebeians. She concentrated on a dish of dormice, sprinkled with honey and poppy seeds, which had been placed on the low table and tried to regulate her galloping thoughts.

When it came to Gawain, it made no difference where she lived. Except if she stayed in Camulodunum the chances were high that she would continue to see him. How could she not, if she and Carys maintained the tenuous friendship that was forming between them?

She would see him with other women. A hard knot formed deep in her breast. *It did not matter.* Yet she knew it did. Because the harsh truth was—she didn't want Gawain to be with any woman but her.

Antonia acknowledged that the feast was sumptuous. The praetor had obviously spared no expense and it was clear this was a feast designed to impress. But who was he trying to impress? Surely not her. And in his eyes, her father, a mere plebeian, was tolerated only because his vast network of contacts across the empire enabled him to source any luxury requested.

The tribune, then? She gave Maximus a surreptitious glance. It didn't seem likely. Although Carys' husband came from one of the premier families of the Senate, so too did the praetor.

"When are you returning to Rome, Maximus?" the praetor asked as slaves served the next course—a magnificent swan accompanied by a dozen different imported vegetables. "You are well overdue for promotion. I cannot fathom why you've remained in Britannia for so long."

"Extraordinary circumstances," Maximus said. "But I'll be taking my wife and daughter to Rome very shortly."

Of course. Antonia had forgotten that Carys would soon be leaving Camulodunum. So much for the friendship she had imagined them forging. But wasn't this better? At least then there would be less chance of accidentally crossing paths with Gawain.

It was better. But she couldn't embrace the knowledge.

"Your beauty will dazzle the jaded in Rome, my lady," the praetor said, bestowing a benevolent smile in Carys' direction. Carys offered him a tight smile in return, but Antonia knew that beneath that calm façade the other woman was seething.

A prickle of sympathy for the praetor shot through her breast. He was condescending to those he considered his social inferiors but, conversely, Antonia also knew that he was sincere in his compliment to Carys. Unfortunately for him, he had no idea that his perception of what constituted a compliment struck at the heart of Carys' true nature.

A shiver trickled along her spine. What did she mean by *her true nature?* Antonia knew the Roman noblewoman persona that Carys presented to the world was merely a guise. But it was no great secret that Carys was a foreign princess of a conquered land. So why had that thought not only slid into her mind but remained with insidious intent?

As if there were more to Carys than Antonia imagined?

Gawain restrained himself from responding to the pompous old goat's remark, but only by filling his mouth with food that he didn't even recognize. He looked over at Antonia but as always, she looked perfectly serene. Whereas he'd been battling a cursed erection from the moment he'd seen her in the atrium, she had remained cool and aloof, bestowing barely a chilly glance in his direction.

Gingerly he shifted position on the couch, but it scarcely eased his discomfort. Only Antonia could do that. And he had every intention of ensuring she did so before this night was over.

It gave him dark amusement to know how responsive and uninhibited his reserved Roman noblewoman was when there was no one else around. Erotic images burned his mind, and it was only with difficulty that he dragged himself back to the present.

Time enough later to indulge his fantasies.

The praetor was still droning on. "But doubtless in time you'll provide Rome with many fine sons."

Gawain choked and hastily tipped his goblet of wine down his throat. Intentionally or not, the Roman had just unforgivably insulted Carys by insinuating her daughter was less worthy than a son might be. There was no way she would let that comment pass.

"If the gods decree it," Maximus said, sliding his fingers through Carys'. "If not, then I consider myself more than blessed to have a beautiful, healthy daughter."

It galled, but the longer Gawain spent in Maximus' company the more he could understand why Carys had fallen for him. From his experience, not many Roman men would defend their daughter in such a way.

He glanced at Antonia. She was staring at Maximus, a stricken look on her face, as though he had just predicted the end of the empire.

His senses sharpened. He knew Antonia had borne children, but he'd never asked her about them. Did they reside with her at her father's?

Or had she been forced to leave them behind in Rome?

Whichever the outcome, her reaction told him volumes. Her former husband had not considered his daughters a blessing.

He wrenched his attention from her and looked at the praetor. "In our culture, our daughters are valued as highly as our sons."

The praetor offered him a perfunctory smile. "I'm fortunate that the gods blessed me with three sons. But I have always privately wished for a daughter to dote upon."

Gawain watched in disbelief as the praetor glanced at Antonia. Disbelief surged into outrage. Was he seriously suggesting that he wanted to sire a daughter with *Antonia*?

He glared in her direction, but she was focused on her hands and once again, her true feelings were masked by that serene façade. She appeared unaware of both the praetor's implication and his own ire. But one thing was for sure—whatever Antonia might imagine, the praetor wanted far more from her than mere friendship.

The interminable feast continued through the evening. Antonia dutifully tried each dish, but everything tasted of ashes. She could try to fool herself, but the truth was painfully clear.

The praetor had declared his intent.

It wasn't merely the way he kept glancing at her or brushed his fingers across hers at every opportunity. He had openly stated his desire for a daughter, when he knew of her past history, and of Scipio's reaction to the daughters she had struggled to give birth to.

The thought of enduring another pregnancy, only for it to end in heartbreak and disaster, caused nausea to roil in her breast.

But that would never happen. She would never remarry and be at the mercy of another man's obsessive desire to produce a son.

Or daughter.

The conversation flowed over her, a distant murmur. Several times the praetor attempted to engage her but the most she could manage was a polite, monosyllabic response. With every moment that passed, her unease mounted. If she didn't manage to deflect his interest before Cassia arrived, how could she hope to keep her child's existence a secret?

"Gawain." The praetor's voice jolted her back to the present. "You are blood kin to the tribune's wife, is that correct?"

"Kin, but not blood bound."

Antonia pushed her fears to the back of her mind. There was plenty of time to dwell on them later. But for now, she hoped she didn't look as enthralled as she felt. In all of their many discussions, she had never outright asked Gawain about his connection to Carys. She'd simply taken it for granted that he was, indeed, her blood kin.

Why else would Maximus allow him to reside under the same roof as his wife?

Clearly the praetor thought that too, if his raised eyebrows were anything to go by. "And you have been in Camulodunum for how long?"

Gawain looked perfectly relaxed. But, as impossible as it should be, Antonia could feel tension spiking from him. It reminded her, with an uncanny ripple of alarm, of the way he'd looked earlier that day in the forum.

"I come and go," Gawain said, which didn't answer the question at all.

"This is merely an extended visit, then, not relocation?" The praetor eyed Gawain over the rim of his goblet. Antonia's glance darted between the two men. It sounded suspiciously as though the praetor were interrogating Gawain.

"Gawain was kind enough to bring me news of my mother," Carys said. "I haven't seen her since before my marriage."

"Ah." The praetor turned to Carys. "Your mother still resides in Cambria?"

"Yes. She remained behind to care for elderly relatives."

Carys' gaze didn't waver from the praetor. There was nothing controversial or strange about her statement. And yet Antonia had the absolute certainty that there was far more to the simple explanation than Carys' words apparently conveyed.

"So you're now a messenger, Gawain?" The praetor waved for a slave to refill his goblet. His eyes remained fixed on Gawain. "That must come hard to a man with your obvious warrior background."

What was he doing? Antonia glared at the praetor, but he appeared oblivious. Of course Gawain was a warrior. He had likely fought against the legions as they'd marched across Cambria. But why was the praetor bringing it up now? It wasn't a crime to fight for your people. Gawain hadn't been captured and sold as an enemy of Rome at the time. Those who accepted the rule of the empire, no matter how reluctantly, were not punished. Therefore, what was the praetor attempting to prove?

"Warriors," Gawain said, his voice giving nothing away of his true feelings, "adapt."

The praetor's eyes narrowed, so slightly and so fleetingly Antonia almost missed it. But it was obvious from that telling reaction that Gawain's response had not been what he expected.

So what *had* he expected? For Gawain to leap to his feet, dagger in hand, and demand that the praetor retracted his not-so-subtle insult? Why was he trying to undermine Gawain? Wasn't it enough to know that the empire had conquered his land and people without rubbing Rome's victory in his face?

"One must learn to adapt to survive," her father said. "It is, after all, far better than the alternative."

"Unless, of course, one is Roman." The praetor smiled but it didn't reach his eyes. "Surrender is never an option for the Eagle."

Tension crackled in the room, causing the hair to rise on the back of her neck and along her arms. The praetor was deliberately baiting Gawain. Did he imagine Gawain such a savage that he would forsake good manners and attack his host in his own home?

Yet where were the praetor's manners? She'd known him for many years, and he'd never displayed such overt hostility in a social situation before.

"To the continuing good health of the Eagle." Maximus raised his goblet. He still held Carys' hand. As everyone followed suit, Antonia noticed Gawain's hands remained planted on his knees. His face was impassive, but he radiated coiled fury.

She didn't blame him. She was furious with the praetor on his behalf.

"Excellent wine, Praetor," Maximus said before he turned to her father. "Is this part of your latest shipment, Faustus? Remind me to place an order."

Her father responded and the conversation once again navigated calmer waters. But the animosity between Gawain and the praetor seethed beneath the surface, a poisonous serpent waiting to strike. And Antonia had the chilling certainty that tonight was just the beginning.

CHAPTER SIXTEEN

*T*he final extravagant course had barely been cleared away when Gawain made his excuses and rose to his feet. Not that he really bothered with an excuse. He merely stated his intention to leave without regret or false apology.

"You're not staying overnight?" The praetor lounged back on the couch. "You are most welcome." Insincerity dripped from every word.

"I have a prior engagement." Gawain inclined his head. "Thank you for your hospitality. It's been most...illuminating."

Antonia could feel heat flooding her face at his choice of words, but at least he didn't glance her way. His gaze was intent on the praetor. But she knew Gawain was really speaking to her. Why else would he have chosen to use the same word she had after the first time they had made love?

Sex. It was only sex. But the reminder did nothing to calm the frantic beat of her heart. Because she knew that Gawain was now fully aware that the praetor regarded her as more than merely an old acquaintance.

She wasn't even sure why that revelation angered him. But it did, and she had known it would, and that was why she'd attempted to allay his suspicions the other day.

Why had she thought it exciting, at the start of the evening, when Gawain had glared daggers at the praetor for taking her arm? She wasn't a foolish girl who found pleasure in having two men vie for her attention.

She had no wish for the praetor's attention. But she desperately longed for Gawain's. And the tragic truth was, his obvious ire at how the praetor had lavished his attention on her throughout the evening had thrilled her feminine pride.

Until that last conversation. Dynamics had shifted, as though the praetor changed battle tactics and went on the offensive. And while his attitude and questions angered her on Gawain's behalf, it was more than that. She didn't know what, didn't even know why that thought was so adamant in her mind. All she knew was something fundamental had shifted and it went far beyond the events that had unfolded this night.

Gawain made perfunctory farewells and strode from the room and Antonia fought the suicidal desire to leap to her feet and follow him. He was meant to be only a distraction. A means to educate herself on the pleasures of sensual seduction. He wasn't supposed to invade her mind at inconvenient moments of the day and night, and he certainly wasn't supposed to interfere with her shield of self-preservation.

The answer was obvious. She should end this liaison before she became more entangled in his hypnotic web. But even as the thought thudded through her head, she knew she had no intention of following it through.

Not yet. She couldn't bear to lose him just yet. Another week or two and the memories they made would sustain her through the years ahead, when her life revolved around Cassia.

The praetor was laughing at something Maximus had said. "You are too noble, Maximus," he said. "I know that look on a man's face, and he was most certainly going to find the sweet comfort of a woman's embrace."

Antonia's stomach churned. She kept her gaze fixed on the table and ignored the pounding of her temples. Gawain was not going to see another woman.

But how do I know? He'd never said she was his only lover. He could have several. After all, they hadn't been together for two days. Yet it had never occurred to her that he might have slaked his lust elsewhere.

How bitterly ironic. Her relief had been overwhelming whenever she'd discovered Scipio had taken a new mistress, since it meant she could enjoy a brief respite from his demands. But the thought of Gawain entertaining another woman caused nausea to rise.

Finally, she couldn't stand it anymore. The conversation, the musicians, or the dancers the praetor had hired to entertain his guests. Everything pounded in her mind, a cacophony of colliding noise. If she didn't leave now, she feared she might scream, and she couldn't embarrass her father in such a shocking fashion.

She pressed her fingertips against her temple and thankfully her father picked up her cues and made their excuses. The praetor held her hand, helped her to her feet, and his concern for her welfare appeared so very genuine. As he led her into the atrium, she caught sight of Carys' face. She looked mutinous. Clearly the thought of staying the night under the praetor's roof didn't appeal to her in the slightest.

"I trust you had a pleasant evening, Antonia?" he said as a slave brought her palla.

"Yes, thank you, Praetor. It was most enjoyable." *Illuminating.* The word mocked her, but she ignored it.

He smiled, but oddly appeared ill at ease. "There's no need to be so formal, Antonia. I've been your friend for many years. I would be honored if you would once again call me Seneca."

Her chest constricted and throat tightened. It was true that in the past she had addressed him more intimately. But she hadn't seen him for months, and in the meantime, he'd been promoted. Calling him by the title of his office gave a semblance of detachment.

She needed to maintain that detachment. Now that she was no longer married, she knew he would look upon her use of his given name as a tacit agreement to his… advances.

"You are very kind." She allowed him to take her hand and remained rigid as he kissed her fingers.

"We trust you will allow us to return your hospitality, Praetor," her father said.

"I would be delighted." The praetor's voice was stilted. He hadn't missed how she had deliberately not used his name, but she was too tired to care.

It was only a short journey home and in the flickering light of the carpentum's lantern, she gave her father an exasperated glare. "Why do you encourage him? You know of my feelings on this matter."

Her father sighed and took her hand. "If your heart is set on adopting this child you told me about, then I'm certain the praetor will have no objection to embracing her as your daughter. He even said how much he longed for a daughter. It's as if the gods themselves bless this match."

She stared at him as horror clutched her breast. She didn't want the praetor knowing she was adopting a child at all—a child who was the exact same age as her own, supposedly dead, daughter—but the scenario her father painted was nothing short of a nightmare.

It would never happen. She took a deep breath and tried to calm her mind. When her father entertained the praetor, she would affect feminine indisposition and not join them. It was unforgivably rude, but surely the praetor would finally realize she wasn't interested in what he offered her?

❄

Elpis met her in the atrium and with relief, Antonia made her way to her bedchamber. The thought of having relaxing incense burning as soothing oils were rubbed on her temples was seductive.

It might even take her mind off the thought of Gawain with another woman.

"Domina." Elpis' whisper was scarcely audible as she paused outside Antonia's bedchamber. "I'll be here if you should need me."

Antonia blinked and frowned. Her headache was worse than she thought, since she could make no sense of Elpis' comment.

"Where else would you be?" Elpis had slept in her bedchamber up until her marriage, and ever since her divorce.

Elpis smiled and opened the door. A low golden glow bathed her bedchamber from the lamps. "Here, domina," she whispered. "I will be right here."

Antonia's breath caught in her throat and a quiver of delicious alarm skated through her breast. *Surely not?* But she didn't ask Elpis the question hammering through her mind. Instead, she stepped into her bedchamber, and Elpis gently closed the door behind her.

From shadows beyond her bed, Gawain emerged, like a warrior god from the beginning of time. Her mouth dried and heart lurched against her ribs. He was here. In her bedchamber. Waiting for her.

"Are you speechless with delight or horror, my lady?" His low, mocking voice wrapped around her, as sensuous as the incense from the Temple of Venus. "Will you scream in pleasure or disgust at my touch?"

"I cannot believe you're here." Her voice was scarcely above a whisper. Her heart thundered too hard to draw enough breath into her lungs. "If my father discovered you, he would..." She wasn't sure what her father would do. Run a dagger through Gawain's heart or die of shame at her feet?

"Then we had best ensure your father never finds out." He took another unhurried step closer to her, and her foolish heart twisted at the magnificent figure he presented. The glow from the lamps heightened the bronze of his skin and dark blond of his hair, and enhanced the breathtaking muscles of his biceps. If Celts sculpted images of their gods in marble, Gawain would be their chief deity made flesh.

She walked over to him until merely a hair's breadth pulsed between them. She longed to wrap herself around him, breathe in his unique scent and forget the outside world in his arms. But she feared if she did so, he might guess that her feelings were deeper for him now. And she didn't want to give him any reason to end this insane liaison any earlier than fate had already decreed.

"How are you here?" Of course, Elpis must have assisted him. But even so, the dangers of evading the guards, of being seen to slip into her room, were immense.

"I have my ways." His teeth flashed in a mirthless smile and with a jolt, she realized that he still seethed with fury. "It was not so very difficult for a man with my talents."

His self-scathing comment lashed across her heart. How many times had he evaded capture to meet an illicit lover in her bedchamber? Why had she imagined this was something as shocking and novel to him, as well as for her?

She smothered the questions before they consumed her. It didn't matter how many times in the past he had done this. At least he was with her now, and not with a strange, faceless woman. The knowledge eased the ache in her heart, and she cradled his jaw with one hand, rubbing her thumb across his light stubble.

"Your talents," she whispered, "are impressive."

His lips quirked in obvious reluctance. "Don't flatter me with pretty words, Antonia."

"Why not?" She trailed her fingertips along the strong line of his jaw. "You flatter me most charmingly."

His large hand covered hers. For a moment, she thought he was going to thrust her from him, but instead his fingers threaded through hers.

"No." His voice was harsh. "I don't. It's one of my irresistible traits. I'm blunt to the point of barbarity."

His self-condemnation caused her heart to squeeze. She took that final step and sank against the hard ridges of his body. "I have yet to see this barbarian of whom you so freely speak."

Tension radiated from him, coiled and waiting to spring. Did he truly imagine that she compared him to the praetor—and found Gawain wanting? How could he be so blind?

How could she prove how wrong he was?

"That Roman." Gawain's breath seared her ear as he wound his arm around her waist and held her in a punishing grip. "Every time he looked at you, he stripped you with his eyes. His lust polluted the air. He will not rest until he has you in his bed."

Unease shivered along her spine at his words, but she forced it aside. She wasn't as easily manipulated as Gawain appeared to think.

"I've no intention of sharing his bed. But I have every intention that you will share mine this night."

She felt his body shake in a silent laugh and then he pulled back so he could look into her face. "I am enraged. How dare you attempt to mollify me with false promises?"

"It's not a false promise. It is night, you are here, and my bed is beside us."

He glowered at her, even as his tempting mouth fought to smile. His frown lost the battle. "You are an enchantress. There's no other explanation. What magic have you cast upon me, my lady?"

"A lady never shares her secrets." And then she laughed at the absurdity of her comment, at the relief Gawain was no longer vibrating with repressed fury and the knowledge that, for a short time at least, she could hold him close and savor each precious moment.

He grunted and began to pull the pins from her hair. "As long as I'm the only one you enchant. I don't share what is mine."

A foolish frisson of delight ignited deep in her heart. She knew he spoke purely from lust when she—ah, she could no longer deny the truth. It was so much more than lust for her. But what did it matter if she hugged his words close and gave them a meaning he didn't intend? "And am I yours?"

For a second he paused, his hand in her hair, his gaze boring into her as if he wanted to peel back the layers of her mind and read her most secret of desires.

"Yes." His voice was raw, primitive and another delicious tremor claimed her sensitized flesh. "Tonight you're all mine. I intend that you'll never forget what we shared together."

There was little chance of that when Gawain had slid, unbidden, into her heart. She would remember him until her last breath.

"But will you forget, Gawain? Will I be simply another Roman woman you passed a few pleasant weeks with? Will you even recall my name a year from now?"

Somehow she kept her voice light, playful, as though she didn't mean every word from the bottom of her soul. It would do no good for him to discover just how devastated she'd be if he forgot everything about her as soon as their liaison ended.

Gawain stared into Antonia's ice-blue eyes, eyes that had captivated him from the first moment they had met. He knew they would haunt him until he continued his journey in the Otherworld, and perhaps their beauty would haunt him even there.

Forget her? How he wished he could be certain that he could. But every time that Roman had fawned over her, pawed her, and attempted to denigrate Gawain in her eyes, the tarnished truth had clawed through his chest.

She was more than a fleeting liaison. She always had been, but until this night, he hadn't realized just how much she meant to him.

They had no future. He knew that. But the thought of her marrying the praetor, as she was sure to given her status and the Roman's obvious interest, curdled his guts.

Antonia was in his arms, smiling up at him and driving him out of his senses with lust. It should be enough. With any other woman, it would be enough. But with Antonia he wanted more. He didn't want her to blithely mention the short duration of their affair. A few weeks? Was that all she was willing to give him?

Savagely he flung her hair pins onto the floor and tugged her ringlets over her shoulders. Now she looked untamed, unregimented. *Un-Roman*. But it didn't matter how she looked. Because her blood was still the blood of patricians and she belonged to the empire.

"Perhaps I'll engrave your name on the inside of my torque." He offered her a sardonic grin. "Then I'll never risk forgetting our enjoyable encounters."

For a moment, her lips trembled as though his words wounded. But perhaps it was a trick of the lamp light. Perhaps he had merely imagined it. Because her smile now was more blinding than ever.

"Do you engrave the names of all your conquests on your torque?" She traced her finger over the images of Lugus but her gaze didn't waver from his. He almost told her yes, he did, but somehow he could not.

"The torque of my forefathers is sacred. I would never desecrate it in such a manner."

Her finger slipped to his bare throat. Her light touch burned his flesh.

"Have you ever been in love, Gawain?" Her voice was soft, persuasive, but anger flared that she dared to ask him such a personal question. Then he looked into her eyes and instead of idle curiosity, he saw those elusive, haunting shadows, and his anger fell to ash.

"Once." More than two turns of the wheel ago and yet it felt like another lifetime.

"Was she of Cambria?"

He unclasped the brooch that held Antonia's gown at the shoulder. "She was a warrior."

The tip of her tongue moistened her lips. "Of course."

He studied the precious gems encrusted in the brooch as it lay in the palm of his hand. He couldn't fathom why, but Antonia's response speared through his chest. And the pain was not for the loss of Morwyn.

Antonia's gown pooled at her feet, leaving her clad in only a knee-length tunic. She looked oddly vulnerable, alone, as if the slightest harsh word from him would send her crumbling into dust.

Three things Morwyn had never looked in her life.

"She saved my life." The words thudded in the air between them, shocking him. He had never spoken them before. Not even to Carys, and she and Morwyn had been the best of friends.

"Yes." Antonia's voice was faint, and she was no longer holding his gaze. Instead she stared at his chest as her fingers unlaced his shirt.

He realized she didn't understand. He tossed her brooch onto the end of the bed and covered her hand, stilling her fingers.

"No." He wasn't sure why it was important she understood. Only that it was. "The last time we saw each other she gave me a warning. That treachery awaited in the land of the Brigantes. If she hadn't, if I had ignored her words, I would've been cut down by those I considered my allies."

Antonia swallowed. "Then I owe her a great debt of gratitude. Because of her foresight you're here with me now."

Whatever he had imagined she might say it hadn't been that. Incredibly, a laugh huffed from his throat, and he cradled her face. She was so fragile, not only physically but also in the way she had so little control over her life. The knowledge seared him, and a wave of raw protectiveness surged through him. A sensation he had never once experienced while he'd been with Morwyn. "You're so different from her."

Her smile seemed strained. "Alas, it was thought more prudent for me to learn Greek than how to wield a dagger."

"There you have me." He began to slide her tunic off her shoulders. "I don't know a word of Greek. Perhaps you should teach me."

She shrugged free of her tunic and stood before him in all her naked glory. His cock thickened with anticipation. She was the most beguiling vision he'd ever seen in his life.

"I cannot imagine why you would wish to learn Greek." She tugged ineffectively at his shirt, and he obliged her by ripping it over his head and dropping it to the floor. "How do you speak Latin so well?"

Other Romans had asked him that. He'd always been aware of the incredulity behind the question, as though they distrusted the fact he spoke their language so fluently. But there was no such undercurrent in Antonia's words.

"There was a Gaul in our clan who spoke perfect Latin. He taught us all." No need to explain that the Gaul had also been a Druid with Roman blood in his veins.

"Hmm." She appeared distracted by his torso, and he flexed his muscles for her viewing pleasure. The breathy sigh she emitted stoked his male pride to new heights. She was always so appreciative. "I could speak Greek to you now, if you wish."

He buried his fingers in her glorious hair as she began to strip him with tantalizing concentration. "I would rather know what you say to me in the throes of passion, Antonia."

She gave a breathless laugh as she sank to her knees, exposing him to her avid gaze. He gritted his teeth, forced his fingers to relax against her head. His fantasy of Antonia sucking his cock into her wet mouth would remain only that—a fantasy.

It didn't stop the tortured groan from escaping, though.

Her hands slid along his thighs and down the back of his calves. Her uneven breath teased his flesh and his erection throbbed with unfulfilled need. She was so cursed close. He imagined the tip of her tongue sliding across his wet slit, imagined her lips wrapping around his swollen glans.

Involuntarily he tightened his grip on her head and battled the primal urge to jerk her forward. To force his shaft between her parted lips and take her as she knelt before him. Did she think he was made of stone? Did she deliberately tantalize him with every ragged breath she took, every teasing stroke of her fingers?

"Stand up." His command was guttural, and he emphasized the urgency by tugging on her hair. She looked up at him, a vision of feminine innocence and earthly desire. A combination that should be impossible, that should never exist. Yet Antonia embodied it all without a trace of artifice or manipulation.

Then she smiled. It wasn't a smile of triumph that she could drive him so easily to the edge of his endurance. It was a smile that speared through his chest, paralyzed his lungs, and hypnotized his enslaved gaze.

He'd never seen such a smile before. It illuminated her face in the glow of the lamps and in that moment, it would be easy to believe she possessed immortal blood. Surely no mere human could look so bewitching?

"Your body enthralls me." Her seductive whisper weaved

through the heated air as she slowly, sensuously rose from her knees. "I want to worship every glorious inch of it."

A tortured laugh escaped, and he sculpted her shoulders, the dip of her waist and irresistible flare of her hips.

"Another night, my lady." In the back of his lust-fueled mind, the leering face of the praetor lurked, mocking him with the knowledge that, sooner or later, Antonia would belong to him.

His banked rage once again surged through his veins and pounded against his skull. Antonia was *his*. He would give her pleasure such as she had never imagined. Would give her a memory that seared her senses forever; a memory that would never fade with the passage of time or become lost in the demands of a new husband.

He cupped her delectable arse, felt a delicious tremor claim her body. He leaned in close, her nipples hard against his chest, and breathed against her ear. "Tonight, sweet Antonia, I will make good on my promise and take your virginity."

CHAPTER SEVENTEEN

Gawain watched Antonia's eyes darken with desire, anticipation—apprehension. But not fear. She didn't pull away but instead mimicked his stance, her hands splayed over his arse, and seductively meshed her body against his.

"I am ready." Her whisper was breathless and stoked his ravening need.

"No." He molded her smooth, rounded buttocks and she trembled in his embrace. "But you will be."

She rose onto her toes and dusted her lips across his in a barely there kiss. Yet the softness of her mouth, the fleeting probe of her tongue, scorched an erotic tattoo through his chest and groin and wrapped around his balls in a thunderous embrace.

Her tender touch would be the death of him.

He took her hand and led her to the bed. While he'd waited for her to return home, Elpis had shown him Antonia's vast selection of scented oils. He'd picked one that reminded him of sunshine and spring, and it waited beside the bed for easy access.

"How do you want me?" She glanced at him and the blush on

her cheeks enchanted him. "I'm not familiar with…the right position." Her blush deepened but she didn't break eye contact.

Despite the rock-hard agony of his cock, he couldn't help a twisted smile. He knew she wasn't familiar with what they were about to do. It was the reason why she would always remember it.

Why she would always remember him.

"Lie flat on the bed on your stomach. First, I'm going to seduce you until you can barely recall your own name."

"I can barely recall it already." She flashed him a smile that constricted his chest, but obediently did as he'd commanded. With her head cushioned on her folded arms she continued to gaze at him with a look on her face he could not decipher.

She looked at him as though she looked at one of her heathen gods. As if he were her world.

He expelled a jagged breath and straddled her hips. When had he started to care how she looked at him? When had he ever cared how a woman looked at him?

In the past he'd only cared about Morwyn. And she had never looked at him in the way Antonia did.

He brushed her hair from her shoulder. A golden chain was around her neck, and she hadn't removed any of her bracelets. The lamp light gave her skin an ethereal, golden glow and for a moment he merely stared, mesmerized, at the smooth perfection of her back. Gently he trailed one finger along the length of her spine and a delicate shudder rippled over her. He leaned over her and kissed her sleek shoulder, savoring the scented haven of her skin and the way she quivered beneath his touch.

His cock throbbed in exquisite agony against the small of her back and her constricted wriggles and uneven gasps were the most erotic sensations of foreplay he'd ever experienced. He captured her earlobe between his teeth and then nibbled kisses along the shell of her ear. "I imagined doing this while you sat so sedately at the praetor's table."

"I'm thankful you had the willpower to restrain yourself." Her breathless response and the way her lush lips curved in a smile caused him to almost lose what little restraint he retained. "Although I wondered if you had even noticed me. You scarcely looked at me all night."

He branded her flushed cheek and aristocratic jaw with hard, possessive kisses, bracing his weight on one forearm so he wouldn't crush her. But gods, the silken warmth of her back and curve of her buttocks as their bodies melded all but incinerated his reason.

Not noticed her? She had filled his vision the entire night. "If I'd looked at you, your father and the praetor would be in no doubt as to exactly what my intentions were towards you." He scraped his teeth and the tip of his tongue along the fragrant flesh of her throat and a delicious tremor claimed her. "Your reputation would be in tatters, and I would be hanging from a tree."

She stiffened. "Don't say such things, Gawain. Even in jest."

He grinned against the curve of her shoulder and trailed his finger along her finely defined biceps. "Do not fear, sweet Antonia. I'd never do anything to besmirch your good name."

She twisted futilely beneath him and finally gave up, but the glare she arrowed his way was still filled with dark alarm. "It's not my reputation that I fear losing."

His grin faded and an odd pain filled his chest. "Then you have nothing to worry about. I've no intention of ending my days in such a manner."

Her rigid muscles relaxed, and she sighed as she once again rested her head on her arms.

"I shall worry, regardless." She whispered the words into her pillow, as though they were not for his ears. Her concern touched him in a way he couldn't explain, didn't fully understand, but again the overpowering, primal urge to protect her surged through his blood.

He raked his fingers through her hair, pulling her curls over her head and exposing the vulnerable nape of her neck. He kissed her there and she gave a delicate shiver, and his fist tightened in her hair.

The knowledge pounded in his mind, no matter how he tried to deny it. Even when their affair ended, he would retain this insane urge to protect her. It wasn't something superficial he could cast off at will. It was bone-deep, insidious, and had permeated the fabric of his existence without him even realizing.

He relinquished his grip on her hair and forced himself upright. She lay before him, his virgin sacrifice, and the thought hammered through his mind. Taking a virgin had never interested him before but when it came to Antonia, the knowledge did something primitive to his reason.

With slow deliberation, he reached for the oil and saw Antonia raise her head to watch him. He poured the oil onto his hands and the delicate spring fragrance drifted in the heated air. It wasn't an exotic concoction from the mystic East or a feted aphrodisiac from the dawn of creation. But as he massaged Antonia's shoulders, the innocent notes of the scent enveloped them in a sensual cocoon.

He worked her tense muscles, the sensation of oil and silky-smooth skin an erotic combination. She sighed and melted, and he moved down her body, lavishing the same concentrated care over her back.

"Your talents are many and wondrous." Her voice was languorous, her eyes closed, and a blissful smile curved her lips.

He shifted position, moving farther down her body, so that her luscious arse was displayed to view. He dripped oil from the bottle onto her rounded buttocks and she smothered a giggle and wriggled her behind. Fascinated, he watched the oil slowly trickle over her flesh and slide into her exposed crack.

His mouth dried and cock jerked with desperate need. How easy it would be to give in to the lust thudding through his blood.

With torturous effort, he tore his gaze away and began to massage her thighs. He'd promised her a night to remember. He would ensure it would be a night she would remember with pleasure and nostalgia and without the faintest trace of regret or unwarranted pain.

He would take her only when she was incoherent with lust, boneless with need and mindless with primal desire. Gods give him strength to survive that long.

"Gawain." Her breathy voice lingered over his name, stretching it out, making it sound unimaginably seductive. He gritted his teeth and glided his fingers along the inside of her taut thigh. "You have forgotten to tend to my bottom."

She wiggled her bottom as if she imagined he might need reminding as to where it resided. All he could see was her delectable behind. It was all he could think about. He dragged his hypnotized gaze from her taunting arse and redoubled his efforts at sculpting her perfect calves.

"I have forgotten nothing." His voice was raw. Still she mocked his self-restraint by swaying her buttocks in his face. He palmed one teasing cheek and forced her flat on the bed. "We're doing this my way, Antonia."

She gave another of her seductive sighs and continued to shift beneath his restraining hand.

"But I'm ready for you now. You are teasing me beyond endurance."

Although fire consumed his groin and licked through his veins, he laughed and squeezed her buttock in a possessive grip. She hitched in a shocked breath and shot him a startled look over her shoulder.

"You can endure more." He rubbed her abused cheek with the palm of his hand and caught tantalizing glimpses of the dark entrance to her untouched tunnel. The thundering desire to *take her now* scorched his mind. Only the force of his Druidic will enabled him to unpeel his fingers from her tempting arse.

His lust would not rule him this night.

Antonia squirmed in helpless delight as Gawain massaged first one calf and then the other, his fingers sure and firm. The scented oil heightened every magical touch and her skin tingled from his torturous ministrations.

He grasped one ankle and lavished as much care and attention on her heel and toes as if they were the most enticing part of her body. She thrust her knuckles into her mouth to prevent her moans escaping, but they escaped regardless. His body shook with silent laughter as he released her foot and began on the other.

She pulled her knuckles from her mouth. "You're killing me with eroticism." Her words were jerky, inelegant, and she couldn't stop her fingers from flexing in a futile attempt at release.

"Not quite my intention." His voice was gravelly and insanely arousing. She groaned and wriggled her bottom again. Perhaps he would grip her the way he had just now. It had been unexpected, but the look on his face as he had gazed on her captured arse had been riveting.

Instead, he straightened and loomed over her. The lamps cast shadows that defined the sculpted perfection of his biceps and shoulders, and his earring and torque glinted with mystical allure.

She forgot how to breathe as anticipation constricted her chest and closed her throat. *Will he take me now?*

"On your hands and knees." It was a harsh demand and her pampered limbs trembled as she attempted to comply. He wrapped one strong arm around her waist and held her steady, his wide chest an erotic wall of living muscle against her back.

"Don't tremble." His raw whisper against her ear caused

another delicious quiver to claim her body. "This night is for your pleasure, sweet Antonia. I'll take it as slow as you need."

She wasn't sure *slow* was what she wanted. "I'm not afraid."

Still holding her around her waist, his other hand cupped her mound. She sighed and ground herself against him. Needing the pressure. Needing him *inside her*. His finger teased her sensitive bud and liquid warmth trickled from her.

Slowly he eased up from her, and his hand skimmed the slippery curves of her waist and hips. Her head dropped and she gazed, mesmerized, along the length of her body to where Gawain spread her intimate folds and continued to tease her swollen clit.

Oil dripped onto her bottom and slid with sensuous intent across her flesh. Gawain palmed her arse cheek and then rubbed in a circular motion, the heat of his hand and slide of the oil warming her buttock with delicious promise.

Each rotation brought him closer to her crease and when the tip of his finger slid into the valley between her cheeks, she gasped and jerked involuntarily.

"Relax." Gawain didn't sound relaxed, but his finger continued to stroke, and the sensation was beyond anything she had ever imagined. "Don't think, Antonia. Just feel."

She drew in a shuddering breath. How could she relax when Gawain teased her without mercy and lubricated her rear with his oil-coated finger?

Surely she couldn't hold out much longer. "I need to come," she gasped.

"You will." It sounded more like a threat than a promise and as he dipped into her wet sheath, he worked one finger into her tight anus.

She bucked in shock, and he instantly stopped his invasion. "Antonia?" It was a rasp in the charged air, and she sucked in a strangled breath as her body accommodated his penetration.

He had fingered her there before. But this time he was

behind her. This time he was watching. And knowing that he watched as he pushed his finger inside her body was unnerving. But although she tensed, cream trickled from her core. *I want this.*

"I'm all right. Don't stop."

A second finger joined the first. "I have no intention of stopping." He tweaked her throbbing clit and pushed his oiled fingers into her.

She panted, fisting the bedcovers, her muscles rigid. The burning sensation wasn't too bad. Through glazed eyes, she watched him continue to tease her, dipping into her cleft and coating her juices over her mound. A low moan vibrated through her body, and it took a moment for her to realize the moan didn't originate from Gawain.

"That's it. Let me hear you, sweet Antonia." Gawain's growl stoked her passion and she backed into him, wanting more. He rotated his finger and she shuddered, lost in sensation, and when he withdrew from her, she gasped in protest.

"Wait." He sounded rabid and with her head hanging down she watched him, from between her parted thighs, lubricate his magnificent shaft. "I'm going to have your tight virgin arse, Antonia. I'm going to make you mine."

"Yes." She wanted him to take her. She wanted to belong to him. Most of all she wanted to tell him, but coherent words were beyond her. "*Yes.*"

Gawain gripped his cock and slid the swollen head into her luscious valley. Her erratic gasps filled his mind and the shudder that claimed her ricocheted along the length of his shaft in torturous delight. He nudged, felt her stretch around his penetration and she went rigid.

His breath came in harsh pants, his blood pounded in primitive need. He slid his arm around her, held her close, found her silken, swollen clit.

"Antonia." It was all he could manage but she gave a jerk of her head as though she understood.

"Yes." Her voice was hoarse. It was the most erotic sound he had ever heard. He teased her clit until she squirmed, her beautiful bottom rubbing against his engorged length. He pushed in a little farther, and the tight clamp of her muscles expanded, granting him entry.

A groan seared his throat. She held him in a mind-shattering vise, her tunnel so tight and hot the urge to *thrust* and *possess* splintered his reason.

The gods only knew how he held back. How he remained motionless while her body adjusted to his invasion, to his size. Her uneven breath stoked his lust, and the vision of his cock embedded in her sweetly puckered arse caused every fantasy he had ever harbored to crumble to dust.

He forced words to form. The hardest thing he had done in his life. "Still with me?"

For answer, she slowly raised her hips, adjusting her position, and his cock sank deeper into her tight embrace. "Gods." It slipped from him, unintentionally. "That feels so good, Antonia."

"Take me." Her words were jagged, and she backed against him a little more, forcing him farther inside her. "Make me yours, Gawain."

Air hissed between his gritted teeth. She was his. She would always be his. He pushed two fingers into her wet slit and teased her clit with his thumb as he thrust into her, and his balls slammed against her vulnerable flesh.

His other hand cradled her breast. She fit so perfectly into the palm of his hand. He pinched her erect nipple and her ragged gasps and seductive little moans licked across his senses like molten fire. His beautiful Roman noblewoman, so reserved in public, was on her hands and knees. Impaled on his shaft. Her body undulating with lust, her hair wild and abandoned.

Then she contracted around him, and the sensation sent lightning splintering along his cock, into his balls and deep into his groin. Primal demand thudded through his veins, glazed his vision. All he could see, all he could feel, was Antonia as she writhed beneath him, every movement an exquisite lesson in uninhibited pleasure.

He abandoned her breast and gripped her hip. Still she writhed, still she whimpered, her choked moans stoking him beyond endurance. He fought to go slow. But his body rode her the way he needed to ride her, and her tight tunnel gripped each possessive slide of his cock with eager submission.

Her back was arched. Her body slick with scented oil and sweat. Her tangled hair tumbled over her shoulders and his grip on her hip became brutal.

Crimson ribbons streaked his world, as everything but Antonia faded to black. He cupped her sex, pressed his finger against her clit and tried and failed to avert the inevitable.

The pressure built. From the base of his spine, the dark pit of his soul. Primal need thudded. He possessed her virgin arse and the feel of her body constricting his cock pushed him over the edge.

A guttural roar tore his throat as he buried himself deep inside and came with frenzied need. As he irrevocably made her his, her hot cream spilled over his fingers as Antonia's climax entwined with his, and they became one.

CHAPTER EIGHTEEN

*F*or long moments, Gawain held Antonia close, his body enveloping her back, his head against her shoulder. Her uneven breath and the erratic thunder of her heart cocooned him in a false sense of serenity. A haven of bliss, where nothing existed but the two of them.

Only when her legs began to shake with fatigue did he finally, reluctantly, withdraw from her addictive embrace. She whimpered and he nibbled kisses along her damp throat. He might have left her body, but he had no intention of leaving her.

Not just yet.

He draped a sheet around her, and they lay on their sides, facing each other. He brushed her tangled hair from her face, winding the stray curls around his fingers. His gaze never left hers. "Was it how you imagined?"

Her smile was tired, but dazzled him all the same. "It was beyond my wildest imaginings."

With her hair enmeshed between his fingers, he stroked her flushed face with his knuckles. "Something you would like to do again?"

She gave an exhausted laugh and flattened her hand against

his chest. "Very much." She stroked him with the tips of her fingers, and it was oddly comforting. "But I'm not sure I could manage that again this night."

He laughed and kissed the tip of her nose. He'd had no intention of doing any such thing. "Another night, then."

"I shall look forward to it." She shifted, and a fleeting frown marred her brow.

"Are you uncomfortable?" He propped himself up on his forearm. He hadn't intended to finish so brutally. But her ragged gasps, her seductive writhing, and the way she had clenched around him had all served to shatter his self-control.

No excuse. She had been a virgin. He should have taken more care.

She trailed her fingers along his jaw and across his mouth. He resisted the urge to suck her finger inside.

"Why the glower?" She traced the outline of his lips and then sighed, as if resigned that he had no intention of bypassing the question. "I'm not uncomfortable, Gawain. I feel pleasantly," she hesitated for a moment and then shot him a sultry glance from beneath her lashes, "ravished." Her blush deepened but a smile teased her lips. Enthralled, he couldn't tear his gaze away. She truly was an enchantress. "But I must confess. I'm relieved I don't have to spend all day tomorrow in the saddle. I fear my bottom would violently protest."

"Next time I will not ride you so roughly."

"Oh." Her breath feathered across his hand as he cradled her jaw. "I was hoping that next time you might lose control earlier."

Speechless, he stared at her. Despite her enchanting blush, she didn't drop her gaze. She knew exactly what she meant and the knowledge that she didn't consider herself a fragile piece of spun glass caused his cock to thicken in delicious anticipation.

His beautiful Roman might not be a warrior but she was far from the pampered, spoiled patrician he'd first imagined. Hadn't she told him, the first time they had made love, that she wasn't made of spun glass? But it wasn't only her sensibilities that were tougher than he'd first assumed.

A satisfied smile curved his lips. "Beware of what you wish for. Are you sure you could handle me if I *lost control?*"

She tugged him down beside her once again. "There's nothing about you that I couldn't handle."

He threaded his fingers through hers and pressed their hands against her heart. Her words touched him, but it was a bitter-sweet sensation. Antonia might think she could handle anything that concerned him but what would she do if she discovered he was a Druid?

Gods, what was he thinking? There were some things that could never be shared.

They lay in companionable silence, content to merely look in each other's eyes. When was the last time he'd done this?

Never. Not even with Morwyn. Yet he couldn't bring himself to move, to bring this strange sense of harmony to an end. Instead, he traced a finger over the bracelets that adorned her wrist. They were of exquisite quality, but he expected nothing less from a family as wealthy as hers.

The gold locket around her throat drew his attention. When-ever they had met her earrings and bracelets had complemented her gowns, but her locket remained constant. Idly he picked it up in his free hand and examined it as it lay on his palm. Antonia didn't say anything, but he felt her tense, as though he had just crossed an invisible and incomprehensible barrier.

He met her eyes. She stared back, oddly defiant. Intrigued by her attitude he didn't allow the gold chain to slide through his fingers as had been his original intention. "This is a beautiful piece of craftsmanship."

For a moment, he thought she wasn't going to answer. Then she sighed and broke eye contact. "Yes. My father gave it to me on the day of my birth."

He knew there was a genuine bond between Antonia and her

father, but her reaction didn't ring true to him. His thumb grazed the clasp and once again she stiffened. Why was she so alarmed at the prospect that he might open her locket and see what secrets she kept within?

Memory stirred. At the praetor's insufferable feast, Antonia's calm façade had cracked when Maximus had defended his daughter's honor. Gawain knew Antonia had been pregnant in the past and from her reaction earlier this night, he guessed she had at least one daughter. Was it her children's portrait she kept close to her heart? Had she been forced by her despicable former husband to leave them in Rome?

He allowed the locket to slide from his fingers and once again nestle between her breasts. Just days ago, it hadn't interested him one way or the other whether Antonia had children, or how many. But now it mattered. He wanted to know. Because whether they shared her life now or not, they were still a part of her.

She stared at his chest, deliberately avoiding his gaze. He lifted her chin with one finger and made her look at him. There might be secrets they were forced to keep from each other, but this wasn't one of them.

"Would you allow me to look on the faces of your children, Antonia?"

The blood drained from her face, and she stared at him in what looked abject horror. What had he said? Had he made a terrible mistake?

"*What?*" Her voice was a tortured whisper and she clutched at her locket as though she imagined he might snatch it from her. Unease snaked through his gut. This was far from the reaction he'd expected.

Why had he asked her? Why did he want to see her children? It could mean nothing to him. And yet it did. They were hers, and he wanted to know everything about her.

That realization did nothing to calm his rising unease.

"You do have children, don't you?" Why was she being so evasive? Why didn't she want him to know of them? Most of all why did her reluctance to share something so important with him sting?

"I—" Her voice was husky. With a stab of shock, he realized she was vibrating with fear. "I conceived five babies. I lost my two sons during the sixth month of each pregnancy."

Horror crawled along his spine at what she had suffered, and the crass insensitivity of his invasive questioning. Words were inadequate but he tried regardless. "Antonia. I'm sorry."

She licked her lips, and her fingers gripped his in a punishing vise, yet she seemed unaware that they still held hands. "I lost my daughters during the fifth and seventh months of pregnancy."

Ice froze his veins. He'd imagined her daughters had survived. But she had lost them all. Not only lost them, but had been forced to go through the hazard of childbirth each time knowing, in her heart, they had no chance of survival.

Gods. No wonder shadows haunted her eyes. No wonder she wrapped herself in a façade of aloof detachment.

He stared into her lovely face and saw grief etched into every curve and shadow. How had he not seen it before?

He tugged her rigid hand up and kissed her knuckles. She hadn't mentioned her third daughter and he didn't have the heart to ask. It was clear what had happened. Her former husband had kept her in Rome.

"My last child was also a daughter." Her voice was low but at least she no longer trembled. He tightened his grip on her hand, trying to infuse her with his strength. Trying to let her know, without the need for awkward words, that he was there for her. "I carried her to term."

She was the child whose likeness Antonia carried against her heart. He still wanted to see her, but knew he would never again ask. By his thoughtless questioning, he had forced Antonia to relive the worst thing a woman could imagine. Yet those tragic events, that he couldn't even begin to comprehend, had shaped her into the woman she was today. The woman he couldn't shift from his mind.

The gods, no matter who they were, or which people worshipped them, were cruel, callous, and entirely self-serving. What harm had Antonia ever done that she should be so brutally punished?

"She lives in Rome?" His voice was hushed and while he was certain she did, there was always the chance Antonia had brought her to Britain. Perhaps, after all, her daughter did live with her.

Antonia expelled a harsh breath and once again he felt her body tense. "When my daughter was presented to her father, he turned his back on her and ordered her death."

CHAPTER NINETEEN

Something dark and ugly twisted deep inside Gawain's chest. There could be only one reason why Antonia's daughter had been condemned to die. It happened in his culture too. He didn't have to like it to acknowledge that it happened. Such decisions were never taken lightly. Who was he to judge another in such a matter?

But for Antonia to have lost four children, only to have her fifth born with such severe deformities that death was considered a kinder option, sickened him to the bottom of his soul.

There was nothing he could say to make her feel better. There was nothing he could do to wind back time and prevent him from asking the question in the first place.

"The gods play vicious games with us at times."

"The gods had nothing to do with it."

Something in her tone pierced the fog of recrimination that gripped him in a wraithlike vise.

"It wasn't your fault, Antonia." Was that what her bastard of a husband had told her? Blamed her for their child's frail clasp on mortality?

She stared at him. "My fault?" She sounded confused, as

though his words made no sense. He resisted the urge to wrap his arms around her and seduce her into forgetting this excruciating conversation. He had started it. He would not dishonor her pain by pretending it didn't exist.

"That your daughter was…" The words lodged in his throat. In the past, before the invasion of Cymru, he had counseled his people in times of need. But that had been different. They had not been Antonia and their loss had not clawed through his chest the way Antonia's loss did now. But still she stared at him and somehow he forced the word out. "Damaged."

The silence after his words thundered between them and for a moment, he thought he'd gone too far. That he had pushed her beyond her limits, and she'd crumble before him. But even as the thought formed, it disintegrated. Because she wasn't looking at him as if she was about to fall apart. She looked at him as though he spoke in the sacred language of the gods.

"My daughter," she said, and there was a fierce and terrible pride in her voice that unaccountably caused the spirits of his ancestors to drift over his arms. "Was perfect in every way. Her only flaw was that she was not a boy. My husband refused to acknowledge her existence to spite me, Gawain. To punish me for the sons I had lost." Disbelief seared him, yet he knew she spoke the truth. She bared her teeth and for one eerie moment looked like a Celtic warrior going into battle. "As if their deaths do not haunt me every moment of every day."

Disbelief surged into rage. It scarcely even registered that the man was Roman. All that thundered through Gawain's mind was her husband had murdered his own child, simply to hurt his wife.

"It's as well he's in Rome. If I ever came across him, I'd run him through with his own sword."

"That notion crossed my mind more than once." He felt the tension seep from Antonia as her fingers relaxed their death grip around his. "Had I possessed the strength that night I would have cut his throat with a fibula if nothing else had come to hand."

Again, the ethereal touch of his ancestors raised the hairs on his arms. Something was infinitesimally out of balance, although he couldn't fathom what. Antonia's heated fury of just moments ago had cooled and while he was relieved his thoughtlessness hadn't caused her to tumble into hysteria, her current state of calm was...unnerving.

She had just confided that her husband had killed their newborn daughter. Admittedly, he had no idea how long ago it had happened although it couldn't be that long, given her age and the length of time she'd been married. But even so, her attitude baffled him. Was it because the only way she could get through each day was to bury the pain so deeply that she could pretend it had never happened?

It seemed logical. But he couldn't shift the feeling that something else had happened that night, something significant that she hadn't told him.

He could think of nothing to say that didn't involve deadly force against her former husband, and so he remained silent. But it was a healing silence as the tension that had held Antonia in its merciless grip faded and she hugged his hand against her breast.

"I vowed I would never conceive another child." Her voice was so low he scarcely caught her words. He wondered if she even meant for him to hear. He buried his face in her silken hair and closed his eyes. There was nothing he could do to ease the pain she'd suffered. How he wished there was.

It was late. Every moment he stayed increased the chance of him being caught. But the thought of leaving her bed held no appeal.

Just a little longer. There would be no harm in that.

"Gawain." Her whisper penetrated his thoughts, and he brushed a kiss across her brow.

"What is it?"

Her sleepy gaze caught his. "I know it's impossible for you to stay all night, but would you mind—could you stay with me for just a short while? Until I go to sleep?"

"Yes." His response appeared to both surprise and delight her, if the look on her face was anything to go by. She bestowed a luminous smile at him, sighed and then snuggled against him, as though that was the most natural thing in the world for her to do.

Propped up on his elbow he watched as her breathing became regular and her muscles fully relaxed. With her hair tangled over her shoulders and spread across her pillows she looked untroubled, untouched by the harsh realities of life.

How deceptive appearances could be.

No wonder she didn't miss life in Rome, when so much tragedy had befallen her there. Was it really her fate to return, as the wife of the praetor?

She would never return to Rome if he had anything to do with it.

The thought filled his mind, and it didn't thunder with heated fury, but chilled his blood with iced conviction. Antonia deserved more than to become the chattel of another arrogant Roman, but what was the alternative? What could he offer her? A life on the run with a displaced Druid, a life filled with lies when he'd have to keep his true nature a secret from her?

What was he thinking? Antonia would never—could never—share his life, even if he lost his mind and asked her to.

No woman could share his life. There was no room for a woman in his future. If Rhys remained adamant about not inciting the other Druids to rebellion, then when Carys left Camulodunon so would he.

He'd travel north, beyond the land of the treacherous Brigantes, into the territories of the Picts. They, at least, still defied the insidious spread of the cursed Eagle.

But instead of anticipation flooding his blood at the prospect, an odd hollowness gnawed in his gut. It was the right thing to do.

The only way forward for a warrior who no longer lived in his homeland. Why then did it feel so wrong?

Perhaps, despite his best intentions, he fell asleep because from the depths of black he jerked awake, heart pounding. For a moment, he had no idea where he was, until he realized it was Antonia in his arms. Antonia whose breath came in uneven gasps, whose body trembled and whose fingernails dug into his forearm in unnamed terror.

"Antonia." He brushed her hair back from her sweaty face. She was in the grip of a nightmare and unintelligible words spilled from her lips. He leaned closer and brushed a kiss across her mouth. "Sweet Antonia, wake up. You're safe. I'm with you."

She went rigid and her eyelids sprung open. He began to smile in reassurance until he realized that she was still asleep. An eerie shudder inched along his spine as her fathomless eyes bored into him. And then she spoke.

"Embrace your destiny. Bring them home to me."

Her words were clear, commanding, directed at him. But it was none of these things, or even the way she continued to stare, unseeing, that caused his stomach to clench and chest contract.

It was because Antonia spoke in the sacred language of the gods that *only Druids understood.*

CHAPTER TWENTY

*L*ate the following morning, as Gawain made his way over to the main villa, Antonia's words echoed in his mind. She'd woken up soon afterward and had been so distressed at the thought he'd witnessed her having a nightmare, that he hadn't told her she had also spoken aloud.

What could he say in any case? She was obviously merely a conduit his gods had used to get his attention. He wouldn't upset her further by telling her such a thing. Especially when he had no idea how to answer the inevitable questions she would ask him.

Why? And how? She was a Roman, not a Celt. But she was a Roman he cared for and like it or not, the tactic had worked.

His gods had his attention. Curse them all, it was not he who had turned his back on them in the first place. Could he be blamed for his loss of faith after the way Lugus had vanished the moment Gawain had left the Isle of Mon?

But unless he wanted to risk Antonia suffering from more nightly visitations from gods that were not of her culture, he'd have to swallow his anger at their manipulative ways and attempt yet again to reconnect with Lugus.

Before dawn had broken, he'd left Antonia in the care of Elpis and although he and Antonia had made arrangements to meet tomorrow it had still been a wrench leaving her. She'd looked so lost and vulnerable, sitting on her bed, that he'd battled the urge to scoop her into his arms and take her with him.

Carys had been right to warn him from pursuing Antonia. He'd become involved without meaning to, and what had started out as merely another erotic game was now something far more deadly.

Not only to himself. Antonia would suffer too when this dangerous liaison finally ended.

A side door to the villa opened and Branwen, a girl Carys had brought with her from Cymru, hurried to him. "Gawain, Carys asks you to come quickly."

In Cymru, Branwen would never have spoken of Carys, a princess with the blood of the gods in her veins, as though they were equals. But many things had changed since the invasion.

He followed Branwen into the villa, and she nodded her head to the atrium before she vanished in the opposite direction. Frowning, he entered the atrium and instinctively went for his dagger at the crowd that greeted him.

But only for a fleeting moment. Although he'd never expected to see them in Camulodunon, these people were not strangers. He strode forward, where Carys held the hand of her mother as though she would never let her go. He bowed his head in a gesture of respect. "My queen."

"Yes, Gawain," Nia said, a dry note in her voice. "I am here."

"Cerridwen brought them safely to us." Carys' voice shook and tears glittered in her eyes as she once again gazed at her mother.

He folded his arms across his chest. "What happened?"

Nia sighed heavily. "Within days of you leaving Mon, the gods claimed Altair as he ascended into trance. It was seen by many as a sign that his adamant refusal to leave the Isle was...flawed."

Altair, the revered Elder who had been most vocal in his opinions and the one whose word held great sway with their people, continued his journey. And with his passing through the veil to the Otherworld he had allowed Nia and the other Druids who were of like mind to finally leave the Isle of Mon.

It was hardly the mass exodus that Nia had wanted. But perhaps she had finally realized that many of the Druids would never leave the sacred sanctuary, no matter what signs they were given.

Gawain had no idea what his queen planned on doing once Carys left for Rome. Would they all journey north? At least this way he would be among his own people in the land of the Picts.

But that was a discussion for another time. Carys would no doubt want time alone with her mother and going by the shadows cast by the sun he was late for a meeting with Rhys.

He swept his gaze around the dozen or so Druids who had accompanied their queen, and they exchanged silent greeting. Then he returned his attention to Nia.

"By your leave. I will see you later."

"No." Still holding Carys' hand, Nia took one step his way. "You'll remain here, Gawain. There are things to discuss."

"But my queen—"

"It was not a request."

He stared at her, and unease trickled along his spine. "I'm meeting someone."

Nia said nothing for a moment, but tension crackled in the air. Then she drew in a deep breath. "No, you're not, Gawain. You are not to leave here until the eighth hour has passed."

Antonia couldn't throw off the sense of impending disaster that hugged her like an unwanted blanket of fog. She'd gone to the forum in the hope the change of scene would help, but if anything, the bustling crowds and numerous scents and odors from stalls and livestock only increased her disquiet.

It was humiliating enough that Gawain had witnessed her foolish nightmare two nights ago. But she had the unshakable certainty that he'd also witnessed her speaking in the tongue of Juno.

Under normal circumstances that wouldn't matter. A visitation from a mighty goddess, even a goddess he didn't personally worship, was worthy of respect. But they weren't normal, because not only could she never remember what had transpired in her visions, nobody could understand the words she uttered while unconscious.

If Gawain had witnessed that, he would think her weak-minded. But he'd said nothing about her muttering in her sleep and she'd been too mortified to ask.

It was her own fault for asking him to stay with her while she fell asleep. But it had been almost a week since Juno had come to her, and the possibility she would again hadn't even crossed Antonia's mind.

She wouldn't make that mistake again. But oh, how wonderful it had been to close her eyes with Gawain's arms around her.

And how wonderful and strangely liberating it had been to tell him of Cassia. It was something she'd never imagined telling him, and yet the words had spilled from her and as they had, a great weight had lifted from her soul.

He might not know that her precious child was still alive. But at least he knew she had been born, and that she'd been dearly loved. How close she had been to telling him the whole truth of that night. How she longed to tell him the truth. His compassion had been as genuine for her beloved daughters, as well as her sons, and for that alone, he would forever have a place in her heart.

Perhaps, after Cassia arrived in Britannia, she and Gawain might still be able to see each other. He could meet Cassia.

Perhaps, one day in the far future, she might even be able to tell him how she had defied Scipio's cruel edict.

"Domina." Elpis clutched her and pulled her from the path of a suddenly riotous crowd. What had happened? What had she missed while she'd been daydreaming of an impossible future that included both Cassia and Gawain?

She grabbed a young boy as he dashed by. "What is it?"

He twisted in her grasp, caught sight of her and with great reluctance stopped trying to escape. "Crucifixion. Out on the road."

Her fingers slackened and he took immediate advantage to disappear in the throng. Antonia turned and stared at Elpis, her heart thudding high in her breast making it hard to breathe, hard to think clearly. The boy had spoken in his native tongue, but she understood enough to know exactly what he'd said.

She had no idea why panic gripped her heart or why her knees had the terrible urge to buckle. It made no sense that her stomach churned, and skeletal fingers scraped over her arms.

It wasn't Gawain who was being crucified. The praetor, for all his faults, was an honorable man and wouldn't kill another because of something as trivial as a perceived threat to the affections of a woman he was interested in.

She knew this. Yet the horrifying vision of Gawain, bloodied and tortured, blinded her good sense.

"Domina, no." Elpis' urgent voice and hand on her arm caused her to pause and glance over her shoulder. "We should return home. It's not safe for you on the road."

"I have to see." She began to run, holding up her gown so she wouldn't trip over the material, and knew that Elpis was by her side. She followed the milling crowd through the streets, to the triumphal arch that had been constructed to celebrate Emperor Claudius' victorious campaign.

Legionaries were everywhere. Trying to push back the crowd, trying to bring order as they finished their grisly task. Just beyond the arch, by the side of the road, a roughly hewn cross had been erected. Even from this distance she could see the naked man lashed to the wood wasn't Gawain.

Thank the gods. She stood by the arch, panting, her hand pressed against her breast. Muted whispers rippled through the gathered people and a subdued sense of unease permeated the relief pounding through her blood.

Druid.

There were Druids in Camulodunum. And, like he said he would, the praetor was hunting them down.

Now she was no longer sick with terror that it was Gawain enduring such a torturous death, a resigned sense of disgust and regret flooded her veins. Of course Druids had to die. They were a cruel, vindictive race that sacrificed babies on the altars of their gods. She had learned all this as a small child at her father's knee, and her years in Rome had only strengthened the knowledge that Druids had to be wiped from every corner of the empire.

But she hated crucifixions. No matter how many she had inadvertently witnessed, it had never served to change her mind. It was a barbaric death and surely even Druids deserved some dignity even if they were incapable of offering such to their own wretched victims.

She reached out to Elpis, who took her hand. But just before she turned away to return to the litter that would take her home, something tugged in a buried recess of her mind.

It meant nothing. She tried to ignore it but despite her best intentions she once again looked at the man on the cross. *Really* looked at him.

And recognized his face.

He was the huge man dressed in peasant clothing she had seen in the forum. The man Gawain had passed a silent message with.

It was a coincidence. Nothing more. Gawain didn't know this man. And even if he did, it didn't follow that Gawain was aware the other man was a Druid.

She barely felt Elpis gently tug on her hand as another jumbled thought surfaced. Gawain had spoken of the woman he'd once loved. How she had warned him that *treachery awaited in the land of the Brigantes.*

When Gawain had admitted he had once loved another, she'd been too foolishly wounded to understand the significance of his words. It had been more than a simple wish for him to remain safe. Gawain had been specific. She had saved his life with her warning.

Had it been a warning direct from their gods? Was the woman he had loved a Celtic priestess?

A Druid?

Gawain said she was a warrior. But everyone knew Druids were fierce, bloodthirsty savages who took pleasure in leading their people into battle. Yet she couldn't believe that Gawain had loved a bloodthirsty savage. A brave, noble warrior—yes, that she could understand, no matter how much it hurt her heart to admit. Gawain deserved a woman like that by his side, one who could match his strength, one who shared his heritage and could face his future.

Shared his heritage.

The words thundered in her brain.

No. She wouldn't believe it. Gawain was not a Druid. He was kin to Carys, and Carys had led the legions to the mad Druid who would have destroyed them all. She wouldn't have done that if she were related to a Druid.

But Gawain and Carys were not blood kin.

"Domina, we should leave." Elpis' anxious whisper pierced her mind and she stared at the other woman, but all she saw was Gawain's face as he told her treachery awaited him in the land of the Brigantes.

During her last year in Rome, there had been great celebrations when the Briton king, Caratacus, had been captured and paraded through the city in chains. He had been betrayed by the queen of the Brigantes and all the Druids who had fought with him had been slain.

Coincidence. But no matter how she clung onto that answer it felt hollow, and threads of panic weaved through her breast.

Her suspicions were insane. Gawain was nothing like any evil Druid she had imagined. Just because he might have known the man being crucified, had once loved a woman who could foresee danger and had been betrayed by those who had turned on Caratacus didn't mean he belonged to the elite ruling class of Celts who, by all accounts, could even out-rank their kings.

"Lady Antonia." The male voice sounded shocked, and she spun around, heart pounding, to see the praetor frowning down at her. *Does he suspect Gawain of being a Druid?* Was that why he'd asked so many questions the other night? "This is not a sight for your eyes. Come, let me escort you to safety."

He didn't wait for her reply and took her arm in a possessive manner, allowing Elpis to follow behind. Short of creating a scene—although would anyone notice with the gruesome entertainment on offer? —she had little choice but to go with him. Words were beyond her in any case. What could she say? Ask him outright if he suspected Gawain of being Rome's bitterest enemy?

He took her to the basilica that flanked the forum, led her across the mosaic-floored antechamber and ushered her into what she presumed was his private office. Elpis stood a few steps behind, and Antonia resisted the urge to reach for the other woman's hand.

"Please, sit." The praetor placed an ornate stool before her. She remained standing behind it and somehow dredged up a smile.

"Thank you, but no. I must return home before my father worries."

"Of course." He stood there, hands clasped behind his back, his gaze fixed on her in an unnerving stare. She forced herself not to fidget. She would do and say nothing that might cause his suspicion to fall in Gawain's direction.

A shiver raced over her arms. Was that why he'd brought her here? To interrogate her about what she knew of Gawain? Did he know of their liaison?

Nausea roiled and her heart slammed a heavy tattoo against her ribs, but she kept her face impassive. There was nothing the praetor could say that would induce her to betray the man she loved.

She swallowed and stiffened her already rigid spine. What a time to acknowledge the truth. Even the possibility that Gawain was a despised Druid did nothing to change the fact.

"Antonia." His voice was gruff. "I deeply regret you saw that crucifixion."

Breathe. "It's not the first I have witnessed." She sounded as though such things were an everyday occurrence that didn't disturb her in the least. She hoped that was how she sounded, anyway.

"And yet I would protect you from such distasteful aspects of life if you would allow me to do so."

Too late, she realized the trap into which she had fallen. Why had she accompanied him into his private office? She should have insisted that he take her directly back to her litter. But it was too late to berate her stupidity now.

Either the praetor was going to ask for her hand in marriage, or he wished to make her his concubine. She had no intention of agreeing to either but the thought of an unpleasant confrontation, on top of her horrifying suspicions about Gawain, churned her stomach.

She forced herself to meet the praetor's gaze. "You are too kind, but I am more than capable of looking after myself."

He took a step towards her, and she was relieved that the stool remained between them. "You must know how I feel about you."

Shock stabbed through her breast. Yes, she knew he had lusted after her for many years, even though he'd always behaved with the utmost decorum in her presence. But for him to state the fact so baldly—she hadn't expected that.

"I—" Words lodged in her throat, and she hitched in a shallow breath. "You've always been very kind to me."

His jaw tightened. "Kind?" He appeared to consider the word and find it greatly lacking. "I would certainly be kind to you, Antonia. You deserve that at least after the mockery of your first marriage."

"Praetor—"

"Seneca. At least grant me that honor once more, my lady."

Heat seared her skin. This was becoming worse by the moment. "Seneca. I have no wish to discuss my marriage with anyone. Not now and not at any time in the future."

"I respect you for that." He glanced at the stool, clearly regretting its strategic position. "I respect you for many things. Your conduct has always been impeccable. Let me assure you that as my wife your life would be one of untold luxury and indulgence. You will never want for anything again."

He hadn't thrown her tainted heritage in her face as a way of underscoring the great honor he was offering her, the way Scipio had. At fourteen, she had been awed by the handsome, arrogant Roman and overwhelmed that he was prepared to overlook her father's common bloodline.

That tactic wouldn't work now, of course. But how much easier it would be if the praetor had only wished her to be his concubine. She could have used the excuse of affronted pride to refuse him. Now, she had no choice but to tell him the one thing that would be sure to dampen his desire to take her as his wife.

"I'm honored by your offer, Seneca. But I fear I cannot accept. I'm unable to have any more children." She'd almost died giving birth to Cassia and while no physician had told her she should not attempt another pregnancy Antonia had made the decision herself. She would never put herself through such heartrending agonies again—unless the outcome was as perfect as Cassia. And who could guarantee such a thing?

She only hoped the praetor concluded it was a medical directive. No man would take the word of a mere woman in such a matter.

"I have three sons. That is more than enough for any man."

Speechless she stared at him. Was he actually saying that, if he took her as his wife, he didn't expect her to breed for him?

Certainly, three sons were admirable. But a man always wanted more. Desperately she clawed through her mind to find a counter maneuver. And recalled their conversation from the other night.

"But you've always wanted a daughter, Seneca." Most men did, once they had sired a good few sons. Daughters were, after all, a valuable asset when it came to strengthening allegiances through their advantageous marriage. "I would be unable to give you one."

A taut silence stretched between them. Unease fluttered in her belly. Why didn't he say something?

Finally, he cleared his throat. "There would be no need for you to endure another pregnancy. I know what you did, Antonia. I know your daughter is still alive."

CHAPTER TWENTY-ONE

*G*awain stood in the shadow cast by the monstrous Roman arch at the outer edge of Camulodunon and his hands fisted in impotent fury at the sight of Rhys. It was obvious the other man had been tortured before this final indignity, and equally obvious he hadn't betrayed his fellow Druids.

But threaded through the anger was a sense of shaken disbelief. Because if Nia hadn't arrived when she had, if she hadn't forbidden him to leave the villa, then he would have been with Rhys when the legionaries had come for him.

If not for Nia there would be two Druids being crucified this day.

He knew it was a sign from the gods. Knew he was being warned that if he didn't follow the right path, this was the fate that awaited him. But, although he would never admit it to anyone, least of all his gods, he no longer knew his path. But more than that, he no longer possessed the belief in Lugus to show him the way.

Yet he could no longer ignore their command. For them to use Antonia in the way they had was bad enough. To take Rhys as an example was sickening. He had to find a way to communicate with Lugus before they did anything else.

He made his way back to the market and leaned against one of the columns of the bathhouse. This evening, after he'd met with Antonia, he would make the necessary preparations and request the counsel of his god.

Frustration seethed at how carelessly the gods used whoever crossed their path to fulfill their wishes. It was something he'd barely acknowledged before the Roman invasion yet since leaving Mon it had plagued his mind.

He had to calm his thoughts before approaching Lugus, otherwise the god would likely strike him down before he even had the chance to take a breath.

Antonia would calm his soul. He didn't know what it was about her, but she had the ability to soothe him with merely a glance or a few inconsequential words. Except nothing about her was inconsequential. Being with her gave him a sense of purpose, as though he could accomplish anything he set his mind to. And that was insane. Why would he feel such a thing when he was with her? What good was it, when fate had decreed at the moment of their births that their futures could never be one?

In his peripheral vision, he saw movement at the entrance of the basilica, the administration building where the local tribal aristocracies allegedly took responsibility for their own decision-making. As far as he could see, it was little more than a focus for the military occupation. Yet something snagged his attention, and he glanced across the square. And froze.

The praetor was leading Antonia from the building. He held her arm and there was a predatory air about him as though he already owned her. Savage fury blazed through Gawain, raw and ugly, as he watched them approach her covered litter.

What had she been doing in there? The basilica wasn't a place for Roman women.

But he knew why she had been in there. It was because of the praetor. And the way he helped her into her litter, the way he kissed her hand and then stood and watched the slaves carry her down the road, all pointed to one distasteful fact.

In the Roman's eyes, he did own her. Had Antonia promised to marry him? *How could she do such a thing?*

Rage boiled through his veins, but it was more than rage, a primal emotion he had never before experienced. He couldn't name the fire that scalded his blood and scorched his reason, and caused his body to burn as though in the grip of a fever.

He couldn't name it, but he'd be damned if he would just stand by and let Antonia be pushed into marrying a man she didn't love. Because she didn't love the praetor. There had been no reciprocal lust or attraction in her eyes or manner during that feast whenever she'd looked at the Roman.

Was it her father pushing for the marriage? Would Antonia really give up any hope of happiness just to please the old man?

So what was he thinking? That Antonia would give up every-thing, her pampered lifestyle, her ties with her father—and follow *him*?

The thought slammed through his brain, a frigid blast of winter ice that cooled his fury but didn't extinguish it. Instead, the thought solidified; became tangible. With Antonia by his side, he could embrace a life in the harsh lands of the Picts.

The litter stopped and Antonia got out. What was she doing? Going back to the Roman? He looked back to the basilica, but the praetor was nowhere to be seen. Frowning, he watched Antonia and Elpis enter the market and savage pleasure speared through him.

She'd fooled the Roman into thinking she was returning home. Somehow, that gave him hope that she wasn't yet fully committed to the praetor.

He marched across the square and followed her through the market. She didn't appear to be inclined to shop and instead sat on a stone bench, Elpis by her side, in the shade of a despondent-looking tree.

Anticipation surged through him. He would persuade her that her path was entwined with his. That was the message the gods had given him the other night. Why else would they have spoken through Antonia? She was meant to be by his side. He could keep the secret of his heritage from her. What use was his heritage in any case, in the land of the Picts?

Antonia took a deep breath and took Elpis' proffered hand as they sat on the bench. Her stomach fluttered with nerves and her throat was parched but there was an odd sense of calm in her heart.

She was doing the right thing.

"Domina," Elpis whispered. "Will you accept the praetor's offer?"

Her fingers tightened around Elpis'. "If I refuse him, do you think he would inform Scipio of Cassia's existence?"

"I don't know." Elpis sounded reluctant to admit it. "He seemed genuine in his desire to adopt your daughter and love her as his own blood."

Yes, he had. As she'd reeled in shock at his disclosure that he knew Cassia was alive, the praetor had continued to speak of her beloved child as though he couldn't wait to claim her. At her prolonged silence, he'd then assured her that he would present Cassia as his own bastard daughter. Antonia's actions would never be known to anyone. She would be Cassia's mother in the eyes of Rome and Cassia would enjoy a lifestyle that was her birthright.

It was unnerving to learn how close an eye he'd kept on her in Rome. Unbelievable that he knew how she'd arranged for her daughter to be saved and brought up by trusted former slaves of

Scipio. The couple were elderly, of no further use to him, but their loyalty for Antonia had never wavered. She had ensured they never went without necessities, and when Cassia's life was threatened, they had been only too happy to take the baby in.

The praetor knew all this. Yet her own former husband, Cassia's father, didn't have the first idea.

"I believe he would love her." Antonia curled her fingers around her locket and saw Cassia's sweet face, when she had gone to say goodbye to her just before she left for Britannia.

But what right did she have to deny Cassia knowledge of her heritage? Every child deserved to know of their true blood lineage.

Her resolve strengthened. For more than a year, she had denied her daughter's existence to the world. But once Cassia was in Britannia, under Antonia's care, what could Scipio do? He had no jurisdiction over her now. He had already denied Cassia's right to live. Therefore, he had forfeited any further rights over her upbringing. And if he tried to assert those rights, Antonia would fight him with every means at her disposal.

She had no doubt that, if she married him, the praetor would keep his word and protect her and Cassia from any vindictiveness Scipio might harbor against her. But they would be living a lie. And always in the back of her mind, whether she agreed to the praetor's proposal or brought Cassia up in Britannia by herself, would be the fear that one day her deception would be revealed.

Until the other night with Gawain, she'd never imagined telling anyone in Britannia about the bloodied events surrounding Cassia's birth. But the events had happened. She couldn't change the past. And she wouldn't face the future burdened by a guilt that was not hers to bear.

She was proud of her child. She wasn't ashamed of what she had done to save her life. When Cassia arrived in Britannia, she would arrive as her blood daughter.

"My lady." The deep masculine voice sank into her senses like warm honey, and it took a moment to realize that the voice was real and not a figment of her imagination. Fierce joy speared with raw denial thundered through her and she turned to see Gawain standing by her side.

He is not a Druid. But he was here, when she had not thought to see him for hours. If that wasn't a sign from Juno to trust him with her most precious of secrets, then what was?

He sat beside her on the bench without waiting to be asked. Something no Roman noble would ever do, and yet where it mattered Gawain treated her with more respect than any of her fellow countrymen ever had.

Yet it was tempting the Fates to meet so openly, even if there was a decorous distance between them. She smothered the urge to wrap her arms around him, to feel his body against her, to reassure herself that he was alive and well and not in danger of being crucified for his beliefs.

"Anyone might see us here, Gawain."

With his legs stretched out before him and hands splayed across his thighs, he looked deceptively relaxed. But she could feel coiled tension radiating from him, and surely no one who glanced his way could be deceived that he was anything but a warrior on full alert.

"Anyone?" His intense gaze scorched her. "Or someone in particular? The praetor, for instance?"

Had he seen her with the praetor? Had Gawain followed her here to confront her?

She wasn't sure whether the knowledge thrilled or dismayed her. And threaded through every thought was the devastating suspicion of what he might truly be.

Once again, she thrust the suspicion aside. "If word got back to my father, he—" The words locked in her throat as, for the first time, she questioned what exactly her father could do. She wasn't a young girl whose reputation needed to remain pristine to make an advantageous marriage. And while she would never wish to shame him with her behavior, speaking in public with Gawain, kin to Carys, wasn't something that would besmirch her name and reflect badly on her father.

"But your father wouldn't mind that you had been alone with the praetor, is that what you're saying?"

If her father knew what the praetor had asked, he would be delighted despite the fact she'd been alone with him. But she had no intention of telling Gawain of that conversation. She had no intention of telling her father, either.

Before she could stop herself, she leaned closer to him, and the horror of the morning smashed through the defenses in her brain. Panic churned through her breast, constricting her breath as she recalled those terrifying moments when she'd feared it was Gawain who hung on the cross.

"I witnessed the crucifixion. The praetor merely saw me there and escorted me back to the forum."

Gawain's jaw tensed. "You saw the crucifixion?" From the corner of her eyes, she saw his hands fist on his thighs. Was it because he didn't like the thought of her seeing such a thing? Or because the Druid had been a friend of his?

Don't go down that path. She had to stop thinking that way. Yet with Gawain by her side, looking at her as though he wanted to drag her into his arms and never let her go, she could think of little else.

"They say he was a Druid." The words were out, stark, and sounded like an accusation. Gawain's expression didn't alter, but since his face was a chiseled mask to begin with, that meant nothing.

"Who are *they*? The Romans?" Contempt edged every word, but it wasn't condemnation she saw in his eyes. She couldn't decipher what she saw in his eyes, but it made her want to take him into her arms and shield him from all harm.

What a foolish thing to think. As if she could ever protect Gawain from anything.

She gripped her fingers together on her lap before she made an exhibition of herself.

"If there are Druids in Camulodunum they will be hunted down and destroyed." Juno, what was she doing? Was she trying to make him convince her he wasn't a Druid or warn him that if he was, he needed to flee?

I don't want him to flee.

"Because your emperor fears their ancient knowledge." His words were no longer filled with contempt but with a strangely weary acceptance.

Startled, she gazed at him. "No, of course it's not for that reason." She hesitated. No, surely that wasn't the reason. It was because Druids incited fear in their people and stirred up rebellion against the mighty Eagle.

Unease quivered through her heart. Stories her father had told her of the long-departed Druids in Gallia haunted her mind.

"They steal the babies of their enemies," she whispered, as an unformed dread knotted the pit of her stomach. "They drink their blood and offer sacrifice to their gods."

Gawain didn't answer. He just continued to look at her, and there was no condemnation in his gaze. He looked at her as though her words didn't surprise him. As if her beliefs were something he had already resigned himself to long before she had spoken.

The dread bloomed with every beat of her heart. She had no personal experience of what Druids might or might not do. But her own husband, a Roman patrician, had been willing to spill the blood of his own child on the altar of his pride.

She hitched in a shallow breath as her world tipped into uncharted waters. She had never questioned her father's words. He told her only the truth as he saw it, as it had been related to him. As it was proclaimed by Rome.

Her father was ruthless in his business dealings. He wouldn't be such a successful merchant if he was not. But at home, with her, he was nothing but gentle and considerate. Yet now, with Gawain sitting silently by her side, she thought of her father's attitude when it came to Druids with a new perspective.

He loathed them. It was personal. A chill crawled along her spine and across her arms. What had happened in the past to make him so sure of their evil nature?

Still Gawain regarded her. A treacherous certainty slid into her mind.

She didn't care if he was a Druid. She would stake her life that he had never mutilated a child in a sacred ritual or embarked on a savage trail of rape and murder of innocents. She realized she was clutching her locket and her thumb traced over its familiar gold surface.

Time hung suspended between them. Gawain still waited for her response, and she imagined her next words would tell him whether their liaison could continue—or finish this day.

Slowly she unclasped the locket and pressed it against her breast. She could ask him outright if he was a Druid. He might even tell her the truth.

But she didn't want to hear it.

She looked back at him once again, the face of a man who might be her worst enemy, but saw only the man she no longer wanted to live without. They might not have a future together. But she could give him this.

"There's something I did not tell you, about the night of my last daughter's birth."

Emotion flickered in his eyes. Whatever he'd expected her to say, it had not been that.

"Is there?" He sounded cautious but his entire focus was on her and although a sedate space remained between them, she could feel his comforting heat embrace her.

Any remaining doubts she might have harbored about telling

him of Cassia vanished. "Yes. I defied Scipio's orders to leave Cassia to the mercy of the gods. She's alive, Gawain. And will be arriving in Britannia in a little over two weeks' time."

Gawain stared at Antonia and hoped his shock wasn't apparent on his face. He'd been bracing himself for her to ask if he was a Druid. Had convinced himself that lying to her was the only thing he could do. Yet, as she so often did, she'd turned the conversation in a direction he'd not foreseen.

His conviction had been right. This was the something significant that had happened the night of her daughter's birth that he'd been unable to put his finger on. Of anything he might have imagined, the truth had not been it.

She'd gone against the word of her husband, the perceived wishes of her gods and, presumably, the laws of Rome to save her newborn daughter. She might be a Roman noblewoman, but she had the heart and the strength of will of a warrior.

There was an odd constriction in his chest as he watched her cradle her locket in the palm of her hand, before she offered it to him. He looked at the opened locket, and saw two perfect portraits. One of a woman, the other of a beautiful baby.

"My daughter, Cassia." Antonia's voice was barely above a whisper as she traced the tip of her finger over the face of the child. Then she did the same to the portrait of the woman. "I named her after my mother."

Remorse burned through him as he recalled his scathing thoughts on the day they had met. Antonia had appeared scandalized that Carys had named Nia after her mother. He'd leaped to conclusions. They had been absolutely wrong.

Antonia hadn't been shocked at Carys breaking with Roman tradition. She had been shocked only because Carys was so open about it.

He, who had once prided himself on his ability to judge others in the name of Lugus, was guilty of unfairly judging Antonia based solely on his own prejudices. He'd known many fearless women. Yet Antonia was the bravest.

He kept his gaze fixed on her locket. "I should like to meet your daughter, Antonia."

The silence after his words razed his senses. If she had no wish for him to meet her child, then why had she told him about her? Finally, he looked up at her, and caught the sparkle of tears in her beautiful eyes.

She sniffed, blinked rapidly and gently closed her locket. "I would like that too."

After leaving Antonia, Gawain made his way through the back streets. He'd met several of the underground Druids but after Rhys' arrest they had all vanished without a trace. But, without Rhys, would they be willing to change their tactics?

He turned into a dingy alley, his mind working on various scenarios whereby the legions fell, and Antonia remained safe. And in that moment when his concentration shifted from his surroundings, the hair on the back of his neck rose in warning.

He swung around, dagger in hand. Two cutthroats stalked him, identical leers on their faces. As one, they leaped at him and he ducked, spun around, and barreled into the closest one, sending them both crashing into a stone wall.

As the first man staggered to his feet, the second one attacked Gawain from behind. He shoved backward and plunged his dagger into the other man's neck. Blood bubbled over the hilt, over his hand, and he slammed his foot against the cutthroat's chest. The man crumpled to the ground, just as the second man smashed his fist against the side of Gawain's head.

Pain exploded through his brain and caused his vision to

double. He staggered, used the momentum, and wheeled back to his attacker.

His hand was slippery with blood, but he clung grimly onto his weapon. The man had a length of chain and he flicked it, like a whip, and Gawain's dagger went flying.

Gawain bared his teeth, grabbed the chain, and yanked his assailant forward. He used his fists, his head, every part of his body was a honed weapon and the only sounds that filled his ears were harsh breaths, heavy thuds, and the thunder of his blood.

With a final punch, the cutthroat fell to the ground, blood dripping from his nose and mouth. Gawain staggered back a couple of steps, his breath searing his lungs, sweat and blood distorting his vision. When he was sure the other man had no intention of finishing the fight he swung around, looking for his dagger.

And at the end of the alley saw the praetor, flanked by two foreign mercenaries.

CHAPTER TWENTY-TWO

Gawain straightened, every battered sense on full alert as the praetor and his mercenaries strolled down the alley to him. His dagger was out of reach, the chain wrapped around the second cutthroat's legs, and he didn't rate his chances high against another three men—who were all armed.

"Celt." The praetor swept his autocratic glance over him, as though Gawain was a leper. "Do I have your attention?"

Gawain spat blood at the praetor's feet. "I'm listening." Not that he had much choice.

For long moments, the praetor continued to stare at him. It was like looking into the soulless eyes of a serpent. Finally, the Roman raised his hand and the mercenaries stepped back, allowing the two of them privacy.

"If I dig deep enough," his voice was low, ensuring they were not overheard, "I'll discover the evidence I require against you. Your relationship with the tribune's wife will not be enough to save your neck."

Gawain stifled the urge to retaliate. Physical violence would get him nowhere in his current circumstances and he couldn't bait the praetor with words, because words could incriminate not only himself but Carys and all her blood kin.

He battened down his frustration and forced the foul lie from his lips. "I don't know what you're talking about."

The praetor's smile was deadly. "Do not waste my time, Celt. If not for Lady Antonia, you would already be feeding the crows on a cross."

Gawain's heart jackknifed. His ribs hurt as he struggled to draw breath into his lungs. He couldn't allow the Roman to see Antonia's name meant anything to him. "You mean the merchant's daughter? What does she have to do with this?"

"I told you not to waste my time." The praetor no longer bared his teeth in a mockery of a smile. "I'm not blind, Celt. I saw the way you looked at her the other night. I saw you sit beside her in the forum just now. Do you really think you have a chance of enticing a woman as refined as she?"

Despite the pounding imperative to smash his fist between the Roman's eyes, relief thundered through him. The praetor didn't know of his and Antonia's liaison. Her reputation was unsullied.

"We're merely acquaintances. She's a friend of the tribune's wife."

The praetor's unblinking stare bored into him as though he sought answers to unasked questions. Gawain stared back. The Roman would learn nothing of Antonia from him.

"Lady Antonia is blessed with the gentle heart of her sex." The praetor puffed out his chest and Gawain battled the need to dive for his dagger and thrust it through the Roman's throat. Condescending bastard. Antonia possessed the brave heart of a warrior. "It would distress her to see an acquaintance condemned as Rome's bitterest enemy. I would do a great deal to avoid causing her such distress. Do you understand me, Celt?"

The dank stone walls that flanked the alley contracted around him and it was hard to draw a breath. A buzzing cacophony filled his head, and the smug face of the Roman imprinted on his mind.

The only reason he was still alive was because the praetor knew his death would upset Antonia. Evidence didn't matter when it came to Druids. Mere suspicion was enough to convict. But the Roman knew Antonia cared for Gawain. And the Roman cared enough for Antonia to warn her barbarous lover of the consequences of continuing their ill-fated liaison.

It didn't matter what the praetor did to him. But it was imperative he didn't suspect Antonia was his lover. Rome set such stock by their noblewomen's unblemished reputations.

"Lady Antonia does not return my regard. If she did, your threats would mean nothing to me."

The Roman took another step closer. "I do not threaten. I'm telling you how it will be. Leave Britannia and never return." He punched Gawain in the face, his heavy ring of office tearing flesh. Gawain staggered but refused to give the bastard the satisfaction of falling to the ground. "Should we meet again when Lady Antonia is my wife and far from this primitive province, my benevolence may not be so accommodating."

Carys stood by his side in the room dedicated to preparing meals in the villa, arms folded, as one of the Druids who'd arrived with her mother tended to his injuries. He'd protested they didn't need looking at, and Carys had threatened him with further violence if he didn't comply.

Only when the other Druid left the room did Carys let out an infuriated breath. "Cutthroats, you say?" Disbelief dripped from every word, and he shot her a black glare. "And you were a random victim they picked upon?"

"Don't worry. They'll never pick on another."

"I don't doubt that for a moment." She unfolded her arms and made a despairing gesture, clearly for Cerridwen's benefit. "But I'm certain the praetor has many others he can call on."

He should have known Carys would see through his attempts to fog the truth. "I won't leave Antonia at the mercy of that bastard. When I leave Camulodunon she will be by my side." Antonia and her daughter. But Carys didn't need to know everything.

Carys returned his glare. "What happened to the brief affair, Gawain? You were supposed to forget about her within the turn of a moon. Not make insane plans to take her with you to the gods know where."

He rolled his shoulders and ignored the pain that spiked into every particle of his body.

"You knew it would never be a brief affair, Carys." She'd warned him against pursuing Antonia. Yet even if he'd possessed this foreknowledge, he would have continued on the same path. The threat of death from a jealous Roman was a small price to pay for the hours he'd spent with Antonia.

"I knew it would cause you great pain." Her voice was no longer accusatory, and she gently brushed her fingers over his shoulder. "And I'm not talking about these physical injuries."

He'd been injured far worse in the past. But the thought of Antonia seeing him, bruised and bloodied, didn't appeal. "Will you send a message to Antonia canceling our meeting this afternoon?" He'd send a message himself, but it was better if it came from Carys, for the sake of propriety.

"You should send her a message ending this liaison." But there was no rancor in Carys' voice, only resignation. "Even if Antonia agrees to go with you, her father will never allow it. He'll search for her and hunt for you until his dying breath."

She told him nothing he didn't already know. Yet his mind was set. When he left for the land of the Picts, so would Antonia and her child.

After Antonia watched Gawain leave the forum she turned to Elpis. "I should tell my father of Cassia."

Elpis remained silent, an oddly brooding look on her face and Antonia clasped her hand, needing the comfort. Surely Elpis didn't think her father would reject Cassia if he knew the truth?

Finally, Elpis looked at her. "Yes." Her voice was soft, but Antonia detected the faintest hint of despair in that one word. "A child should know her own blood kin, domina."

There was no condemnation in Elpis' response, but guilt stabbed through Antonia all the same. Elpis had been taken from her family, her land and everything she'd ever known when she was a small child. She had no idea if her parents were alive or dead, or whether she had any brothers or sisters.

If she were free, would she search for them? If Antonia was in her place, wouldn't she long to know the truth of her heritage?

Antonia had escaped the shackles of Rome. So too had her precious daughter. How could she not offer the same freedom to her faithful slave?

Antonia handed her father her locket and watched him look down at the portrait of his granddaughter. After leaving the forum, Antonia had returned to the villa and found her father here, in the courtyard. And so she had told him of Cassia.

He hadn't interrupted her. Had not said a word. But she'd watched him age ten years and guilt ate into her heart.

She couldn't take the words back. Would not, even if she could. She had once feared her father's heart wouldn't survive learning of Scipio's treatment of her. But her father deserved to know the truth. Cassia deserved the truth to be told.

Finally, he stirred, his finger tracing over the delicate

portraiture. "You named her after your mother?" His voice was hushed. He appeared incapable of tearing his eyes away from her locket.

"Yes."

"She's the image of you at that age." He looked up at her and her heart twisted at the tears she saw glistening in his eyes. "She's beautiful, Antonia."

"Father." She reached out and took his hand. "I'm sorry I didn't tell you of her birth before."

He continued to stare at her and with every passing moment, his features hardened, and eyes grew colder. A shiver trickled over her arms, and she squeezed his fingers. Despite his obvious desire to see and welcome Cassia, did he condemn her for defying Scipio's command?

"Your former husband had best not set foot in Britannia, Antonia. He would not last a day here."

Relief washed through her. Her father was completely on her side. "He considers Britannia a primitive outpost of the empire. He would never come here willingly."

"My contacts spread far. I'm owed a great many favors. Perhaps even in Rome he is not safe."

There was an icy note in her father's voice that she had never heard before. Alarm spiked. She wanted him on her side, but she didn't want him putting himself in danger to exact vengeance against a powerful patrician.

This was why she hadn't wanted him to know the details of her marriage.

"Only one thing matters. That you're happy to acknowledge your granddaughter. Promise me you won't attempt retribution."

Not that she cared if an excruciating accident befell Scipio. She'd often fantasized that he suffered agonies through disembowelment or even crucifixion. But fantasies were safe. Put into reality and the repercussions could be fatal.

Soon she would have Cassia. That was all that mattered.

Her father was once again staring at the portrait of Cassia. "He sired a perfect child. May he rot in Tartarus for all time."

She agreed with every particle of her being. But she didn't wish to discuss the fate the gods had in store for her former husband. Now she knew Cassia's welcome was assured, there was another matter she needed to ask her father about.

"There was a crucifixion on the road today."

He looked up. "Yes. Another filthy Druid has met his just end."

Growing up he'd encouraged her to question and investigate everything. Everything except when it came to Druids. It was as though an invisible barrier surrounded the subject and she had never been inclined to penetrate it.

Until today.

"Perhaps not all Druids deserve such a fate."

He stared at her as if she had just blasphemed against Jupiter himself. "They all deserve to die." His voice vibrated with fury and Antonia gazed at him, aghast at his vehemence. "Never doubt that. Every last one of them must be eliminated from the face of the earth."

"But why?" Her voice was little more than a whisper. "What have they ever done to you, Father?"

For a moment, she didn't think he was going to answer her. His eyes became glazed, as though he no longer saw her but, conversely, his fingers curled around her locket in an oddly protective gesture.

Unease crawled along her spine, and she had the insane desire to retract her question, to change the subject. To wipe that unnatural expression from her father's face.

Finally, he drew in a long breath. "I've not been fully truthful with you, Antonia. About your mother—it was not giving birth to you that killed her. She was murdered by the hand of a Druid."

❄

Antonia remained in the courtyard after her father left to attend to his business. Disjointed thoughts and jagged memories collided in her mind and when Elpis entered the courtyard, her father's words spilled from her lips.

Shock scorched Elpis' face. At least she hadn't known of this great and terrible secret. But although Antonia's heart thundered against her ribs and nausea roiled in her breast, denial hammered with relentless insistence in her mind.

She did not believe her father.

Could not.

He'd refused to go into any details. Had swept her incredulous questions aside. His face had become a rigid mask and only the anguish in his eyes had prevented her from telling him she didn't believe him to his face.

It was terrifyingly obvious that he, at least, believed every word.

"You heard no whisper of this from the other slaves when you were a child?" She gripped Elpis' hand and pulled her onto the stone seat. "How could such a thing be kept so secret?"

"I heard nothing, domina. But who would confide in me, a Greek slave girl?"

There was no recrimination in Elpis' voice. She simply spoke the truth. Why would slaves and servants who had served her father for years confide in a foreign newcomer? Besides, by the time Elpis had joined the household Antonia's mother had been dead for eight years.

The silence wrapped around her, suffocating. She took a deep breath, but it didn't help calm her racing thoughts. She chanced a sideways glance at Elpis, but the other woman remained serene, as she always did.

I should free Elpis. Again the thought twisted through her mind. Antonia had been born free, but her marriage to Scipio had been little more than slavery embellished with luxury and the blessing of Rome. She had been given her freedom. Did Elpis, who had also suffered at the brutal hands of Scipio, deserve less for her loyalty?

A part of her heart would break if Elpis decided to leave her. They weren't related by blood, yet she was the nearest thing to a sister Antonia had ever known.

Indecision gnawed through her gut, yet she knew she had no choice. Tomorrow. She would arrange for Elpis' manumission tomorrow. Despicable relief licked through her at the unavoidable delay.

Another slave came into the courtyard. "Apologies for interrupting, domina. A message arrived for you from Lady Carys. She deeply regrets she has to postpone your visit this afternoon."

Disappointment seared through her. She'd been looking forward to seeing Gawain again.

But why couldn't Gawain see her later? Had something happened to him? No. Surely Carys would have found a way to let her know. There were a thousand reasons why Gawain couldn't see her, and none of them had anything to do with him wishing to finish their liaison.

Her afternoon was now free. She glanced at Elpis and knew she could no longer put off the inevitable. Elpis, who had remained by her side for seventeen years without complaint, deserved the chance to choose her own future, not have it dictated for her.

CHAPTER TWENTY-THREE

*T*he following morning Antonia answered her father's summons to the atrium without Elpis by her side. After the formalities of her manumission had been completed, Antonia had arranged for Elpis to be given her own quarters in the townhouse. She had offered her clothes appropriate to her freed station, jewelry—even her own personal slave girl if she wished.

Elpis had remained oddly subdued by her enhanced status, as though everything Antonia offered her to persuade her to stay did not quite touch her.

What else could she do to ensure Elpis didn't decide to leave? She'd imagined—hoped—the other woman would continue to accompany her as she always had. But Elpis hadn't offered, and she hadn't liked to ask. Not when she had just granted Elpis her freedom.

With a heavy sigh, she entered the atrium. Her father had appeared to be avoiding her since his shocking disclosure the previous day. Had he changed his mind, and now wanted to share more details of her mother's untimely death?

A thought stabbed through her mind. Had he called on the

mysterious wisdom of Druids in a last attempt to save her mother's life? And when the Druid in question had been unable to prevent the inevitable, instead of berating Juno, goddess of childbirth, her father had laid the blame at the Druid's feet.

Although the scenario was scarcely credible, it *was* possible. Surely more possible than the idea her mother had been murdered in cold blood.

But if her father now wished to confide, why had he summoned her here? This was where they greeted guests, not where they—

Her thoughts severed as the praetor turned to her. Did he want his answer already? He'd said he would give her a few days to consider his offer. Not that she had needed a few days. Her decision had been made before she even left his office.

"Antonia." Her father walked over to her and took her arm. "The praetor has requested permission to speak with you alone. Is this something you also wish?"

From the corner of her eye, she saw the praetor shoot her father a shocked glance. Clearly, he hadn't expected her father to ask her opinion on such a matter. But there was a thread of granite in her father's voice that had never been apparent in his dealing with the praetor before, and Antonia knew why.

It was because her father knew the praetor was acquainted with Scipio. And for that, the praetor no longer existed on a pristine patrician pedestal in her father's mind.

Rome had lost her glow.

It was better to get this over with sooner rather than later, and it wasn't fair to keep the praetor waiting in hope for something she had no intention of doing. "Yes."

He stared into her eyes for a moment longer than necessary, then nodded and left the atrium. But instead of disappearing, he sat on a bench that gave him visual access. It was obvious he no longer trusted the praetor at all.

She turned back to the praetor and the two slaves who

remained in the atrium retreated to the far wall to allow them some degree of privacy. He came to her, kissed her hand, and visibly stiffened when she firmly withdrew her hand from his prolonged clasp.

"My lady. I trust you have given my proposal some thought."

She couldn't put it off any longer. "I have, Praetor."

His jaw tightened at the use of his title, but he said nothing. She swallowed and wished Elpis' comforting presence was by her side. "I thank you for the great honor you offer me, but I must refuse. I have my daughter's well-being to consider and will never remarry."

But how I would love to call Gawain my husband. A foolish dream, fit only for young, naïve girls. But still she wished it, with all her heart.

"Your daughter's well-being is of paramount importance to me, also." His words were stiff but the very fact he'd uttered them and not either arrowed a withering remark her way or gathered his pride and left, astounded her.

She struggled to find her voice. Clawed desperately through her mind for a suitable response. It was unheard of that a man of his status should attempt to persuade her, a plebeian in the eyes of Rome, to accept his hand in marriage.

They could dance with words for hours. The thought sent a shudder of horror along her spine.

"Seneca." Her voice was hushed. For all his faults, he had never been anything but thoughtful with her. "I'm sorry. I endured one loveless marriage. I could not bear to embark on another."

The silence screamed in her ears as his unblinking gaze bored into her. She resisted the urge to squirm, to look away, to call her father to her side. Why didn't the praetor accept her word and take his leave? Why did he insist on prolonging this excruciating encounter?

"In time, my lady, I believe you could grow to love me."

Her knees shook and she gripped her fingers together as his words echoed and overlapped in her mind. Was he saying what she thought he was?

Juno, no. The praetor could not love her. She didn't want his love. She must have misunderstood.

"There's no room in my heart to love another but my daughter." Even as she said the words, Gawain's face swam into her mind, and she felt blood heat her cheeks in damning denial.

The praetor's lips thinned, and a chill trickled along her arms. Instinctively she stepped back, and instantly his features returned to their normal mask of civility.

But nothing could erase that fleeting moment and a terrible suspicion surfaced. Did the praetor know of her affair with Gawain?

Nausea churned her stomach. She hoped she was mistaken. The praetor was a powerful man. He could have Gawain killed in an instant if he so desired.

"I'm a patient man, Antonia." He sounded perfectly reasonable, but the unease persisted. "I've waited more than ten years for you. I can wait a few more for your love. But when I leave Britannia, you'll be by my side as my wife."

She let out a ragged breath. "I have no intention of leaving Britannia or becoming your wife."

If he continued, she would have no recourse but to call for her father. The praetor clearly didn't believe she meant every word. But a refusal from her father—that would carry all the weight needed.

Again silence stretched between them. He didn't move and yet his presence loomed over her. Finally, he spoke. "I understand your reluctance in this matter. But you have the rest of your life ahead of you. You cannot fill your entire future with dangerous... infatuations."

A skeletal claw closed around her heart and an eerie echo filled her mind. He couldn't know for certain. He was merely playing with words. She fought the overwhelming urge to collapse on the nearest couch.

"Infatuations?" Her voice sounded oddly high-pitched. She sounded utterly guilty.

His mouth smiled but his eyes did not. "The savage lure of a barbarian can be seductive. I don't blame you in this matter, Antonia. But you must know it can go no further. The risk is too great."

He knows. The words pounded against her skull, amplifying every panicked beat of her heart. She didn't much care if he threatened to drag her reputation through the mud, but she knew that was not his intention.

For Gawain's sake, she had to persuade the praetor his suspicions were unfounded. "You speak in riddles, Praetor."

His jaw tensed. "It would be unfortunate if my investigations uncovered certain... criminal activities associated with a Cambrian of our mutual acquaintance."

The thinly disguised threat wrapped around her like a poisonous fog, sucking the strength from her limbs and filling her mind with a hammering terror. Somehow she forced words around her paralyzed tongue. "Criminal activities?"

He could mean only one thing. And they both knew what it was without the need to say the word aloud.

Druid.

"The last thing I wish is to cause you unnecessary distress." He reached out and took her unwilling hand between his. "As my wife, any acquaintance whose company you may have enjoyed in the past will naturally be above all such suspicion."

The fog coalesced into a hard, unforgiving knot in the center of her breast. "And if I refuse?"

He brushed his lips across her knuckles, but his eyes never left hers. "There will be another crucifixion within the week."

Gawain stirred on his pallet and winced at the pounding in his head. His entire body throbbed but that wasn't the reason he was lying down in the late afternoon. It was because that interfering healer had given him something that had knocked him out.

That morning he'd intended to visit a nearby village whose inhabitants had been ousted from their land when the Romans had taken Camulodunon. Unlike the Iceni, they hadn't received bounty from the invaders, and he'd wanted to gauge the extent of their discontent. If the praetor believed their previous day's encounter had cowed Gawain into submission and flight, he was deluded by his own sense of grandeur. The clumsy threats had merely fueled Gawain's obsession to stir any embers of rebellion he could uncover.

He'd accepted the cup of herbal tea from the healer, assuming it would ease his aches. Instead, it had stolen his senses.

He was under no delusion that the sleeping draught had been given to him to help him sleep off his attack. It had been a deliberate measure to prevent him from seeking retribution. He was going to throttle the bastard healer the next time they crossed paths.

No one dictated his movements in such an underhanded manner. There was still time to get to the village and request audience with the Elders before it grew dark. With a grunt, he forced himself upright and leaned against the wall, his legs outstretched along the pallet.

He needed to get word to Antonia. Had intended to earlier this day, before he'd been outmaneuvered. There was no physical reason why he couldn't see her today. Yet he knew he'd wait another two or three. Because he didn't want her to witness the aftermath of his encounter with the praetor's hired men.

She wasn't used to the brutalities of the street. She'd be horrified by his battered state. But even as the excuses thudded through his mind, a mocking grin twisted his lips.

He'd never imagined avoiding a woman because of personal

vanity. But no matter how he tried to convince himself it was because he wanted to protect Antonia from seeing a seedier side of his life, he knew it was more than that.

Of course she could cope with seeing a few bruises and cuts. She had coped with far more in her past. She'd see far worse in the future they would share. The truth was he didn't want her to see how the praetor had bettered him. It stung his pride.

His attempt to communicate with Lugus last night had also gone badly. The god had remained elusive, disdaining Gawain's sacrificial rituals and naked worship. Perhaps the sight of Gawain's battered body had offended the god. Or perhaps Lugus deemed the attack had not been sufficiently severe to compensate for Gawain's lack of faith recently.

Maybe he'd simply been unable to hide his anger that the gods had chosen to use Antonia in the way they had. Yet why would they go to all that trouble only to ignore Gawain when he answered their summons?

What in the name of Annwyn does Lugus want from me?

A knock at the door jerked his attention back to the present. He darkened his features into a scowl, waiting for Carys to enter. She would've known of the healer's intention. The order to prevent Gawain from leaving the villa earlier today had likely come from her in the first place.

"Enter," he growled when it became apparent she had no intention of opening the door until he invited her to do so. How unlike her normal disregard for his privacy. The door slowly opened, and his heart jackknifed against his ribs at the familiar silhouette.

Antonia.

She stood at the threshold. In the distance behind her was the newly constructed villa that encompassed her Roman world. And if she took a single step forward it would bring her into his.

Time slowed and his breath tangled in his chest. She was a vision in her pale blue gown with her blonde ringlets framing her face and dusting the elegant curve of her shoulders. Beyond the door, sunlight cast a golden glow and dark shadows across the wild grasses and ancient trees, somehow enhancing the absolute stillness of the woman caught between two opposing cultures.

He couldn't drag his mesmerized gaze from her. And yet with every thud of his heart the sordid baseness of this wattle and daub roundhouse—*his hut*—dug deeper into his heart.

No matter how noble his heritage or that the blood of the gods ran through his veins. He could never offer her the kind of lifestyle she was accustomed to. Even with slaves or servants to undertake the menial tasks of living, they would never possess the type of wealth patricians took for granted.

For a moment, his conviction wavered. But only for a moment. Antonia was his light in a world of dark and he wouldn't leave her behind.

"Gawain." There was a catch in her voice and then she stepped into his world and closed the door on her own. *She's made her choice.* Even if she didn't know it. The tension in his shoulders eased and he released a breath he didn't even realize he'd held. "Oh gods, Gawain. What happened to you?"

He hadn't wanted her to see him like this. The pain in her voice speared through him. Yet her concern enveloped his chest with fierce warmth that flooded his veins and vanquished any lingering doubt.

She'd never entered this dwelling before. He had never even pointed it out to her. Somehow that was significant. That she had not only taken a chance on his being here by journeying to the villa without prior arrangement, but had then wanted to see where he slept.

He rolled onto his knees before standing. The ache in his bones diminished as he rolled his shoulders and flexed his biceps. "A minor skirmish. The back streets of Camulodunon seethe with such bloodlust."

She made no move to him, simply stood on the rammed earth

floor, looking as out of place in the dingy surroundings as a displaced moon goddess. The only light came from the smoke hole in the roof and from where parts of the thatch had disintegrated over time and yet Antonia seemed to radiate an ethereal glow of her own.

His head must have been hit harder than he realized to imagine such fanciful notions. But the possibility didn't stop him from enjoying the way her gown draped over her shoulders and clung to her curves. He ached to reach out and cradle her breasts, rub his thumbs over her responsive nipples and once again hear her breathy gasps as desire consumed her.

He shifted, trying to ease the pleasurable discomfort that throbbed between his thighs. He would have her. But he wouldn't grab her like a starving man with no thought but to slake his hunger.

"You should be resting." She came to him, one hand outstretched as though she intended to push him back down onto the pallet. The thought made him grin.

"I've rested enough."

She didn't return his smile. "You're in pain." She sounded distraught although the only outward sign of her evident distress was her raised hand and the oddly intense expression in her eyes.

He threaded his fingers through hers and tugged her closer. Surprisingly, he detected a slight resistance but that made no sense. Why would she be here if she didn't want to be in his arms?

"I'm in pain because it's been too long since I felt the silk of your skin beneath my body." Just saying the words aloud caused his muscles to tense in anticipation. Her tempting scent of woodland flowers drifted in the air, innocence and seduction combined in an irresistible bouquet. "You torture me with your icy Roman reserve when I know it's nothing but a façade. When I know I'm the only man you allow to stir your hidden passions."

Her eyes glittered and for a brief, uneasy moment, he thought she was going to cry. But then she reached out with her free hand and gently trailed her fingers along his jaw.

"Your face." She choked on the words and curled her fingers into a fist. He covered her hand with his, pressing her knuckles against the damaged skin that so distressed her.

"I have no injuries that won't heal, Antonia."

"You could have been killed." Her voice was low but vibrated with fear and a dark suspicion gnawed through his gut. Did she know who was behind the attack? Or did she merely suspect?

His male pride didn't want her to know. The fight might not have been a fair one between him and the Roman but nevertheless, he was the one who had been bloodied, not the praetor. "It would take more than two desperate drunks to kill me."

"Please. Promise me you'll take more care, Gawain." Her ice-blue eyes beseeched him in a way they never had before, and his dark humor drained away. In its place, a raw protectiveness blazed through him. For her he would curb his recently acquired inclination to seek out danger at every opportunity.

The irony wasn't lost on him. Before the Romans had invaded Cymru the only dangers he'd faced were those any warrior would. And now, because of another Roman, he would temper his thirst for vengeance. It was not the right time, and the people of Camulodunon were not in the right frame of mind. He wouldn't risk his life, wouldn't risk losing Antonia, in attempting to stir apathetic Britons to revolt.

An odd sense of peace weaved through his chest, as though a great weight had lifted from his heart. Antonia did this to him. Centered him. Gave him the clarity of mind that was so essential for a warrior. A clarity that, since he'd left his homeland, he'd found so hard to recapture.

He smiled down at her, his unlikely Roman savior. "I promise."

CHAPTER TWENTY-FOUR

*A*ntonia knew she should pull away from Gawain's touch. She hadn't meant for them to touch. Yet all along, she'd known it was inevitable that they would.

How could she not touch him when every inch of her skin, every breath she took, and every despairing beat of her heart called for him? When her body craved to feel his strong arms around her, when she wanted nothing more than to bury her face against his shoulder and pretend the world outside this primitive dwelling didn't exist?

Yet she remained where she was. Trapped by the hunger in his eyes, the raw need that pulsed between them and the feel of his scarred fingers interlocking with hers. But even as desire coiled between her thighs, crimson terror raked through her breast.

There was no doubt in her mind who was behind Gawain's attack. It was a warning. For them both. If she hadn't already made the decision not to tell Gawain of the praetor's threat, seeing Gawain's injuries would have been enough to keep her mouth shut forever.

He would bow to no Roman. He would confront the praetor. And Gawain would die.

A shudder racked her, and her fist shifted along his jaw. His stubble grazed her knuckles and her skin tingled at the abrasive contact. The fierce desire to rub his jaw across her face, over her breasts and belly and between her thighs pounded through her. She wanted him to brand her with his rough day-old beard, to mar her flesh the way she had inadvertently marred him.

She wanted to stay with him forever. He and Cassia were all she wanted. It was a fantasy, had always been a dream, but lately she'd harbored the secret hope their liaison might continue indefinitely, regardless of outside forces.

The torn flesh on his aristocratic cheekbone and the myriad bruising across his face and naked chest caused every fragile dream to crumble. And she acknowledged the harsh truth.

She had come here today to end their affair. But buried deep in her heart, where she hardly dared to venture, the tiniest of hope had continued to flicker. The hope they could somehow evade the praetor's power that encompassed her world like a vindictive spider's web.

But the time for foolish delusions was over. And a delusion was all this affair had ever been. She was of Rome through the blood of her mother, and Rome did not relinquish her captives so easily.

Slowly she pulled free of Gawain's possessive grip. He didn't attempt to stop her and instead of severing contact as quickly as possible she lingered, savoring the way their fingers caressed. Until this moment, she had never realized how sensitive her fingertips were, how her flesh tingled at the languorous touch.

She focused on their hands as she sculpted each of his fingers and then laid her palm flat against his. His size dwarfed her. He could crush her in the blink of an eye and yet for all his size, for all that she knew, in her heart, he was a Druid, she trusted him with her life.

"I won't break, Antonia." There was a thread of amusement in his voice as he dragged her fist to his lips. "Like you, I'm stronger than I appear."

She managed to smile as he nibbled kisses across her clenched knuckles. His intense gaze never left her face. "If that were true, you would belong on Olympus and not here among us mere mortals."

His eyes crinkled. He clearly wasn't offended that she compared him to her gods and not his own. "You flatter me outrageously, my lady. What are you after? A few mind-shattering orgasms? I assure you that I intend to give you them regardless of your pretty words."

She didn't want to think of the orgasms she'd shared with Gawain. Yet they sparkled in her mind like the stars at night, causing quivers of primal need to grip her whenever she recalled them.

How had she ever imagined that she would be able to let him go with barely a shrug at the end of their liaison? How had she imagined that only the memory of their times together would be enough to sustain her throughout the rest of her life?

How could she tell him that it was over, and walk away without taking one more glorious, heartbreaking memory with her?

She circled her forefinger over his palm, spiraling downward to his wrist. She manacled him with her hand, but her hand was too small to enchain him. Instead, she brushed the pad of her thumb across his pulse, secretly enthralled by the unexpected silkiness of his skin there.

A glimpse of masculine vulnerability. And instantly her pleasure died. She didn't want Gawain to be vulnerable in any way. And the only way to ensure he remained the invincible warrior she cherished in her mind was if she left him.

"Antonia." His voice had lost its bantering tone. He cradled her face and gazed into her eyes as though she was the only woman in the world. Her heart would shatter irrevocably if she didn't leave right now. But why was she trying to blind herself to the truth? Her heart had already shattered.

He sighed and his thumbs caressed her cheeks in a gesture so tender she wanted to weep. "Don't be afraid. I've given you my word. I won't seek retribution."

He could read her mind, her fears, too easily. They both knew who was behind this attack. And neither would say the name aloud. As though, by acknowledging it, it would force them to face the harsh truth that the praetor had won.

She couldn't let Gawain believe that. Because, no matter what he had promised her, if he believed she went to the praetor against her will, his pride would demand justice.

He would die. His blood would be on her hands. She gripped his wrists, intending to pull free of his embrace, but it was impossible.

This was their last time together. Tonight her betrothal to Seneca would be made public. She would never again enjoy the freedom she had experienced since arriving in Britannia.

She was under no delusion. She would never see Gawain again, either.

"I know." She refused to allow her voice to crack and somehow managed to give him a smile. He would never guess that she could read his mind in this matter as easily as he could read hers. "You're the most honorable man I've ever met, Gawain."

The words came straight from her heart. She prayed he would always remember them, when he remembered her.

For a moment his eyes clouded, as though her words had inadvertently wounded him. He didn't say anything for several heartbeats, and she thought the moment had passed. Then his fingers tensed against her face.

"My honor is tainted, Antonia." The words were low, as though he spoke against his better judgment. "A warrior is judged by his victories." Bitterness tinged his voice, but he didn't look at her with condemnation.

And then she knew. He wasn't referring to the invasion of his homeland. He spoke of the capture of Caratacus in the land of the Brigantes.

Her heart squeezed with empathic pain. He was a Druid and had been charged with protecting the Briton king. He'd escaped the fate of his fellow warriors only because his gods had fore-warned him.

Without honor, a warrior was nothing. Roman, Celt or Druid. Was there really that much difference between them?

"A warrior is judged by his actions." She slid her hands from his wrists, over his forearms and gripped his powerful biceps. "He cannot be held responsible for the betrayal of those he thought his allies."

"Yet still, I was the only one who escaped." There was no mistaking the self-contempt in his voice and his hands dropped to her shoulders. "The one who witnessed the defeat of Britain's last hope."

It was true. After Caracatus' capture, Britain had accepted the might of the Eagle. Cambria still rebelled, and a treacherous corner of her heart rejoiced in the knowledge that Gawain's homeland continued to cling onto their tenuous freedom.

But she couldn't bear to see the recrimination in Gawain's eyes. Perhaps her words would mean nothing to him. But perhaps they would help ease the guilt that she could now see fueled his every action.

"Caratacus gave a mighty speech in Rome, Gawain. The emperor was so impressed, he pardoned Caratacus and his queen and family. They weren't executed or enslaved. They are...admired."

She saw the question in his eyes even as relief skated across his features. And then she remembered. He'd never mentioned who had been betrayed. He was clearly surprised she'd managed to put the pieces together.

"I'm not entirely ignorant of politics." She had been educated in politics since she was a child, and it was just as well. Patrician women might give the impression of being empty-headed vessels in thrall to their husbands. But a noblewoman who had no concept of the politics of Rome was rare indeed.

It all came down to survival.

"You're not ignorant at all, Antonia." There was an oddly wary note in his voice. "It never occurred to me Caratacus would be freed. I assumed he'd been executed with great triumphal ceremony."

As the Druids who had accompanied Caratacus to the land of the Brigantes had been executed. And she realized Gawain wasn't shocked that she had known he'd been charged to protect Caratacus. It was because he feared she might jump to the conclusion that Gawain was also a Druid.

Did he think she would turn her back on him? Did he imagine she would betray him, as was her duty as a Roman?

It hurt to know he didn't trust her enough to share such an important aspect of his life with her. But at the same time, she understood his reasons. No matter what they had shared over the last two weeks, she was still a Roman. And only the day before she'd displayed her prejudiced ignorance before him by repeating what her father and others had told her. Why should he confide in her, when he believed she thought Druids murdered babies and drank their blood?

"The emperor appreciates a stirring speech." She wouldn't let her wounded heart taint her memories of the time she had spent with Gawain. Just because she'd told him her secrets didn't mean he had to tell her his. "Perhaps if people talked more to each other there would be less bloodshed."

He laughed, and while she loved the sound of his laughter and the fact she amused him even at a time like this, a part of her balked. Her words had not been said in jest. Why could a warrior see no option but to fight?

What other life was there for a warrior?

"You should be a politician." He tugged on one of her ringlets. "But since Rome doesn't acknowledge women in their precious Senate perhaps you should consider using your powers of persuasion in a Celtic court."

She stared at him. Was he mocking her? Or was he serious? Sometimes it was hard to tell when Gawain made a passing comment about women, because his views were so different from those of Roman men. She mirrored his actions and twined a length of his hair around her finger. How she would miss playing with his hair. But not as much as she would miss their strange, exhilarating conversations.

"I'm sure your Celtic chieftains would be only too eager to take advice from a woman with the blood of Rome in her veins."

"You might be surprised." He smiled down at her, a smile filled with warmth and laughter and something else. Something so infinitely tender it made her heart ache and chest constrict.

No man had ever looked at her in such a way. But she had dreamed of this since she was a young girl. And now, when she had found what she had always yearned for, it was with the knowledge that she could never claim his love.

When this day was over, it wouldn't simply be Gawain's pride she injured. Had she really thought it would be? His warrior pride was one thing. But now she knew, in her heart, that he loved her, it was more important than ever that he never discovered the depth of her own love.

Let him believe she'd merely used him as a diverting dalliance. At least then he would let her go without swearing vengeance upon the praetor.

She leaned forward and pressed her lips against his chest, so he could no longer look into her eyes and guess the truth.

"I would be astonished." Her voice was husky, and she

wrapped her arms around him, a gentle hug, mindful of his bruised body. His skin was warm, his muscles taut. His evocative scent of wild forests invaded her senses and desire pooled between her thighs. *Juno, how can I bear to walk away from him?*

"I look forward to astonishing you on a regular basis, my lady." Amusement vibrated through every word, as he continued to toy with her hair as if her ringlets bewitched him.

She closed her eyes, but the impossible vision of sharing a life together shimmered in the darkness. He was a Druid. A leader. A fearless warrior. Among his own people, she knew his word would carry great weight. Was he also a chieftain? Had he once presided over a Celtic court of his own?

There were so many things she wanted to ask him. The questions remained locked in her heart. Already she knew too much about him. If she learned any more, she feared she might never recover from losing him.

And she had to get over him. For the sake of her beloved Cassia.

CHAPTER TWENTY-FIVE

*A*ntonia pressed her cheek against Gawain's chest and trailed the tips of her fingers along his back. His heart thudded against her face, strong and reassuring. His hand cradled the back of her head, an endearingly possessive gesture and involuntarily her fingers dug into his hips.

He groaned and she instantly pulled back, guilt eating through her.

"I'm sorry." Her fingers fluttered over his naked hips, where his braccae had slipped revealing not simply his irresistible body but also more livid bruising. "I didn't mean to hurt you."

"Antonia." His exotic accent caressed each syllable of her name, and she forgot about not looking him in the eyes again. "You didn't hurt me. It's impossible for you to hurt me." He paused, and his beautiful mouth curved into a teasing smile. "Unless you stop touching me."

She flattened her palms over his bronzed chest, and tried to ignore the evidence of his recent attack. In the years to come, she wanted to remember him as he truly was, not recall the superficial injuries the praetor had inflicted as a demonstration of his power.

"I cannot stay long." She'd brought another slave woman with her, as Elpis once again hadn't offered to accompany her. And while the slave was loyal, Antonia hadn't confided the real reason she had journeyed to the tribune's villa.

For a brief goodbye to the man who held her heart. How foolish to imagine anything with Gawain could be brief. But while she longed to stay in his arms for the rest of the day and night, her time was short.

If the praetor found out about this illicit visit, he would never believe it had been an innocent meeting between her and Carys. A shiver crawled along her spine. Had he set spies on her here in Britannia, the way he had in Rome?

"One day, you will never leave my side." Gawain cupped her bottom, his strong hands warm and firm and quivers of need claimed her. *I can't leave without loving him one more time.*

"One day, perhaps." Every day in her dreams. She forced a smile to her lips so he couldn't guess her thoughts. "But alas, that day is not today."

"No." His eyes darkened. "Not today." He made it sound as though the fact she would one day remain by his side was a foregone conclusion. Or was she so blinded by her own love and need for him that she was seeing more in his every word and gesture?

In the end, it didn't matter, except to her heart. The outcome would be the same, however he felt about her.

She slid her hands beneath his braccae, her fingers clinging to the taut curve of his backside. Still clasping her bottom, he tugged her against him, and his erection dug into her belly. The proof of his arousal sent swirls of need pulsing between her thighs, a desperate need that after today would never again be satisfied.

She sank against him and felt his cock thicken farther. His grip on her became predatory, unyielding, and her body throbbed for his possession. She rose onto her toes, deliberately sliding her body against his rigid shaft, and his groan of frustration echoed through the room.

"I'm going to make love to you." Her promise whispered against his lips, and he grinned in clear appreciation. Their affair had begun through pure desire and the need to experience something other than her former husband's selfish touch. It was only sex, the joining of a man and woman for mutual satisfaction. How little she had truly known. Had she really imagined she could walk away at the end of this liaison with nothing but enhanced sexual knowledge to show for it?

When she left Gawain today, he would despise her. But in time, when he recalled their last encounter, she wanted him to remember it with fire in his blood and passion in his heart. Even if the fire was nothing more than lust and the passion stoked with fury, she wanted, more than anything, for him to never forget her.

No matter how selfish that desire was.

"You read my mind." His hands molded her waist, his heat scorching through her gown and branding her flesh. How easy it would be to let him make love to her, to savor every touch and cherish every demanding kiss.

She still intended to savor and cherish but for once, he would not be in control.

"No." She tugged his braccae over his thighs, her breasts crushed against his broad chest. "You're going to be under my command, Gawain. All you have to do is suffer my touch."

He laughed, and with a swift movement ripped his braccae down his legs and tossed them across the floor. She smiled and shook her head in mock displeasure at his instant response to take over.

"Then make me suffer, my lady. My body is in your hands." Amusement threaded through every word and to underscore his surrender he took a step back from her.

Her gaze traveled over his beloved face. Beneath the torn and bruised flesh, his proud, aristocratic bearing was plainly visible. His dark blond hair hung loose to his shoulders, and the enchanting amber flecks in his irises were all but obliterated as desire darkened his eyes.

His muscled shoulders were worthy of the greatest warrior, but she knew only too well how comforting it could be to lay her head against them. His chiseled chest, scored with old scars and discolored by his recent abuse, would strike fear into any enemy. Yet how tenderly he had often held her against him, when the thud of his heart soothed her wounded soul.

"And what a beautiful body you have." Hunger gnawed the pit of her stomach as she devoured the hard planes of his abdomen. A hunger she knew would torment her for the rest of her life.

"My body isn't beautiful." He sounded on the verge of laughing again, but didn't attempt to pull her into his arms. "Now your body, that is a different matter. And you're not playing fair. Why are you still dressed when I'm naked for your blatant delight?"

For a moment, she caught his gaze. His eyes were warm, not only with lust. He had taught her that sex could be fun and even if she hadn't been foolish enough to fall in love with him, for that reason alone he would always hold a special place in her heart.

"Who said I intended to play fair?" And because she knew how much he enjoyed touching her hair, she slid one finger into a ringlet that fell over her shoulder. He watched, mesmerized, as she gently tugged on her curl with her thumb while her finger rotated inside the silken threads.

"I see you plan to torture me before I'm subjected to your touch."

"Such a cruel thought had never crossed my mind." She pulled her ringlet to the limit of its endurance before letting it spring back into place. Gawain's gaze remained riveted on her hair, and she took the opportunity to admire the perfect musculature of his flat stomach.

And his thick, glorious cock that jutted proudly upward across his belly. She wanted to press herself against him, rub her tender lips along his swollen rod and gain a measure of instant satisfaction.

But if she did that, he would wrap her in his arms. Sweep her onto his bed and worship her body in the way only Gawain knew how. And she would let him, and forever curse her lack of resolve.

Instead, she stepped closer and slowly speared her fingers through his hair, tugging at his temples, letting the soft strands caress her palms. Once again she rolled onto her toes, and this time brushed her lips over his.

He cupped her hips but didn't tug her forward. He seemed content, at the moment, to endure whatever form of torture she devised.

She nibbled his bottom lip and felt him smile, but he didn't open his mouth for her. Her fingers tightened in his hair, holding him still, although he'd shown no indication of moving.

She slid the tip of her tongue along the seam of his mouth, sculpting his shape, probing for entry. Finally he opened for her and a breathy sigh escaped as she delved inside.

Their tongues touched. His fingers trailed up from her hips, molding the dip of her waist. Knife sharp prickles of sensation shivered over her skin, even though she wasn't even naked. Her nipples pebbled and she struggled against the primal urge to flatten herself against his hard body for momentary relief.

His tongue invaded her willing mouth, intent on possession. She wound his hair around her fingers, loving his length, the silken strands, the way he growled in her mouth as she tugged on him.

She loved the feel of him inside her, the tip of his tongue exploring. Gently she sucked on him, and a feral need awakened deep within her aching cleft.

I want more.

Panting, she pulled back and stared into his dark eyes. His breathing was ragged, and his hands curled around her rib cage, his thumbs grazing the undersides of her breasts. She dragged her fingers through his hair and cradled his face, the roughness of his unshaved jaw prickling her palms.

She stretched up and brushed a butterfly kiss across his torn flesh. With tender dedication, she kissed his bruised and battered skin, as though by doing so she could somehow help him heal.

"Do you intend to kiss every injury with such devotion?" His voice was husky as he angled his head so she could gain easier access to his throat.

"Yes." She breathed the word against his pulse, inhaling his evocative scent and this time detecting the underlying hint of astringent that had been used to clean his wounds. She screwed her eyes shut for a moment, forced the shadowy fears away. Gawain was safe. He would remain safe. She had the praetor's word.

"Do you wish me to show you my most severe injuries?" His cock jerked against her belly as he spoke, and she gave a soft laugh at his unvoiced hope.

"No. I can manage by myself, thank you." She chanced another look into his eyes and the potent combination of amusement and desire made her heart ache. She stirred restlessly then stilled as Gawain rubbed his thumbs over her throbbing nipples. "Do you wish me to stop?"

He groaned in mock defeat and abandoned her nipples to cradle her bottom. She wasn't sure that helped. His hands on her body were a delightful distraction no matter where he put them.

"I'm at your mercy, my lady. Do with me what you will."

CHAPTER TWENTY-SIX

*A*ntonia slid her hands to his throat and then sculpted the rock-hard contours of his shoulders. Gently she pressed her lips against his bruised chest and Gawain shifted beneath her touch.

"Am I—?" She didn't have the chance to finish her question as his fingers dug into her bottom and jerked her roughly against his erection.

"No." His voice was as rough as his actions. "You're not hurting me. But I wish to the gods that you would."

"Oh." She offered him a wicked smile and before he could react to that she dipped her head and sucked his nipple. Hard.

"Enchantress." It sounded like a curse.

He tasted of the forest, wild, fresh, with intriguing salty undertones. She tantalized him with her teeth and scraped her nails along his rigid biceps. She knew he wanted her to bite harder, to gouge his flesh. And although she also knew that no matter what she did it was unlikely she could ever hurt him, she simply couldn't do it.

And so her fingernails teased him and her teeth tormented him with a restrained passion. The constraints she imposed fueled her own desire and she pressed her thighs together and squirmed helplessly.

"Remove this gown." Gawain's voice was hoarse as he began to tug her gown up around her hips. She wriggled and slapped his hand, then gripped his wrist in warning.

"Stop distracting me."

"I want to distract you. You're concentrating far too hard. I won't bleed." He paused for a fleeting moment as she attempted to sling him a sizzling look of displeasure. And failed. "Even if I do bleed, I assure you I'll greatly enjoy it."

He had already bled because of her. His face would be scarred because of her. She knew, in her head, this was completely different and yet her heart flinched at inflicting more pain on him. Even if this pain would give him nothing but pleasure.

"It's not your place to instruct your torturer on how to proceed."

"I'm having second thoughts about being your willing victim."

"Trust me." She traced the sensual outline of his lips with her finger and managed to avoid his attempt to suck her inside his mouth. "I'll make it worth your while."

He dropped her gown with a flourish. "Just remember, everything you inflict upon me I intend to repay with interest."

Her throat closed and she couldn't answer. What could she say? Blatantly lie to him that she looked forward to his sexual retribution when she knew it was nothing but an impossible dream?

She avoided eye contact by once again lavishing attention on his injuries. She kissed and licked every graze, every discolored bloom of flesh, while her fingernails raked a featherlight touch across his biceps and forearms. His hair tickled her fingers and as she moved down his body, his dusting of chest hair caressed her cheek and lips.

The head of his cock, slick with desire, rammed against her chin and she froze. Gawain growled, a primal sound that vibrated the length of his hard body. But he didn't grip her head, didn't try to force her to do what he so very clearly wanted her to do.

She swallowed and felt his shaft move against her throat. Slowly she rose, and inched her way around Gawain until she faced his back. The indentation of a chain lash striped across his magnificent shoulders and her stomach clenched in shame.

My fault.

"Do you wish me to pose for your pleasure?" There was a strained note in his voice, although the glance he slung over his shoulder showed dark amusement. Without waiting for an answer, he flexed his biceps, showing the breathtaking contours of his perfect musculature across his shoulders and torso.

Instinctively she stepped back, so she could more easily admire the play of muscles across his lower back and tight arse. Her mouth dried and fingers clutched her gown at the hypnotic show. He moved as if intent on capturing her interest, the way a pleasure slave might.

The thought slapped across her mind, a frigid, unwelcome thought. She gripped his arms, momentarily pressing her body against his back to still his provocative display.

"Enough." Her voice was husky with need. She wanted him to hold her, to tell her everything was going to be all right. If she showed the slightest vulnerability, he would do just that. And she would despise herself for always, even more than she did right now. "You distract me to the edge of my reason."

"And I, Antonia, am barely clinging to the edge of my reason."

Despite her fatalistic thoughts, she smiled. He could always make her smile. She pressed a kiss over his shoulder blade, and he flexed it one more time in arrogant disregard of her command.

She worked her way down his back until she kneeled on the floor, eye level with his buttocks. She had only seen one other male backside before Gawain's, and there was no comparison.

Holding her erratic breath, she ran her finger along his spine and dipped into the crevice between his taut arse cheeks.

He jerked, obviously not expecting such a touch and widened his stance. "Better?" His voice was deliciously raw with frustrated need.

Her heart thundered in her breast and her breath escaped in a ragged gasp. Speech was beyond her. She traced the curve of his firm arse to the inside of his thigh and then repeated the maneuver on his other taut cheek.

His fists clenched against his thighs, the muscles on his forearms and biceps bulging with reined in tension. The knowledge that he was holding back so she could explore and learn his body caused a bittersweet pain to engulf her heart.

She slid her arms around his thighs and pressed her cheek against the firm swell of his backside. He curled his hands around her arms, just above her wrists. It was a light touch, one of tenderness. To convey he wanted to touch her, not command her. No matter how much he might wish to.

The tips of her fingers stroked his shaft. He was hot, hard and the sensation was enhanced because she couldn't see his impressive organ.

Her breath was uneven as she cupped his heavy sac. His light grip on her arms tightened and his arse tensed. Daringly, she nipped his succulent flesh and squeezed his vulnerable balls. His Celtic curse ricocheted around the room and his fingers bit into her arms.

"Be still," she panted, her gaze riveted on the mark of possession she'd inflicted on him. "I didn't draw blood."

His hoarse laugh sounded pained. "I can't promise to remain still. Your methods of torture slay me."

She smiled and couldn't resist giving his backside another leisurely nibble. His cock jerked in her hand and her grip around him tightened. His shaft was so thick her finger and thumb could not meet around him. The memories of all the times he'd filled her hammered through her mind and she quivered with need.

"I haven't finished yet." Her whisper was jagged and in response, he flexed his arse in a deliberately provocative manner. She slid her hand along his rigid length and then brushed her thumb over his wet slit. His moan of appreciation rumbled through his chest.

Slowly she pulled back and curled her hands over his hips. He didn't move a muscle, simply waited for her next move.

Nerves and anticipation fluttered in her stomach. She wanted to do this. *I can do this.* Because he was Gawain, and he expected nothing from her that she was not willing to give.

"Turn around." Her voice didn't sound like her own. She sounded like a sultry siren from ancient myths.

He turned, and she stared in silent worship at his glorious cock. She'd often looked at it, touched it, and the truth was that this part of his body fascinated her. But she had never put her mouth to him. He'd never asked her to, after that first humiliating time when she had made a fool of herself.

"You look like a goddess kneeling at my feet." There was a note of awe in his voice as if he could not quite believe his eyes. "A goddess shouldn't kneel before a mortal man."

His words tore through the web of nerves that threatened to overcome her. She looked up at him and caught the reverential expression on his face. One of them might well have the blood of the immortals in their veins, and it wasn't her.

"You make me feel like a goddess, Gawain." She deliberately allowed her breath to drift across his erection and he swallowed, clearly struggling to cling onto his control. "But more than that, you make me feel like a woman should."

"Antonia." His voice was deep, threaded with desire, and need coiled tighter in her breast. In her peripheral vision, she saw him clench his fists, clearly fighting the imperative to grip her head and force his cock into her mouth.

But Gawain would never do that. It was the reason why she wanted to give him this parting gift. Something he would, she prayed, remember with pleasure when his anger had finally cooled.

She took a deep breath. The indefinable scent of fresh male sweat combined with the heady odor of arousal caused damp heat to slick her tender folds. She wrapped one hand around his shaft and felt him throb against her palm.

"Sit back on the bed." Her voice was uneven, and she pushed ineffectively against the top of his thigh with her free hand. It was like trying to shift a mountain.

"No. If I move, I may break this spell."

"You won't." She couldn't tear her gaze away from the swollen head of his erection. She had the sudden, savage urge to discover his taste. "I promise you won't."

He plunged his fingers into her hair and held her head as he stepped back. She shuffled forward, uncaring of the dirt floor that was surely staining her gown. The bed was lower than she was used to, and when Gawain sat with a pained grunt, he stretched out his legs and trapped her between his granite-hard thighs.

Now she was level with his face. Her thumb caressed his sensitive glans, his arousal sliding across her skin like ambrosia from the gods.

Slowly she bent her head. His fingers were still buried in her hair. She licked her lips, her mouth dry with nerves. But the butterflies in her stomach and the erratic pound of her heart were nothing like the blind panic she'd always experienced before when in a similar position.

I've never been in a similar position.

Gawain's hands cradled her head, his grip firm. But there was no malice behind it. She knew she only had to lift her head and he would never try to stop her.

The knowledge spurred her courage. She held his shaft and

tentatively flicked the tip of her tongue along the underside of his erection. The faint taste of his arousal rippled across her tongue and raw pleasure surged through her core. Even the painful jab of his fingers against her skull, his instinctive response to her wet touch, didn't alarm.

"Your promise was true." His voice rasped with barely contained lust. "This spell continues."

Her breath escaped in a rush, leaving her lightheaded. She couldn't tear her gaze from his cock.

"This enchantment will never end." The words were whispered, not meant for his ears. Not meant to be uttered aloud at all. Yet the pressure of his fingers, the way he hitched in a sharp breath, told her he had heard.

She leaned in closer, one hand splayed against his hip for added balance. The glistening head of his cock enthralled her. This time she would do more than merely look, as she had before. This time...

The thought drifted through her mind, an unimportant distraction. She knew what she would do.

CHAPTER TWENTY-SEVEN

*a*ntonia shifted on her knees and wished she'd taken the time to strip off her gown. She wanted to be naked before Gawain. But it was too late now.

She tried to regulate her erratic breath, but it was impossible. Her fingers twitched around his organ as she carefully eased his thick length closer.

His groan shuddered along his body. "I swear on all the gods of my forefathers, Antonia. *I won't break.*"

She'd held him before. Had avidly studied this part of his body before, much to his amusement. But this time there was added tension in the heavy air. He knew, of course he must know, that today she intended to do so much more than merely look.

"I know." Had she spoken aloud or was her whisper only inside her mind? She didn't know. Didn't care. Her pulses raced and heart thundered. There was no moment in time but this. And this moment would last her for all time.

She opened her mouth. And fastened her lips around the head of his erection.

His strangled moan and the way his fingers tangled her hair heightened the desire that throbbed between her thighs. The tip of her tongue skimmed across his flesh. He was so hot. An elusive saltiness, the essence of Gawain, teased her senses and instinctively her hand tightened around him.

She liked his taste. The revelation flooded her mind, along with a faint sensation of shock. Again, she slid her tongue over the head of his cock, this time lingering. Savoring.

He tasted of wild, untamed man. He tasted of *her* man.

His thighs tensed, enslaving her more securely. But she had no desire to move. Her nails dug into his hip as she lowered her head a little more. He slid farther inside, filling her mouth, but no terrifying urge to gag overwhelmed her.

For a moment she stilled. His hard length compressed her tongue and burned the roof of her mouth. Only her fist around his shaft prevented her lips from sliding farther along his cock.

Her sheath clenched and liquid heat bloomed between her thighs. She wanted him there, stroking her clit, filling her aching cleft. But she couldn't move. Didn't, in truth, want to move. Because, despite the need thudding through her, another need hammered with insistent demand.

The need to take him, as he had so often taken her, using only her mouth.

Slowly she pulled up, her lips clinging to his rigid flesh. For a moment he resisted, his hands on her head rendering her immobile, but then the pressure eased. And only the feel of his fingers in her hair remained.

"This feels so good." His voice was hoarse. Feminine power surged from her core, flooding her body. She sucked him deep into her mouth, her cheeks hollowing with effort. His choked curse and savage grip on her hair sent thrills cascading through her.

Was it her imagination or did his hands shake?

"You're killing me." With obvious effort, she felt his fingers release their deadly grip. But she wanted him to grip her hair, hold her still. She wanted everything, now, that she had always feared before.

She growled in the back of her throat and slid her hand down his shaft to his root. With her other hand she cupped his heavy balls. And squeezed.

Gawain's big body jerked at her touch. His hands clamped against her head, holding her still. Her heart hammered high in her breast, her breath came shallow and ragged. His male scent cocooned her as she knelt before him, her face buried between his thighs.

He rocked into her mouth, the drag and push of his shaft over her tongue and teeth insanely arousing. Beyond the erratic thud of her heart, she could hear the harsh, uneven sound of his breathing. Could feel his balls harden with impending climax.

Could feel the possessive clamp of his hands around her head. Holding her immobile for his ruthless penetration. Immobilizing her for his oral pleasure.

A desperate moan razed her throat and shuddered around his thrusting cock. Slick heat tormented her sensitized cleft. She massaged his root, palmed his balls. How she would love to see his face when he finally spilled his seed.

With a guttural curse, he released her head. Shock spun through her. Even now he gave her the choice. She sucked hard, her fingers gripping his root with relentless, single-minded purpose. Blindly she sought his hand, her fingers reaching for him above her head.

He threaded his fingers through hers. She pulled him roughly back to her head, pressing him against her tangled hair. His cock jerked in her mouth, thrilling her. He knew what she wanted.

Once again, his hands cradled her, his fingers biting into her head. She dug her nails into his rigid thigh as he hammered into her mouth. Fast. Hard. The way she wanted it.

She felt his muscles lock beneath her. His entire body vibrated with leashed need. His roar of release thundered through the room, shattered through her mind. And then he came, violent spasms, his hot come filling her mouth.

She swallowed. And swallowed again. Goddess, it felt so good. Greedily she sucked on his pulsing cock, milking him, wanting everything he had.

"Antonia." His voice was uneven. He continued to thrust inside her, as if he never wanted this moment to end. "My sweet Antonia."

His endearment wrapped around her heart. She closed her eyes and savored his taste, the feel of him in her mouth, the scent of their lovemaking in the air. She wanted to hold him like this forever.

After countless heartbeats, the unyielding grip on her head relaxed and his hands slid to her shoulders. Then he gently pushed her from his still hard erection.

But she didn't want to let him go. Not yet.

He gave a ragged laugh at her reluctance and wrapped one arm around her shoulders. He cradled her face with his other hand, and his thumb tenderly caressed the corner of her mouth.

"You have developed new appetites, my lady." He sounded well pleased by the notion. Before she could respond, his mouth captured hers, his tongue sliding between her parted lips.

It was a tender kiss, yet a kiss that claimed and conquered and proved that, for all time, she was his.

Only when he pulled back did she realize she'd wound her arms around his neck and plunged her fingers through his hair. She was still on her knees, and she resisted when he tried to lift her to her feet.

"Antonia." He breathed her name against her ear and shivers of need cascaded along her sensitized flesh. Instead of trying to pull her to her feet again, he began to tug on her gown. She rocked from knee to knee, allowing him to painstakingly drag her gown along her legs until the material no longer hampered his access.

He slid his hand up the inside of her thigh, the tips of his fingers causing havoc to her senses. She squirmed helplessly. This wasn't what she had planned, but she couldn't resist his insistent touch.

When he cupped her sex, she ground against him, unable to stop herself. Not wanting to stop herself. Their gazes locked and she clung onto his hair and drowned in the lust and amusement and *love* she saw glinting in his dark eyes.

His thumb brushed her swollen clit, and she bucked her hips with mindless need. He pressed against the sensitive nub. Her juices flooded her channel, and she contracted around his probing fingers.

"My beautiful Roman noblewoman." Gawain's voice was husky, and she gripped his hair, her only lifeline. "Come for me, sweet Antonia."

"Gawain." She didn't recognize her voice. She sounded parched, desperate. Lust coiled between her thighs, fiery, untamed. Wild need thundered through her blood and tightened her nipples. But still she clung onto his hair. Still she gazed into his dark eyes. And her body and soul came for him, her only love.

CHAPTER TWENTY-EIGHT

*G*awain tightened his hold around Antonia's shoulders as shudders rocked her body. Frantic gasps spilled from her lips, and she clutched his head as though she would never let him go.

Watching her climax caused his cock to thicken once more. Her eyes were dark with passion. Her elegant ringlets were messy by his hands. And her lips were pink and swollen from having taken his cock into her mouth.

The memory caused his groin to throb with renewed lust. His Antonia would never cease to surprise him.

A smile of contentment, of masculine satisfaction, curved his lips as she finally sagged against him. Her erratic breath was warm against his chest, and her nails gouged his scalp, unmindful of whether she might be hurting him or not.

Slowly he slid his fingers from her slick folds and wrapped his arm around her waist. Her shudders became less frequent, but still gratifyingly intense. The urge to pull her down onto his bed, to keep her with him until the morning, drifted through his mind.

Soon such a fantasy would be his reality. Soon, she would

never have to leave him to hurry back to her restricted Roman existence.

Soon he would have to tell her of his plans.

But not right now.

Finally, her breathing eased and her fingers relaxed, releasing her claw-like grip on his head. A few moments later, her hands dropped to his shoulders and then, with clear reluctance, she lifted her face from his chest.

Her cheeks were flushed, her eyes glazed. She looked like a woman who had just been thoroughly satisfied by her man.

He intended to satisfy her further before she escaped him this day.

"Come up onto the bed." He brushed a curl back from her warm cheek. "Your knees must be sore."

She didn't answer him or sit by his side as he indicated. Instead, she stared at him, her gaze roving over his face as though she was memorizing every feature. An odd shudder inched along his spine, although he couldn't imagine why. There was nothing sinister in her appraisal. Yet the feeling lingered, like a malevolent shadow across his soul.

Her hands sculpted his biceps, a languorous caress. Yet inexplicably another prickle of unease skated across the back of his neck.

Instinctively his hold around her waist tightened. She let out a ragged breath and used his arms to push herself to her feet. He held onto her hands and watched her gaze travel slowly down his body until she reached his far from disinterested cock.

The feeling of unease vanished, and a satisfied smile tugged at his lips. "There is something very wrong with this, Antonia." He waited until her startled glance meshed with his. "You're not naked."

She swallowed and whatever spell had held her silent for the last few moments appeared to shatter.

"I'm sorry." Her voice was low, husky. "I shouldn't have—I can't stay."

He sighed heavily and pushed himself to his feet without relinquishing her hands. He looked forward to the day when they'd settled in the land of the Picts, and Antonia had no need to rush from his arms.

"You had best call Elpis, then. You look as though you've been thoroughly ravished." Despite his irritation that Antonia had to leave when he wanted her to stay, he couldn't help the grin he shot her way. She didn't merely look ravished. She looked utterly ravishing.

She glanced down at her gown and her eyes widened in clear horror. He followed her gaze, and a wave of raw possessiveness gripped him.

"Carys will lend you a gown." Lust throbbed through every word. He knew Antonia was distressed by the state of her gown, but he couldn't share it. The dirt smearing her pale blue linen where she had knelt before him reminded him of the feel of her mouth sucking him. And the unmistakable traces of their shared passion that stained her elegant gown made him want her all over again.

She snatched her hands free and patted ineffectually at the ground-in dirt. He laughed, even though he knew he shouldn't, and gripped her wrist.

"Let me call Elpis. She can attend to your needs while I go and find Carys."

"No." The word sounded strangled, and Antonia jerked free from his grasp. She didn't look at him as she continued in her vain attempt to clean her gown. "Elpis is no longer my slave. She didn't accompany me today."

He paused for a moment to consider that. He'd always taken it for granted that Elpis would accompany them to the land of the Picts. She might have been Antonia's slave, but he'd seen the closeness between them. Would Elpis still come with them, now she had the choice?

He wanted Antonia to have someone with her that she trusted. It would take time for her to make new friends in a new country. Especially since, as she so often reminded him, the blood of Rome flowed through her veins.

"Then I will clean you myself." That would be no hardship. Perhaps, for Antonia, he would bury his stubborn refusal to use Carys' ostentatious bathhouse and they could bathe together.

Antonia gave up on her gown and straightened her shoulders. He had never seen a woman look so beautiful, regal—or desirable.

The possibility of sharing the Roman bath with her grew more enticing by the moment.

"I can't stay, Gawain." Her voice was low but infused with a note of finality. "I only came here today to…" She hesitated and broke eye contact to stare instead at his chest. "To say farewell."

Filled with lascivious thoughts of what he would do to her in a bath, he'd only half been paying attention to her words. But her final word slammed through his mind like a thunderclap.

"Farewell?" His voice was ominously quiet. *Farewell* was not a term he cared to use in association with Antonia. "Until when?"

She raised her gaze, but only as far as his nose. "We both know this liaison was only of short duration. I believe—I believe it's time to go our separate ways."

He heard her speech. And that's all it was. A speech. Because the words made no sense.

"Is this a jest?" His voice was harsh, and he took a step towards her. "I do not find it amusing."

She stood her ground, despite how he towered over her. Then again, why would she retreat in fear? She knew, as well as he, that he would never raise a hand to her in anger.

Not that he was angry. They were obviously at cross

purposes. Did she think he wished to end their affair, and this was her way of saying goodbye? But why would she think that?

He'd never given her even the slightest indication that he intended to end their liaison.

"I do not jest in such matters." Still she stared at his nose. He had the savage urge to grip her shoulders and shake her until she looked him in the eyes. He fisted his hands instead. "I want to thank you for your company over the last two weeks. I've found it most enjoyable."

Disbelief pounded at his temples. "Enjoyable?" It was the only word he managed to force through the constriction in his throat. She'd found the time they spent together *enjoyable*?

"Yes." She inclined her head in a way that was so familiar, a sharp pain stabbed through his chest. He'd once thought her so cold and aloof, until he had discovered the passionate woman beneath. But now all he saw was her chilly, brittle façade.

It was only a façade. She didn't mean for them to part.

"This was more than a casual dalliance, Antonia." She wasn't the kind of woman to embark on meaningless affairs. Why then was she trying so hard to give him that impression?

"Oh, Gawain." She gave a brief, insincere laugh that lacerated his guts. "What else could it be?"

He gripped her shoulders. Couldn't help himself. But he stopped short of shaking her.

"Don't lie to me." He glared at her, but she refused to meet his eyes. "Look me in the face if you mean your words."

For a moment, he thought she would refuse. Then she looked up at him, and the look of anguish on her face made him almost wish she hadn't.

Her ice-blue eyes sparkled with unshed tears and her lips trembled. Gods, she had no intention of leaving him. She thought this was what he wanted. He'd tell her his plans for their future. Then there would be no doubt in her mind that he wanted her in his life.

"I'm sorry, Gawain." There was a heartbreaking catch in her voice. "I don't want us to part in anger. I'll always remember you with great fondness in my heart."

Fondness? The word was a foul curse. A woman could be fond of her horse or silk or jewelry. Not her godsdamned lover.

The tip of her tongue moistened lips. He couldn't drag his gaze away. She lied. And then, with sickening certainty, the reason punched into his mind.

"It's the praetor." It wasn't a question. "I've told you, Antonia, you don't need to concern yourself about him. There's nothing he can do."

There was a great deal the Roman could do, but now wasn't the time to dwell on that.

"No." Antonia's voice was eerily calm, and a strange blankness descended in her eyes. "He has nothing to do with this decision. You are a Celtic warrior. I have the blood of Rome in my veins. We always knew our time together was short. How could it be anything else? It was never our fate to be together."

She sounded so reasonable. As though she believed every word.

Frustration ripped through him. Everything she said was true. Yet so much had changed since that day he'd first decided he wanted her in his bed.

And then a chill rippled along his spine. Things had changed for him. But had they changed for Antonia? It had never occurred to him before that she might only—still—see him as an entertaining diversion.

But he'd stopped believing that about her from the moment he'd discovered she had never taken a lover before him. She was nothing like the other Roman women he'd had. In any way.

"If Rome had never invaded this isle, then you're right. It would never have been our fate to be together." He gentled his grip, slid his hands along her arms and grasped her hands. "But

Rome did invade. We did meet. We can forge our own destiny, Antonia."

She shivered but before he could take that as a good sign and wrap her in his arms, she straightened her already rigid spine and pulled her hands free.

"That is nothing but a foolish child's fantasy." Her voice was pure ice and her eyes glittered like a frozen woodland stream. "I haven't once imagined we could ever share anything more than this fleeting affair. I cannot believe you have, either."

Fury churned through his chest that she dared compare him to a foolish child. And in this matter, no less. The last thing he'd wanted was to grow to care for her. Yet he had.

Even as his heart pounded against his ribs, he knew it was more than rage. More than wounded warrior pride. He refused to acknowledge the ache in his heart and focused on the anger.

Because he knew how to handle anger.

"Spoken like a true patrician." Contempt dripped from every word. But the contempt was for himself. Had he really been so blinded by Antonia's sweet nature that he'd imagined she felt more for him?

"Except I'm not a patrician, Gawain." She gave him an oddly vulnerable smile that shattered his previous thought. He hadn't been mistaken. She did feel more for him than she admitted. "In the eyes of Rome, I'm but a merchant's daughter, tainted by the blood of my father."

He knew her mother had been noble-born. In his eyes, she was a Roman patrician by virtue of her maternal heritage, but he had no compunction in using the empire's prejudice to his advantage.

"Then you have no blood ties to Rome. We can forge our own life together in the far north."

It wasn't the way he'd imagined telling her of his plans for their future. But surely she would agree with him.

She had to.

"The far north?" There was a wistful note in her voice and her eyes lost focus for a moment, as if she was lost in the possibility of a new life in a new land. "The mountains of Caledonia?"

"Yes. The land of the Picts. We can leave as soon as your daughter arrives in Britain."

The prolonged silence after his words thundered in his ears. Antonia had once again broken eye contact and was staring at his chest. He fought the urge to pick her up, fling her onto his bed and take her until she could think of nothing but him. Until the thought of living without him was forever erased from her mind.

And then she spoke. "My daughter is a patrician."

The rage burst through his veneer of calm. "Her despicable father would have murdered her. I will cherish her, as though she were my own."

Her face was so pale, for a moment he feared she might faint. But he should have known better. Antonia might look fragile, but at her core she possessed the strength of a warrior.

"But how will you cherish her? Should my daughter suffer the life of a peasant, simply because I enjoy your sexual prowess?"

Her softly spoken words rammed through him, ugly and offensive. But there was no condemnation in her eyes. She spoke only the truth.

What life could he offer her or her daughter? They would be fugitives from Rome. He would be hunted as an abductor. A primitive hut was all he could promise her until his warrior skills provided them with better.

"We may not have the luxuries you're used to." His voice was stiff with pride. "But we will never live like peasants."

But in the land of the Picts, would his noble heritage and ancient blood links to the gods be enough to elevate him through their ranks? He had never doubted it before. But how could he ask Antonia to give up her pampered lifestyle for one when she might never own anything more than a rammed earth floor?

If she loved him, none of that would matter.

The question thudded in his mind. *Unanswered.*

"I've learned something else since coming to Britannia." Now she didn't look at him at all. Her gaze was fixed on one of the many holes in the wall, where sunlight spilled through. "I miss the vibrancy of Rome. This far-flung province has its merits, but I have no desire to remain here permanently. I wanted to tell you myself, before you find out from someone else." She hesitated and glanced at him, before once again focusing on the broken, dirty wall. "I've decided to marry the praetor."

"You don't love him." He flung the accusation at her. Denial hammered through his brain. She couldn't marry the praetor. The very thought of it disgusted him.

Devastated him. He shoved that thought aside.

She made a dismissive gesture with her hand. "Love has little to do in such matters. It is an advantageous match, for the daughter of a merchant. I'll no longer be a burden on my father, and my daughter will be raised as the patrician she is."

Her arguments were reasoned. Logical. Marriage was often nothing more than a strategic maneuver to bring more power or prestige to those involved. It happened in his society, between the royal families and chieftains of various tribes.

But not between Druids.

"You can't marry him, Antonia." He would sink to the lowest depths and make her confront her deepest fears, if it meant she'd change her mind. "All he wants is a brood mare. He'd never accept your decision to have no more children."

Unlike him. Had he ever told her that? How could he tell her that now?

For a brief, heartbreaking moment her lip trembled. He hated himself for causing her more pain. But he would make it up to her. He would spend the rest of his life making it up to her.

If she only gave him the chance.

And then she spoke. "The praetor already knows of my decision. He has no desire for more children. He merely…wishes me to be a mother to his sons."

His chest tightened. Antonia had no intention of discussing this matter, or trying to find a solution. Their affair had been, as she'd always maintained, nothing but a brief liaison.

"You've obviously thought this through." His tone was bitter. "You're a true Roman noblewoman, whatever your precious empire might think."

She flinched, as though he had physically struck her with his barbed words. The knowledge he could hurt her did nothing to salve the ache consuming his chest.

"I don't want us to part with angry words between us." For a fleeting moment, she caught his gaze. "I'll never forget you, Gawain. I hope one day you'll remember me with…kindness."

Kindness was not the way he would remember Antonia. "Perhaps I should carve your name into my torque after all." He allowed his gaze to roam over her, from her messy hair to her dainty sandals and then back up again. "That way I will always recall your name when your face has faded into the mists of time."

Who was he trying to fool? There was not the slightest chance in all of Annwyn that her face would ever fade from his memory. There was no need to carve her name into his torque.

She was carved into the beating core of his heart.

Her fingers clutched her gown, but she didn't otherwise react to his derisive taunt. She didn't laugh with contempt or tell him he was delusional if he imagined she had ever wanted him to be a part of her future.

He could think whatever he wished of her. But the truth was Antonia was as he had always believed.

A strong, honorable woman. She'd never promised him anything. She was doing nothing but trying to give her child the best life possible. How could he condemn her for that?

Yet he did. He understood her motives, but he could not forgive her for it.

"Farewell." Her whisper was so soft he scarcely heard it above the frantic thud of his heart. Then she turned and left his world.

And returned to her own.

CHAPTER TWENTY-NINE

*G*awain remained rooted to the spot, his gaze riveted on the closed door. She would come back. She had to come back.

But he knew she would not.

He turned and slammed his fist through the wall of the hut. The pain gave only momentary satisfaction, and it didn't even touch the pain eating its way through his chest.

His heart.

Except she had taken his heart with her.

He doubled over, his hands grasping his thighs. Blood dripped from his knuckles, and he watched the crimson drops soak into the earthen floor.

She was going to marry the praetor. Share his bed. Allow him to touch her body. And for that, he would take her back to Rome.

Rome. The city where she had endured so much heartache and loss. Where her bastard ex-husband was.

Slowly he straightened. From the moment he'd met Antonia, she had given him the impression she despised that jewel of the empire. After he'd grown to know her better, his first impression had only strengthened.

Antonia did not love Rome. Her father was immensely wealthy, but she had never flaunted that wealth as some daughters might. She was, as she had once told him, easily pleased.

Why would she want to take her beloved Cassia back there, when she had gone to such pains to bring her child to Britain?

He knew the praetor lusted for Antonia. Knew he was the kind of man who would do anything to get what he wanted. But Antonia, to his knowledge, had never given the praetor any encouragement.

It wasn't Rome she wanted. It was the chance to give her daughter a good life. And she possessed the means to give Cassia a good life here, in Britain.

Antonia hadn't consented to marry the praetor of her own free will. It was because that bastard Roman had blackmailed her into it. And the only way she could be blackmailed into doing such a thing was if he'd threatened her beloved daughter.

Gawain took a deep breath and unclenched his fists. No one would force Antonia to do something against her will.

He owed the praetor a visit.

Antonia kept her spine rigid and head high as she walked from Gawain's roundhouse back to the villa. She'd known their final farewell would break her heart. But she'd never imagined Gawain would look so devastated.

He had imagined them sharing a future together. Had thought they could find a life in Caledonia. He'd never know how dearly she had wanted to fall into his arms and beg him to take her and Cassia far from Camulodunum. How she, too, had dreamed of such a future.

She blinked rapidly to clear the foolish tears from her eyes. She had to keep up this despicable façade for Carys.

Her steps faltered and against her better judgment, she turned and looked back at Gawain's roundhouse. She'd desperately wanted them to part amicably but his final taunt had shattered all hope of that.

He despised her, as she'd always feared he would. Yet better that he despised her, believing she would chose the decadence of Rome above him, than for him to guess the truth.

Her throat ached with grief as she entered the courtyard. Gawain's face was etched into her heart and soul. She would never be able to forget him, even if she wanted to. How long would it take for his pride to erase every last memory of her from his mind?

Carys was on her knees, tending to her herb garden. Antonia forced a smile to her lips.

"Sweet Cerridwen save us." Carys' eyes widened as she took in Antonia's appearance. Antonia's face heated. She'd forgotten the state of her gown and hair. But what did it matter? Her palla would hide the worst of the damage until she arrived home.

Carys stood up and planted her hands on her hips. She was once again wearing a Celt inspired gown and looked little like the noblewoman she played for the outside world and every inch the foreign princess she truly was.

"What is Gawain thinking, to let you walk out like that? He should have come and found me for a replacement gown. And you know you're always welcome to use the bathhouse."

"Yes, I know." To her horror, her voice was husky. Until this moment, she hadn't considered that her actions would also affect her relationship with Carys. She liked the Celtic woman. But she knew Carys was fiercely loyal. Why would she want to remain Antonia's friend after knowing how she'd hurt Gawain?

And how desperately she wished to keep Carys' friendship. It seemed they were both destined to live in Rome, after all. How wonderful it would have been to know a noblewoman there who hadn't once turned her back on her when she had most needed support.

"Are you well?" Carys frowned. "What has Gawain said to you?"

She had to pull herself together. "Nothing." At least her voice no longer betrayed her shredded heart. "All is well, Carys. I—I have good news. I am to marry the praetor."

Carys stared at her in disbelief. "The praetor?" Her tone left no doubt as to her disgust. "Antonia, you cannot do this. If you tell your father you don't love him, he will never force you into this."

Carys sounded so certain. How odd. And yet how right she was. After the praetor had left, apparently satisfied that her shocked silence equaled acceptance, her father had barely said a word when she'd told him of her marriage plans.

Perhaps he would have more to say this evening, when the praetor returned to make their betrothal official.

"It has nothing to do with love." Did Celtic nobles only ever marry when their heart was involved? Or was that something peculiar to Druids?

Was Carys a Druid, too? The thought slid into her mind without any shock or denial. It seemed, now, perfectly possible that she was a Druid even if she had married a Roman tribune and lived the life of a patrician.

It was, after all, only one more layer on the façade Carys portrayed to the empire.

"But..." Uncharacteristically Carys appeared lost for words. "But this is not Cerridwen's will."

"Why should your goddess be interested in my fate? I'm not a child of Cerridwen." No, she was a child of Juno. And once again Juno had failed her.

Great goddess forgive me. She didn't mean her treacherous words.

Yes, I do. Juno had let her babies die. And now she merely watched as Antonia walked away from the only man she had ever loved.

From the corner of her eye, she saw a shadow move on the far side of the colonnade. Inexplicably a shiver chased over her arms. How long had the shadow been there, listening to their conversation?

A regal woman emerged into the sunlit court. Her long auburn hair cascaded over her shoulders and her gaze remained fixed on Antonia.

"Mother." Carys appeared flustered, another state Antonia had never before witnessed. "Let me introduce my dear friend."

Before Carys could continue, the woman held up her hand in an imperial gesture. Carys immediately fell silent. Although the woman's eyes never left Antonia's, she had the eerie certainty that the older woman had not only taken in her disheveled appearance but despised her for it.

"I know who she is." There was the faintest trace of contempt in her tone. Obviously, she knew Gawain, and had overheard everything. Antonia tensed her nerves for further insult. "You are Cassia's daughter."

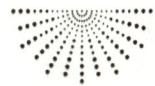

CHAPTER THIRTY

*S*hock punched through Antonia's breast. Of everything she might have imagined the older woman saying, this hadn't even crossed her mind. How was it possible this Celtic noblewoman—*queen*—knew her mother's name?

"You knew my mother?" It was impossible, but what other explanation could there be?

"I knew of her." The queen paused beside her daughter, who looked as staggered as Antonia felt. "Your father spoke of her often."

Antonia clutched her gown in a futile attempt to make sense of the queen's words. But they made no sense.

"How—" She cleared her throat, tried again. "How could you know my father? He lived in Gallia until he moved to Britannia three years ago."

"No, foolish girl. Not the man who raised you. I'm talking about the man who sired both you and Carys." The queen's deep blue eyes glittered. Antonia suppressed a shudder and the urge to back away. She wouldn't allow this woman to intimidate her, even though it was obviously the queen's intention.

"You lie."

"So." The queen raked her gaze over Antonia. When she finally looked her in the face again some of her antagonism had faded. "You truly are ignorant of the circumstances surrounding your birth."

"I don't know what you mean." But her father's recent outburst thundered through her mind. *Her mother was murdered by the hand of a Druid.*

"Is that why Cerridwen sent me visions of Antonia before I even knew of her existence?" Carys' voice was hushed. "Is that why my goddess charged me to embrace a woman of Rome? Because she is my half-sister?"

"I am only surprised," the queen said, turning to Carys, "that Cerridwen didn't share this knowledge of your blood kin with you sooner."

"But my father—"

"He never hid the fact from me that a Roman patrician had captured his heart during the time he lived in Gaul." The queen looked back at Antonia. "He loved me. But I always knew Cassia was his beloved."

"No." Antonia's chest constricted, and she took a step back, her hand raised in denial. She knew who her father was. This foreign queen lied. "*No.*"

"You've always known I had a half-sister?" There was a note of disbelief in Carys' voice.

"Of course." The queen sounded impatient, as though her daughter's question was irrelevant.

"And you didn't think to tell me of this? Even knowing how dearly I've always longed for a sister?"

"I'm not your sister." Panic coiled deep in Antonia's chest, spreading through her limbs, threatening to close her throat. How dare Carys and the queen suggest her mother had been unfaithful with a Celt? "My father is Drusus Antonius Faustus, a merchant from Gallia."

"Why would I speak to you of your father's eldest daughter,

Carys?" The queen angled her head in a regal manner. "His other daughter was nothing to *me*. But I chose to accede to his wishes in the matter of your education. He was adamant you learned Latin like a native of Rome. Not only because of the advantage it would give you when confronted by your enemy. But because he wanted both his daughters to be equally educated."

"I refuse to listen to any more of your lies." Antonia infused her voice with all the contempt she could, but her feet refused to move. She remained rooted to the spot, staring at the queen with rising dread.

She didn't believe a word. Of course she didn't. But a tiny kernel of doubt wormed through her breast, rendering her immobile. Forcing her to listen as the queen spewed more of her insanity.

"I knew this day would come when his daughter of Rome met his daughter of Cymru." The queen paused for a moment, lost in the past. *Lost in the web of her lies.* But why would she lie about such a thing? What could she gain by it? "He told me Cassia's daughter would unite our fractured land."

"You are mad." Antonia retreated another step and glanced wildly around for her slave. She had to get out of here. "I'm leaving."

"Leaving to marry the praetor." The queen gave a soft, scornful laugh. "How like your weak-minded Roman mother you are."

Antonia froze. "Do not speak ill of my noble mother."

"Your father begged her to go with him. She may have loved him, but she didn't possess the courage to face an uncertain future with her lover." The queen raised one eyebrow in condemnation. "In what way are you different?"

But she wanted nothing more than to share her future with Gawain. The queen didn't know everything. The queen would never know everything.

"My mother was scarcely fifteen when I was born. She was

just a girl. You have no right to presume to know what she may or may not have done. Just as you have no right to presume you know the reasons for *my* actions."

Silence screamed in her ears. Both the queen and Carys stared at her with identical expressions on their faces. As though they had never truly seen her before.

Heat washed through her. Had she said too much? What *had* she said?

"Then perhaps you should rethink your strategy," the queen said, and Antonia glared at her. She had no strategy. All she could hope to do was save Gawain's life. "The strength is within you. After all, no Druid gives their heart lightly."

She might have meant Gawain. But Antonia knew the queen was referring to the man she insisted was Antonia's father.

The panic reared again, searing her breast and flooding her veins with a wild frenzy. Before she could stop herself, the words spilled from her lips.

"I'm not a Druid."

The queen's lip curled. "You may possess the blood of one of the greatest Druids of our Age, but unless you are also chosen by the gods then no. *You* are not a Druid."

Her heart hammered in her breast. Her palms were sweaty, breath restricted. She'd not been chosen by the gods, because the queen referred to her heathen, Celtic gods.

But Juno's blessed me with visions ever since I was a small child. Visions that had terrified her. Delivered by a goddess who looked nothing like Juno was depicted in the temples. A goddess who spoke to her in an unknown language. A language that made perfect sense to her until she awoke.

Terror gripped her and she turned and fled from the courtyard.

Back at her father's townhouse, she found Elpis in her room, sewing. She tore off her palla and flung it onto the bed. Elpis' eyes widened and she leaped to her feet.

"Domina, what has happened? Are you all right?"

Antonia whirled on her. "I'm no longer your domina."

Elpis held her hands and Antonia drew in a deep breath, but it failed to calm her shredded nerves. Could it be true? Had her father lied to her all these years?

"You need to bathe, my lady." Elpis was so calm, so serene. For some reason that fueled Antonia's agitation.

"Tell me." She snatched her hands free and twisted her fingers together. "The first time you heard me speak in the language of the gods. How did you know, Elpis?"

Elpis swallowed and refused to meet Antonia's eyes. "I don't understand, my lady."

"Please, Elpis." Antonia took the other woman's hands. "This is so important. How did you know, all those years ago, that it was Juno speaking to me?"

Elpis shifted uncomfortably. "Your father was so panicked, my lady. He feared you had been possessed by evil shades of Tartarus. I told him what I thought would calm him. And...it did."

Antonia stared at her in disbelief. "You lied to him?"

"Not exactly." Elpis finally stopped fidgeting. "I'd heard the language before. In the temples of Athens. But it was not the voice of Juno I heard speaking through you. It was the voice of Hera."

CHAPTER THIRTY-ONE

Gawain entered the massage room in the public bathhouse and saw the praetor sprawled face down on one of the benches. He closed the door and shoved a small stone table in front of it. He wanted no interruptions.

"Finally." The praetor, facing the opposite wall, sounded irritated. "I've been waiting far too long. This standard of service would never be tolerated in Rome."

Gawain flexed his fingers. The image of plunging his dagger through the Roman's throat flashed through his mind. But no matter how much he desired the praetor's death, there was no honor by killing him in such a manner.

Instead, he wrapped his hands around the man's neck, his fingers jabbing into his windpipe, his forearms across the Roman's shoulder blades, pinning him in place. The praetor gagged, struggled, and then clearly realized the futility.

"Just so you know." Gawain leaned over the man and spoke by his ear. "You're at my mercy." He increased the pressure around the praetor's throat to underscore the Roman's vulnerability before relaxing his grip. "Get up."

As the praetor struggled to sit up, Gawain unsheathed his

dagger and pressed the blade against his thigh. It was an unsubtle reminder that the Roman remained weaponless.

"In Rome you would never have got through the security."

"We're not in Rome." Gawain twisted the hilt of his dagger and didn't miss the way the praetor glanced at it. It had been easy enough to bribe his way in. Loyalty to the invaders only extended so far. "I heard a rumor that you intend to coerce Lady Antonia into wedlock."

The praetor stiffened. "You would be wise not to speak Lady Antonia's name in my presence, Celt."

Gawain tightened his grip on his dagger. "She'll never belong to you."

"You think she would choose you above me?" Despite being at a grave disadvantage, the praetor showed no outward fear of Gawain, and it irked. Another man would be sweating, stuttering, glancing around for a means to escape. But the praetor looked him in the eye, and his bearing was proud.

"At least I don't have to resort to base threats against an innocent child to secure a woman's favor." All he needed to do was ensure Antonia didn't wed this man before her daughter arrived. Then, no matter what protest she might raise, she would accompany him north.

"An innocent child?" The praetor stood, his face mottled with affront. "Your sources are misinformed, Celt. Your obsession with Lady Antonia has addled your brain. She makes her own decisions in such matters."

Gawain narrowed his eyes. He wanted to believe the praetor was lying but his gut told him otherwise. Yet if the man hadn't threatened Antonia's daughter, then why was she going to marry him?

"Whatever misbegotten tactics you've used won't work. Your men won't surprise me a second time, Roman. And be assured that I can outmaneuver any security detail you assign to protect yourself. If I decide to have your blood on my hands, there's nothing you can do to prevent it."

"You believe that murdering me will gain you favor in Lady Antonia's eyes?" Contempt dripped from every word.

"No." He knew Antonia far better than to believe that of her. "But at least it will stop you from having her."

The praetor's nostrils flared, and he bared his teeth. "The way you have had her?"

Gawain's grip tightened around his dagger as the inviting image of ripping the praetor's tongue from his throat filled his mind.

"One day she will belong to me, Roman." Barely leashed rage thudded through every word. "And I will have her in every sense."

The praetor gave a harsh laugh. "You delude yourself, Celt. She is of Rome. Even if she returned your infatuation do you really think she would give up everything for you and live like a barbarian?"

Infatuation. The word pounded in his head, fury mounting with every thud of his heart. Raw boys suffered from infatuation. It was a calculated insult, intended to distract him, to give the Roman an advantage.

Antonia's face flooded his mind. The memory of her soft voice calmed his temper. Control balanced. He curled his lip at the Roman.

"It is not I who is the barbarian in this room, Praetor." He gave the man's official title the contempt it deserved. "Lady Antonia is more than the sum of her blood heritage."

"You're wrong." The praetor sounded as arrogant and assured as though he were wearing his full patrician regalia instead of standing naked before his dagger-wielding enemy. Gawain slaughtered the flicker of respect that attempted to ignite for the other man's courage. "We are all the sum of our blood heritage. There's no denying or escaping the call of our forefathers. Do you deny yours, Celt, simply because of current circumstances?"

"I'm not ashamed of my heritage." They both knew what he was. But Gawain would never give the praetor the satisfaction of hearing him say the words.

"And you would willingly drag Lady Antonia into your world, knowing your heritage would taint her as surely as it taints yourself? That a death sentence would hover over her head because of her association with you?"

Denial roared through him. He could protect Antonia. She would never know he was a Druid, and he would never do anything to let such a suspicion arise in her mind. The Romans didn't rule in the land of the Picts. The Picts would not betray him the way the queen of the Brigantes had betrayed Caratacus.

But suppose they did? Suppose Antonia was captured, and her protests of innocence ignored because he had knowingly forced her into danger?

The praetor gave a low, scornful laugh. "I see your lustful plans had not extended that far ahead."

His plan had extended as far as taking Antonia and her daughter away from Camulodunon, to where his heritage didn't have to be concealed.

But he'd always intended concealing it from Antonia. Just as he'd always planned on looking after her and ensuring she wanted for nothing.

It was a grand, noble plan. Except it was hollow. Because he couldn't promise to give her every luxury she deserved. He couldn't even promise to protect her from tenacious, vindictive Romans should they come hunting in the far north.

And how could he expect her devotion when he kept such a vital element of who—*what*—he was a secret from her?

Yet that wasn't the reason why his lungs burned and chest ached. It was because Antonia hadn't even wanted to accompany him. It had nothing to do with the praetor coercing her. She had chosen a life of comfort with a man she didn't love over a life fraught with uncertainty with Gawain.

There was nothing to prevent him from abducting her and taking her north by force. But what would that gain him?

He stepped back. Victory gleamed in the praetor's eyes. He knew he had won.

But there was something the Roman had to know. "Everything your precious empire believes of those who are descended from the ancient gods is but a shallow glimmer of the truth." He sheathed his dagger. Maintained eye contact. Because by all the gods that existed in the Otherworld, he would avenge Antonia if this bastard failed to respect her as she deserved. "If you ever harm Lady Antonia, I will find you. And unleash the wrath of my ancestors on your bloodline."

"I must speak with my father." Antonia turned from Elpis and then realized the other woman wasn't following her. She swung back. She hadn't told Elpis the reason why she needed to find her father. The thought of repeating the queen's words caused her stomach to cramp. It would be hard enough saying them once, to her father. "Elpis, I need you. Please come with me." Elpis had been by her side since they were both young girls. Antonia couldn't confront her father on her own with such a shocking accusation.

"Of course." Elpis obediently went to her side. Antonia stared at her and tried to smother the panic that threatened to overwhelm her at any moment.

Who am I? She was the daughter of a patrician woman who had disgraced her noble family by marrying far beneath her status. Up until this afternoon, she had also been the beloved daughter of a wealthy merchant from Gallia.

Quicksand sucked at the roots of who she was, at everything she had ever believed. If she allowed herself to think about everything the Celtic queen had said, she would go mad.

She had to find her father. She had to hear him tell her it was all lies. There had to be a perfectly logical explanation for why the queen would say such a scandalous thing.

But first she had to ensure that Elpis *understood*. It was of vital importance. She wasn't even sure why, only that it was.

"No." She hitched in a ragged breath. "You don't *have* to come with me. I *want* you to come with me. You don't have to do anything I ask anymore, Elpis. You can go home to Athens if you wish. But—but it is my dearest hope that you choose to stay with Cassia and me."

Elpis looked down at the floor. "What would I do in Athens?" Her voice was quiet. "I lost my blood kin the day I was enslaved." She raised her head and looked into Antonia's eyes. "When you freed me, I thought you wanted me to leave."

How could Elpis have imagined that? Didn't she know how much Antonia cared for her?

But why would she know? It was only over the last year or so that Antonia had finally acknowledged that Elpis was so much more to her than merely a slave.

Tentatively she wrapped her arms around Elpis. They had often held hands, but had never hugged. That was reserved for women of her own social standing. Women like those patricians in Rome.

"I would like you to stay," she whispered. "You're like a sister to me, Elpis." *If the queen speaks the truth, then Carys is my half-sister.* A shiver rocked through her, tipping her further into a maelstrom of confusion as Elpis returned her embrace.

She needed to speak to her father. To put to rest once and for all the queen's lies that were eating through her heart. She changed her gown and Elpis rearranged her hair. And all the while Antonia tried to work out how she could raise the subject of her true parentage with her beloved father without offending his honor.

As Antonia and Elpis hurried through the forum, she caught

sight of the praetor leaving the bathhouse. She quickly pulled her palla over her head and hoped he hadn't seen her. She was in no mood to confront him and his demands.

Her father was in the back room of the luxury merchant shop he owned near the forum and didn't appear especially delighted to see her.

"What is wrong?" He came to her and held her shoulders. "Has something happened?"

He had always been so concerned for her comfort and well-being. Not all fathers cared so dearly for a daughter. Surely he wouldn't care for her at all, if the queen was right and Antonia was the product of an illicit liaison between her mother and a Druid.

A tiny voice in the back of her mind urged caution. What could be gained by raking up the past? She should let it go. Push it to the back of her mind and try to forget the accusation.

But she knew she would never be able to forget it. Because a part of her feared the queen spoke only the truth.

She stared into her father's eyes and her courage wavered. Perhaps she should take the time to think this through, to choose her words with care and practice what she needed to ask.

But there was no easy way to say it. She could have a year to prepare the words, and still she wouldn't know what to say.

"Is it true that I'm the daughter of a Druid?"

CHAPTER THIRTY-TWO

*H*er father's swarthy complexion paled, as though she had struck a mortal blow to his heart. Antonia stared, appalled. There was no need for him to confirm or deny. The stricken look in his eyes told her everything.

"No." His voice was hoarse, and he gave her a small shake. "You're my daughter, Antonia. You have always been my daughter."

She pulled free of his grasp. Panic writhed deep in her gut, a malevolent serpent seething with poison, corroding everything she had ever believed of her life. *My father is a Druid.*

It made a distorted sense. She'd often wondered if her mother would have married a merchant if she had not been pregnant. Now she knew the truth beyond any doubt.

"What did my mother's esteemed family give you for taking her off their hands?" Her voice was bitter, and she scarcely acknowledged how Elpis gripped her hand. How foolish she had been to imagine her parents had been so blindly, completely in love that it had crossed all social boundaries.

"Antonia." Was it her imagination or did her father sound shocked? Why did he sound shocked? Should she remain ignorant of her roots, now they'd been wrenched from the false bed she had lain in for the last twenty-five years?

"Why? Why did you marry her?"

"Because I loved her." Her father let out a pained breath and Antonia's heart ached at the look of desolation on his face. "I loved her. She was intelligent, beautiful, and always had time to speak to me whenever our paths crossed. I always knew I never stood a chance with her."

"Until she disgraced her father's name."

The look of desolation vanished, and her father's eyes gleamed with rage. "She disgraced no one, Antonia. The filthy dog raped her. I was honored to be chosen for her husband. Cassia deserved a life in Rome as befit her noble birth, but instead she was destined to die in Gallia. Because of the barbarism of a Druid."

Antonia reeled at the foul accusation. *I'm the spawn of rape?* Denial pounded through her mind, but before words could form the sound of the door shutting behind her caused her to swing around.

The praetor stood there, his face as hard as marble. "Lower your voice." It was a command. "I could hear you from outside the room."

Her father stiffened. "What did you hear?"

The praetor glared at her father. "Enough."

"Antonia has the blood of one of the premier houses of Rome in her veins." Her father took a step towards the praetor. "She is innocent of the darkness surrounding her conception."

"Of course she is." The praetor kept his gaze fixed on her father. "And as my wife she will enjoy the status into which she should have been born."

"You'll never hold this against her?" Skepticism threaded through her father's words, but Antonia also heard a trace of fear. Fear that the praetor might turn on her because of her tainted blood.

The wild urge to laugh bubbled deep in her chest. All her life she had lived with the knowledge that in the eyes of her mother's family she was not quite good enough because of her father's plebeian blood.

But it wasn't plebeian blood that soiled her veins. It was the blood of Druids. And that heritage was enough to crucify her.

"I give you my word on the names of my forefathers that I will never harm Antonia by word or deed."

Her father drew in a deep breath. "Perhaps, after all, you are worthy of my beloved daughter, Praetor."

The urge to laugh faded and instead a strange, ethereal sense of calm descended. She freed her hand from Elpis and stepped towards the two men who were discussing her fate as though it had nothing to do with her.

An eerie familiarity rippled along her spine. She had been here before. Her future hung in the balance, suspended between the might of two powerful men and the fragile will of a mere woman.

Embrace your destiny. The feminine whisper in her mind was in a language she didn't know. Yet she understood the words.

They were the words spoken in the visions she had when Juno visited.

Juno? Or Hera?

Or another goddess altogether? A goddess from her unknown father's pantheon?

"I am not the product of rape." Her words shocked her almost as much as they shocked the two men, judging by the looks on their faces as they turned to her. She looked into the eyes of the man she had always thought of as her father. The man she would always love as her father, because he was the only father she had ever known. "My mother loved him. You've always known this, Father."

It was the reason he loathed Druids. The reason he'd never allowed her to discuss them. It wasn't because of their emperor's prejudice and extermination decree. It was because a Druid had stolen the heart of the woman he loved.

"Cassia was too young to know her own mind." His voice was harsh but the undercurrent of despair tore through Antonia's heart. Not only for her father. But for the mother she had never had the chance to know.

How terrified she must have been. A young girl pregnant by her illicit lover. How easy it would have been to coerce her into marrying another man. A man who would never be suitable under normal circumstances, but one who was immeasurably preferable to a despised Druid.

Slowly she turned to the praetor. She didn't have the excuse of being a young, inexperienced girl, and yet she had allowed this man to coerce her all the same.

"How could you take me as your wife now, Seneca?" Her voice was quiet but didn't tremble with the aftermath of the recent revelations. The strange serenity still cocooned her and there was an odd sense of detachment. As though she was watching this tableau unfold, yet was not quite a part of it. "You have pledged to rid the civilized world of all who bear my heritage."

The praetor swallowed. "You're not the sum of your heritage, Antonia." He sounded as though the words choked him and he gripped her hand. "When you marry me, my heritage is yours."

It was true. A woman was nothing but the sum of her father's heritage until she married. And then she was her husband's. Yet how proudly the man she loved as her father had always instilled in Antonia the noble lineage she inherited from her mother.

But now she was more than the child of a daughter of Rome. Her Druid father's blood flowed in her veins. If he was half as noble and honorable as Gawain, then how could she allow his legacy to fade into obscurity?

"I love you, Father." She looked at the man who would forever be her father in her heart. He'd concealed the truth from her, but she understood his reasons and couldn't hate him for it. Then she looked back at the praetor. Both men stood shoulder to shoulder. A barricade of masculine power. If she allowed it, they would bend her to their will, in the misguided belief they were doing it for her. She freed her hand from the praetor's grip. "But I will always be the daughter of a Druid."

Their vehement protests flowed over her. She waited until their demands and entreaties finally faded into silence. A silence that clearly grated on both men's nerves but that sank into Antonia's soul and enhanced her sense of calm.

If she returned to Rome, she would never learn anything more of her blood father. Her daughter would remain in ignorance of her true heritage. Antonia's marriage would be a sham and her life a lie.

To save Gawain she would do all that and more. But was this the right path for her to take? Was this truly her destiny, to continue to deny the past and blight the future with yet more fabrications?

Or was her place by Gawain's side, ensuring the truth prevailed? Not simply the circumstances surrounding her birth. But the deeper truth of the mysterious people—*my people*—who were the scourge of the empire?

The Druids.

"Would you crucify me, Seneca, for my foreign blood?"

She saw her father press his hand against his heart, but her focus was on the praetor. His jaw tensed, the only outward sign of his thoughts he allowed himself.

Finally, he spoke. "No."

She took a deep breath. The time for deception by omission was over. "Would you truly crucify the only man I've ever loved, because of *his* foreign blood?"

"What man?" There was a note of fear in her father's voice, but for once she ignored him. Her eyes never left the praetor's. When he had given her the ultimatum before she'd blindly believed it, too terrified that Gawain's life was in danger to question the praetor.

But now she did question. Now, when he was fully aware that Gawain was the man she loved, the man she was prepared to sacrifice her happiness for, she demanded an answer.

She wouldn't allow him to bask in the delusion that he was saving her from an ill-advised liaison or fanciful infatuation. Such tactics could work on a naïve fourteen-year-old girl. But not on a woman of twenty-five.

The praetor's nostrils flared. "You would give up everything—to be with *him?*"

Everything but her daughter. And yet, if she could be with Gawain, she wouldn't be giving up anything.

But the praetor didn't need to know everything. "I would."

Silence reigned. She knew the praetor was doing it deliberately, hoping to unnerve her enough so that she would break the silence by saying something unwary. But the strange sense of peace still cocooned her, and she was content to wait for the praetor's response.

It was her father who eventually broke the deadlock.

"Antonia." There was a heartbreaking catch in his voice. "Think of Cassia."

Before she could respond, the praetor drew in a harsh breath and flung her father a look that suggested he had taken great offense to the comment.

"I was charged to come to Camulodunum and hunt down any Druids who had sought sanctuary within the city. I captured the leader, his followers scattered and the threat to the empire has been eliminated."

Antonia's heart thudded against her ribs. Was the praetor granting her freedom?

"You are to be congratulated, Praetor." Her father's gaze was fixed on the other man. "The emperor will be well pleased by the news."

"I imagine," the praetor said, looking at her father, "there will be no need for me to remain in this primitive province much longer."

He's setting me free.

"You will be glad to return to civilization, I have no doubt." Her father refused to look in her direction and appeared eager to usher the praetor from the room. For a fleeting moment, her gaze clashed with the praetor's. She saw his Roman pride, the arrogance of countless generations. And she also saw a glimpse of desolation for a future that would never be his.

As her father followed the praetor from the room, she took a deep breath. She had to return to Gawain. Explain she was now free to go with him.

To the land of the Picts. *Caledonia.*

Unease knotted her stomach. Would he be willing to listen to her, after the terrible things she'd said to him?

Her father returned and closed the door behind him.

"What man?" His voice was hoarse and once again she heard the fear in his words. "What have you done, Antonia?"

"He is Gawain." She wanted to tell her father that Gawain was a Druid. But it wasn't her secret to share. "I love him, and if he will take me back, I'll follow him wherever he leads."

"No." Her father gripped her hands. The fear vibrated through his body, and she knew that he'd guessed what Gawain truly was. "I forbid it. Do you hear me, Antonia? *I forbid it.*"

"He's my destiny," she whispered, as tears prickled the back of her eyes. Her father had never really had the woman he loved, because of a Druid. And now she knew he feared losing her, because she too had fallen in love with a Druid. "Please give me your blessing, Father. But I must go to him. I have to tell him how I really feel."

CHAPTER THIRTY-THREE

Gawain kept off the Roman road, but for a perverse reason he couldn't fathom, kept it within his sights as he rode across the countryside. It wouldn't be long before dusk fell and he knew he should have waited until the morning before he left Camulodunon, but he'd had to get away.

Carys had urged him to stay longer. Even the queen had suggested he was being hasty, which had only spurred his departure. There was nothing to keep him longer in Camulodunon. Within weeks, Carys and Maximus were leaving for Rome. The queen and other Druids were discussing their options.

He would travel into the land of the Picts. And when he'd gathered the information he needed, he'd return and see if the queen and others wished to accompany him into the mountainous north.

Storm clouds darkened the sky, and a chill wind pierced his skin. A sense of foreboding clung like malignant fog around him, inexplicably urging him to return to Camulodunon.

He dug in his heels. He had no desire to be around when Antonia's betrothal was announced. Or when she wed that bastard. Even now, knowing that she had never imagined a future with him, the thought of her with the praetor turned his guts.

His horse stumbled. Gawain cursed and dismounted. The animal had come with him from the Isle of Mon. Had been his constant companion when he'd trekked the British countryside and not once had it ever lost its footing.

He held onto the reins and took a few steps back, then clicked softly for the horse to follow. It did not appear to favor any leg, but he couldn't take any chances. The creature stood patiently as Gawain ran his hands over each leg from shoulder to pastern. His pressure was firm, his hands sensitive to any sign of soreness or fluid. He examined each hoof, carefully digging the dirt free with his dagger, then using the hilt to press on the sole and sensitive frog area. As far as he could tell, there was no damage.

He straightened and frowned into the distance. The village he'd intended to stay at this night was still some way ahead, but he didn't want to risk riding in this light. He might have missed a small injury and didn't want to worsen it unnecessarily. And so he began to lead the horse forward by the reins.

The silence pressed into him. It was unnatural. He missed the forests of Cymru. Would the mountains in the north be anything like the mountains of his homeland?

With every step, the sense of dread that thudded through his chest magnified. An insidious sense of wrongness permeated his soul, but he couldn't fathom why.

Sanctuary could never be found in Camulodunon. It was too Romanized. Held too many memories he wanted to forget. Even though he knew, in his heart, the memories of Antonia would never fade.

So why did this overpowering need to retrace his steps hammer through his mind?

An ancient Briton pathway caught his eye up ahead. The Roman road had cut across it with callous disregard for the old ways of travel, intent only in reaching another Roman destination with military precision.

His step slowed as he reached the ancient path. Already it was becoming overgrown as locals abandoned their traditional routes and made use of the new. His gaze traveled onward to the Roman made road. It irked him to admit, but perhaps his journey would be faster if he made use of it.

The silence was broken by the distant thunder of approaching horses. Stealthily he began to back away into the encroaching shadows, but his horse whickered and tossed its head in unprecedented mutiny.

Eerie shivers crawled over the back of his neck, and he froze as the Roman horse riders thundered towards him from the direction of Camulodunon. There had to be at least a dozen, but they were not of the Legion.

Disbelief trickled along his spine as he stared at the rapidly approaching leader. *It was Antonia.*

His eyes were playing tricks.

She pulled up some distance from him and raised her arm in a clear signal to halt. The other riders—clearly her guards—obeyed her unspoken command. The sense of unreality expanded as she dismounted without waiting for assistance and began to walk along the road, leading her horse.

Gods of Annwyn it really was her. The thought hammered through his mind and acted as a trigger. He pulled on the reins, but his horse was no longer recalcitrant and followed without protest.

They met at the point where the ancient road vanished beneath the new. Her hair was windswept, her cheeks flushed. She looked like a wild Celtic goddess in the guise of a gentle Roman noblewoman.

Curse all the gods. This woman made him think of the most fanciful, insane things.

"When Carys told me you had left, I was afraid I'd never find you again."

Her breathless voice sank into his heart, as though it had been years since they had last spoken instead of earlier that day. And then the meaning of her words registered.

If his horse hadn't stumbled, he would have already reached the next village. And once there, it was unlikely Antonia would have been able to find him until the sun rose. And by then he would already have left.

He ignored the ripple of awe that feathered across his shoulders. It was a coincidence. Lugus, despite his affinity with horses, had no hand in this. His god remained distant. Gawain traveled this path without guidance and Antonia had made it very clear she wanted to be no part of it.

Yet if that were true, what had possessed her to follow him?

"Why did you wish to find me?" His voice was harsh and his grip on the reins tightened. She was so close to him her elusive scent of woodland flowers drifted in the breeze, intoxicating his senses. If she came any closer, he'd be unable to stop himself from dragging her into his arms.

"I had to see you again. I had to speak to you."

He gave a mirthless laugh and kept his distance from her only by sheer brute willpower. She'd rejected him once. He wouldn't give her the opportunity to reject him a second time.

But why has she followed me?

"I believe we said everything earlier this day, my lady."

She swallowed and straightened. Only then did he realize how intimately she had leaned closer to him. The loss of her evocative scent was like a physical blow.

"I'm sorry for the things I said, Gawain. I hope—I pray you can forgive me."

"Why are you here, Antonia?" He fisted his free hand to prevent himself from grabbing her shoulder and shaking her.

"You didn't ride all this way simply to offer me an apology and beg for my forgiveness."

There was only one reason he could think of as to why she would follow him. *Because she's changed her mind.* But there was no reason why she should have. She had made it very plain where her priorities lay.

"Circumstances have changed since we last saw each other."

His senses sharpened. "In what way?"

She hesitated for the briefest moment. "I would rather not discuss my reasons."

He gripped her shoulder and jerked her forward. From the corner of his eye he saw one of the riders—*her father?* — canter to them, only to pull to an abrupt halt when Antonia raised her hand in warning.

For some reason her action ignited the smoldering fury, frustration—*love*—that had seethed beneath the surface for untold hours. He'd resigned himself to never seeing her again. And here she was, seeking him out. Grinding his pride into the dirt with every word she uttered.

"If you want to keep me as your lover while you marry your Roman patrician then you've had a wasted journey. I decline the offer."

Even in the dusky twilight, he saw the blush stain her cheeks. But she didn't break eye contact or stiffen in affront.

"I came to tell you that I'm not going to marry the praetor."

Shock stabbed through him. She'd been so adamant earlier that day. He'd wanted nothing more than for her to change her mind. But he hadn't seriously imagined she would. So what had happened?

"Why not?" He realized his fingers were biting into her shoulder and forcibly relaxed his grip. But he couldn't release her. Gods, he never wanted to release her. What life would he have in the land of the Picts, if Antonia wasn't there to share it with him?

She angled her head in a proud manner that sent a lingering pain through his heart. "I choose to embrace my destiny, instead of having it thrust upon me by outside forces."

A chill inched over his flesh. *Embrace your destiny.* Those were the words his gods had said through Antonia the night she had suffered a vision. It was sheer coincidence she repeated them here, now.

"And what of your daughter? Does she no longer deserve to embrace her destiny, as a patrician in Rome?" The words seared his throat. The way they'd seared his heart when Antonia had thrown them in his face.

"Please, Gawain." There was a pleading note in her voice that instantly raised his suspicions. What was she hiding? "Can you not simply accept that I was wrong? I've—had time to think it over, and I could never resume another life in Rome with a man I don't love."

He didn't believe her. She'd had plenty of time to think of how her life would be if she returned to Rome. His hand slid along her arm, and he threaded his fingers through hers.

"Tell me, Antonia." His voice was unforgiving. "What happened to change your mind since you left my hut?" He used the word deliberately. Reminding her of the vast differences in their lifestyles. In case she had forgotten.

Her thumb caressed his and despite how she'd trampled on his heart, despite the current circumstances and the anger that seethed beneath the surface, desire flared with rampant disregard.

Desire would always be a facet when it came to Antonia. He gritted his teeth and refused to succumb to the insistent imperative to claim her lips and remind her that *she was his.*

She hesitated for another moment. Then she took a deep breath. "Do you swear on the names of your forefathers that, no matter what I say, you'll not seek vengeance?"

Dull rage thudded through his chest. He'd been right. The

praetor had blackmailed her into agreeing to marry him. And that bastard had looked him in the eye and sworn he had not.

And Gawain had believed him.

"He'll never harm Cassia as long as there's breath in my body." He tugged Antonia closer. He would protect her and Cassia with his life. "How can he call himself a man, to threaten an innocent child?"

Antonia frowned, as though she had not the slightest idea what he was talking about.

"The praetor didn't threaten Cassia." There was an unmistakable note of shock in her voice, and he stared at her as confusion gnawed through his chest. If the praetor hadn't threatened her beloved daughter, then what was Antonia talking about?

He was convinced he was right. That he had always been right in this matter. The only reason she had agreed to the praetor's demand was because she felt she had no other choice.

"Then who did he threaten?" The only other person was her father. So had her father confronted the praetor and somehow released Antonia from her pledge?

The silence ate through him as she stared at him as though she regretted having confided in him. Finally, she spoke.

"You."

CHAPTER THIRTY-FOUR

For a moment Gawain didn't comprehend what she meant. Him? The praetor had coerced Antonia by threatening *him*?

Disbelief slammed through him. "What were you thinking? How could you even imagine doing such a thing?" He resisted the urge to shake her. The need to crush her in his arms. The overwhelming desire to bury his face in her hair and reassure himself that she was here. She was safe. That the danger of her leaving for Rome had passed.

But how could she have agreed to something so vile in the first place?

"Why do you think, Gawain?" Her voice was soft but there was a thread of unmistakable power that pulled him from his jagged thoughts. "I would do a great deal to ensure your safety."

No. This was wrong. Antonia should never have to put her happiness at stake because of him. He'd gut that Roman before he allowed the bastard to put one hand on her.

Above the roar that filled his head and the thunder of his heart in his chest, her words echoed through his mind.

She wasn't going to marry the praetor.

The constriction within his chest eased. It didn't matter what the praetor threatened against Gawain. He could take care of himself. Thank the gods Antonia had come to her senses in time and realized that.

"The praetor," she said, "has concluded his mission for the emperor in Britannia. He's returning to Rome shortly."

Why would he return to Rome when he had vowed vengeance on Gawain? Unease slithered through his veins. There was still something she hadn't told him.

"What did you promise him, Antonia? Why is he leaving Britain without," he'd almost said *crucifying*, "killing me for taking who he covets?"

"Because I confronted him with the truth." She took a deep breath, as though for courage. "There have been too many lies in my past. I don't need to be protected for my own good or because a man considers I'm incapable of making and living with my own decisions."

She looked up at him, her gaze intent, as though she were trying to see inside his head and discover his deadly secrets.

But he couldn't tell her what he truly was. To expose her to that aspect of him could put her in danger. It had nothing to do with him considering her incapable of handling the truth. He simply didn't want to risk her safety by knowing the truth.

"We'll travel north together, as soon as Cassia arrives in Britain."

She didn't answer right away but he saw a flicker of what looked oddly like disappointment in her eyes. Before he could attempt to decipher why he should imagine such a thing, she lowered her head and focused on his jaw.

"Yes." Her voice was low and although she'd agreed with him a sense of unease pierced through him. "I know it will not be an easy life, living with a warrior, but I'd rather be by your side than anywhere else in the world."

"I'm more than a warrior." He raised her hand and kissed her chilled knuckles. "Before the invasion I was a seeker of truth and teacher of my people."

As a Chosen One of Lugus he was a custodian for the sacred history of the Druids. He had upheld their laws and counseled people in times of despair or dispute. While he was, and would always be, a warrior, a part of his soul craved to return to the time when he could also assist his people in a less bloodthirsty manner.

Only time would tell whether the Picts would ever trust him enough to enjoy such a life.

Antonia remained silent and as he stared at her averted face, a sliver of guilt stirred deep inside. He'd just told her he was a seeker of truth. Yet he withheld from her the most important element of who he was.

She'd just told him there had been too many lies in her past. Did he intend to dishonor her courage by lying to her, even if merely by omission, in the future?

Instinctively his fingers tightened around hers. He didn't fear that she would call her guards to arrest him when she learned the truth. Only that she might decide to leave him here on this unlikely crossroads, and return to her own people.

"There's something about me you should know." His voice was gruff. She looked up at him and he forced himself to continue. "Something that may cause you to change your mind about sharing your life with me."

"You can tell me anything, Gawain."

He knew that. But the confession stuck in his throat. There was no easy way to say the words. Only the stark truth.

"I'm a Druid."

The tense expression on her face relaxed and a smile illuminated her face. Stunned, he stared at her. Whatever reaction he'd expected, it most certainly hadn't been this. She appeared *relieved*.

"Thank you for trusting me enough to tell me." Her whisper was scarcely loud enough to be heard, but it wasn't the words that rendered him speechless. It was the meaning behind her words.

She had known. How long had she known? Would she ever have confronted him, if he'd not taken the leap of faith and confessed to her?

He watched her raise his hand and press her lips against his knuckles. He cleared his throat and barely noticed how the storm clouds faded in the sky.

"It was never about a question of trust."

She looked up at him and he realized that wasn't what she had meant. She knew he trusted her not to share the deadly secret of his heritage. It was because he trusted that she was strong enough to accept the legacy of his forefathers and everything it entailed.

"I have a confession of my own." She pressed his hand against her breast. Against her heart. "I discovered today my heritage is more tainted than even Rome imagined. I'm the daughter of a Druid, Gawain. I'm the half-sister of Carys."

Antonia was the daughter of a Druid? She had the blood of the ancient gods in her veins? Awe trickled along his spine as he recalled her nightmare. He'd blamed his gods. Thought they were using Antonia to get to him.

But his gods were as much a part of her heritage as they were of his own. Was it possible they'd not been speaking to him at all that night?

Could they have been speaking to Antonia herself? *Had they spoken to her before?*

"It seems our destinies were always intended to collide."

On the western horizon, a blaze of orange and gold from the setting sun burst through the remnants of the storm clouds, banishing them from the twilight sky. The ethereal glow bathed Antonia as she stood before him. He had often likened her to a goddess. But now, as the golden light illuminated her, a shiver raised the hairs on his arms.

She did possess the blood of the gods. Was she, in her own right, also a Druid?

"Do you still want me to come with you to Caledonia?"

She stood on the Roman road and used the Roman name for the ancient land of the Picts. But she was willing to sacrifice her Roman heritage.

To be with him.

The lingering tendrils of foreboding that clouded his soul faded as he finally faced the truth.

His home was wherever Antonia was. She was the path he had been searching for.

He stepped forward onto the road, leaving the dusty, over-grown trail behind. How could she even ask him such a thing?

An odd thought hit him. He'd never asked her if she would go with him. He had always assumed. She deserved more than that. Gods, she deserved everything, but all he could give her was himself.

And the courtesy of giving her the choice.

"I have no wish to go anywhere without you, Antonia. If I could, I would take you back to the valleys of Cymru." He untangled their fingers and tenderly cradled her face. "But my homeland is fractured. Will you come with me into the far north so we can forge our own destiny together?"

He'd expected her joyful capitulation. At the very least a smile of assent. But instead, she stared at him as though she was frozen. He gently traced his thumb across her cheek. "Antonia?"

"Cassia's daughter would unite a fractured land." Her voice was hushed, and he frowned. What was she talking about? What did her future grandchild have to do with it? *"You must bring them home to me.* That's what Juno has been telling me since I arrived in Britannia, Gawain. The message I've never been able to recall."

The spirits of his ancestors brushed over his arms, and he gave an involuntary shudder. Antonia gazed at him, clearly waiting for his response, but his voice was locked in his throat.

She has no idea that she's just spoken in the language of the gods.

He dragged in a deep breath. How could there be any doubt? Antonia was a Druid, whether she knew it or not.

"Juno has often spoken to you in visions?" He used the same ancient language, but her words thundered through his mind. *You must bring them home to me.* The same words she had gasped in the throes of her vision that one night he'd stayed with her.

"Ever since I was a child." *She understood me.* But she now spoke in Latin. "I remember now, she told me stories of gods I'd never heard of and places I had never seen. But why would Juno speak to me of such things?" She pressed her hand against his heart. "Yet if the goddess is not Juno—*who is she?*"

Before the invasion, he'd often been called upon to decipher the confusing visions of young acolytes, or children who had not yet been welcomed into the sacred fold. But none of them to his knowledge had possessed Roman blood. Until this moment, the only other one he'd known was the ancient one from Gaul who had taught Latin to his clan.

Spectacular red streaks splashed through the deep orange of the dying sun, casting mystical shadows across the land. The knowledge of the Druids was vast and ancient. But even Druids could not know all the secrets of the gods.

"What else do you remember of your visions, Antonia?"

For a moment, her eyes glazed, as though she was searching through half-recalled memories. Then she blinked, and all confusion vanished.

"She is young, like a goddess of spring. Yet she possesses such an aura of power and majesty I've always thought she was the queen of Olympus." She hesitated for a moment. "I've always worshipped her as Juno. Even though sometimes—in my heart—I feared it wasn't her."

A goddess of new beginnings. Yet one that wielded the power of majesty. Suspicion stirred. But surely not. The goddess in his mind was the most powerful one of all.

"What else? Do you recall where the goddess spoke to you?"

"It was dark. But I knew I was standing on the precipice and one false move would send me plunging to my death. And yet..." Her voice trailed off and she frowned, obviously trying to understand her fragmented recollections. "The path I should take was not certain. I had to choose. And I never knew whether my next step would lead to destruction, or a future filled with hope."

"The crossroads." His voice was hushed. For a moment they stared into each other's eyes until, as one, they looked down at their feet.

Where the Roman road crossed the Celtic path.

Lugus was the finder of paths. But the Morrigan stood at the crossroads of life. Yet it was not the great goddess in her warrior aspect that had taken Antonia for her own.

"Your goddess is Blodeuwedd." The Morrigan in her maiden form. The goddess who overcame the manipulations of those who would enslave her—to find her true destiny.

"She wants me to bring you home." For the first time Antonia sounded uncertain. "To Caledonia?"

Caledonia—the land of the Picts—wasn't his home. In his heart, he knew it never would be.

"Cymru is my home. But how can any of us return there? It's infested by Romans."

A small smile touched her lips. "I'm half Roman, Gawain. And I am as proud of my mother's heritage as you are of yours."

"That's not what I meant."

"I know what you meant." She traced her fingertips along his jaw. "But Rome is here. And she has no intention of leaving."

His fingers tangled around one of her irresistible ringlets. "I'll never succumb to the cursed Eagle."

"I would never wish you to." She paused for a fleeting moment. "But that doesn't mean you couldn't utilize what Rome offers for the good of your own people."

"Do you wish me to become a politician?" He might have once

held a position of responsibility among his own people. But until this moment, he'd never considered there was any similarity between a Druid upholder of the law and a Roman official. "I would likely choke on the rhetoric."

"You could speak for your people in the Roman administration, and I could speak for mine in your Celtic courts."

She was jesting. Surely. But he was not entirely certain. "Cymru is a land in revolt. Unlike the Britons we've not surrendered our freedom."

"I've heard the Caledonians are a fierce, warlike people. They might resist Rome, but they continue to fight each other. Their blood feuds are legendary," Antonia said.

The people of Cymru had legendary blood feuds also. But since the invasion, they had buried their rivalries to oust the enemy.

Yet he knew what she meant. If he had to ride into battle, would he rather be among Picts or leading his own from Cymru?

With a sense of disbelief, he stared down at Antonia. From the moment Aeron, the mad High Druid, had unleashed the fury of the gods and devastation had swept across the land two turns of the wheel ago, Gawain hadn't imagined it possible he could ever return to Cymru except in the role of insurgent.

But why shouldn't I?

Didn't he owe it to his people to return to the land of his birth, the land where his ancestors had lived since the time of Creation? Didn't he owe it to all those who had died defending their land to ensure their ways and beliefs were preserved for future generations?

Would he ever have seen beyond his thirst for vengeance and crippling guilt at having failed Caratacus if Antonia hadn't entered his life?

Her quiet strength and courage had opened his eyes.

Lugus had not abandoned him. He was the one who had led Gawain to Antonia.

He pressed the palm of her hand against his chest. His heart ached with everything he wanted to say to her. But in the end, there was only one thing she needed to know.

"I love you, Antonia. You brought the light back into my world."

In the last glowing rays of the sun as it sank beneath the far horizon, he saw the shimmer of tears in her beautiful eyes.

"And I love you, Gawain." Her whisper sank into his soul, a healing balm. "You and Cassia *are* my world."

EPILOGUE

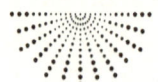

TWO WEEKS LATER, LONDINIUM

*G*awain stood at the dockside beside Antonia as the passengers on the ship bringing her daughter disembarked.

Since that night at the crossroads, he'd spread the word that he would lead any displaced Celt back to Cymru. Several of the Druids he'd met through Rhys had come forward. By the end of this week, they would return to their homeland.

The queen, along with several of her Druids, had decided to accompany them. With her connection to Carys, who had helped avert genocide, and Maximus, whose name carried great weight in the Roman world, they would receive due respect from the invaders when they returned as the exiled rulers.

Gawain caught the stony glare of Antonia's adoptive father as he stood on the other side of her. The older man didn't approve of either Gawain or their plans to move to Cymru. But he had given his daughter his blessing. And intended to join them in their new life.

He looked at Antonia. There was an aura of excitement surrounding her, of anticipation and relief but threaded through there was also a tremor of fear.

Will Cassia still remember me? Her whisper from last night haunted him.

He disregarded Roman protocol and threaded his fingers through hers. Her hand was chilled, but she turned to look at him, and the love in her eyes stilled the breath in his throat.

Tomorrow this woman would be his wife in the eyes of Rome. But she was already his wife in his heart, where it truly mattered.

An elderly couple emerged from the crowds and Antonia stiffened. The old woman held a small child, a replica of Antonia in miniature. The baby caught sight of them, and a smile illuminated her face.

"She remembers you, my sweet Antonia." He squeezed her fingers and she laughed, and finally the last shadow died from the depths of her eyes.

Together, they went to greet their daughter.

ALSO BY CHRISTINA PHILLIPS

Do you like spellbinding historical romance filled with intrigue, passion, and drama? Then you'll love *The Highland Warrior Chronicles,* set in 9th century Pictland and featuring tough Scots warriors and their pagan Pictish princesses.

Her Savage Scot

He'll do anything to protect her from his king...

When Connor MacKenzie rides into Pictland on a mission for his king, he never expects to be captivated by a beautiful Pictish widow. Drawn under her spell, yet unaware of her identity, he risks everything for one passionate night in her arms.

A princess who hides dark secrets in her soul...

Aila, princess of Pictland, long ago turned her back on her goddess, and vowed she would never marry again. But despite how Picts and Scots are sworn enemies, after meeting Connor her frozen heart thaws and she imagines a future filled with love.

A forbidden love that could cost them everything...

When he delivers the royal message, Aila becomes a pawn in a deadly game of politics. Her heart belongs to Connor, but she must marry the prince of Dal Riada – his half-brother. But as dangerous secrets unravel, both Connor and Aila must find a way to outwit their enemies and face the shadows of their past if they want a chance of surviving, together, in this fractured new world.

Her Rebel Scot - Prequel

Her Savage Scot

Her Vengeful Scot

Her Baseborn Scot

Her Wicked Scot

Her Outcast Scot

ACKNOWLEDGMENTS

For Amanda Ashby and Sally Rigby, thank you for everything, fabulous Tiara Girls, and here's to the next twenty years!

To the lovely Cathryn Hein, who answered my horse-related questions with humour and grace, you're a star.

And of course, a huge thanks to my wonderful husband and children. Your patience amazes me!

ABOUT THE AUTHOR

Christina Phillips is an ex-pat Brit who now lives in sunny Western Australia with her high school sweetheart and their family. She enjoys writing paranormal, historical and contemporary romance where the stories sizzle and the heroine brings her hero to his knees.

She is addicted to good coffee, expensive chocolate and bad boy heroes. She is also owned by three gorgeous cats who are convinced the universe revolves around their needs. They are not wrong.

Discover all of Christina's books on her website
ChristinaPhillips.com

AUTHOR'S NOTE

During the first century AD, the languages used in Britain were Brythonic by the native tribal peoples and Latin by the Roman invaders. In *The Druid Chronicles* I've used words not in common usage in the English language until the 1500s and later, on the reasoning these peoples had words of similar meaning in their own languages at that time.

It was likely the Romans who called the ancient peoples of Europe and Britain Celts. They would have called themselves by their own tribal names. For clarity, I have taken the liberty of using the term "Celt" in reference to the ancient tribal peoples of Cymru as a whole.

www.ingramcontent.com/pod-product-compliance
Lightning Source LLC
Chambersburg PA
CBHW050137120726
47903CB00002B/393